Sundays

A. Robert Allen

ISBN: 978-1-0879-4199-8

Slavery and Beyond Series

Volume 5

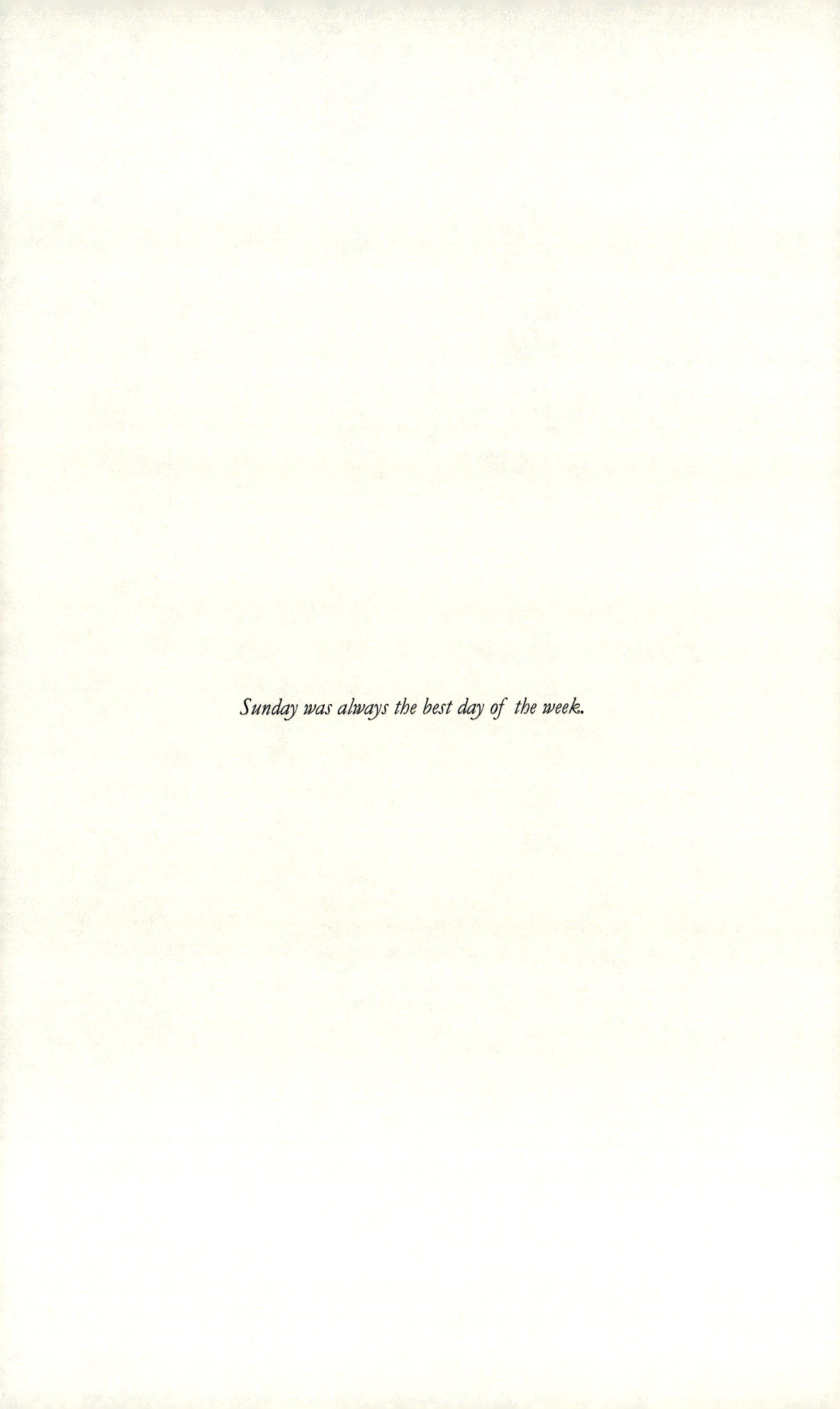

Sunday was always the best day of the week.

Part One

Long Island
2009

CHAPTER 1

The Letter

IT HAD ALWAYS been more of a need than a desire, and nothing in Dustin Murphy's life had led him to believe things would change. The terrace umbrella strained to conceal his broad frame as the first boat passed without incident. Dustin smiled. Clanging beer bottles and laughter announced the next. Once both vessels were almost out of sight, he stepped out from his hiding spot to verify his conclusions: a grandfather taking his grandchild out for a day of fishing and a rented party boat hosting a reunion of twenty-something high school friends. A blaring horn startled him, and his eyes darted back and forth between another approaching craft and the protection of his umbrella. It was too late. The game was over. He exhaled and slumped his shoulders. *Time to get started.*

Dustin began in the hallway closet, packing up coats and jackets his recently deceased Aunt Grace had accumulated over her eighty-three years. Five garbage bags later, he stopped to admire the antique portrait of his great-great-grandfather, which rested on the wall facing the canal. Dustin stared into his ancestor's piercing eyes and wondered about all of the things he had witnessed standing guard over the family for the last hundred and sixty years. A small envelope protruded from the back of the frame. It was dated nine years earlier and addressed to him.

"My dear nephew,

If you're reading this, I'm likely no longer on this earth and I've lost the opportunity to speak to you personally about piecing together the story of our family, which is quite complex with many layers and more than a few sensitivities. Your mother and I planned to talk to you after your birthday party today but she decided that the time still wasn't right. Unfortunately, the time may never be right for my sister to broach certain topics.

Both your mother and I agreed long ago that you should become the next guardian of the family story, as well as the custodian of valuable artifacts like this portrait, but we still worry about whether you're up to the task. I think your problems go back all the way to what I call your lost month when you were ten years old. If you have no idea what I'm talking about, it's time to find out. Speak to your mom about what happened back then as well as the family project, but prepare yourself because she will find both of these topics difficult to discuss.

This letter is attached to the likeness of our ancestor, Joseph Julian, a Sephardic Jew whose family wound up on the Caribbean Island of St. Croix. This line was significant in our family and I've documented everything I know about the Julians in a notebook that I keep in my top desk drawer. Take the painting home with you and find a fitting location for it. Also, go through the contents of my desk carefully, because I tucked away other documents that will help you better understand. We've hidden all of this for far too long, Dustin, and you're the one to bring it out into the open. Good luck!

Aunt Grace"

Chapter 2

Mom

Dustin wiped a tear from his eye as he studied the urn in the center of the dining room table. His mother, Ilva, sat across from him and clutched the arms of her chair. They both placed a hand on the lid and bowed their heads.

Ilva's chin trembled as she spoke. "This might be the last time we're all together."

"There's no rush to move the ashes to the mausoleum, Mom. Aunt Grace can stay with you as long as you want."

"I never expected to outlive my younger sister."

Dustin touched his mother's hand. "Let's play a game. I'll go first." He counted on his fingers. "I see three things, other than the urn, in this room alone that are connected to Aunt Grace. How many can you find?"

Ilva wiped her eyes and pointed to two portraits her sister had painted, a vase given as a gift, and three postcards taped to the side of a cabinet. She smiled. "Grace is all over."

"Yes, Mom, she's everywhere."

Ilva straightened up and raised her finger to punctuate her next word, but nothing emerged from her mouth. Dustin pulled his chair closer and took her hand. They sat quietly without speaking. After a few moments, he said, "Aunt Grace left me a letter that I think we should talk about."

Ilva scowled at the urn and mumbled something under her breath. She turned to her son. "What did she tell you?"

"She said there were things about the family that you never explained."

"It's not that simple." Ilva folded her arms and stiffened her upper back.

"Don't worry, Mom. Let's move Aunt Grace over to the serving cart next to you. This way, she'll be right by your side."

Dustin's eyes locked onto the portrait of his mother as a teenage girl, which was mounted on the wall across from his seat. His breathing slowed and his eyelids fluttered. Ilva placed her hand on his right shoulder and started to hum. Dustin fell into a deep sleep. She whispered, "Rest, my son. You're going to need your energy." Fifteen minutes later, the table was set for dinner and Ilva touched Dustin again on his right shoulder with the palm of her hand. He opened his eyes and said, "Smells delicious."

⊶⊷

Dustin recalled having this dish as far back as his eighth birthday but didn't remember much else from his early childhood. He had focused on the texture of the food as a young boy. Tuna fish casserole with a potato chip crust had been his favorite and he'd tried to magnify the volume of the crunch in his mouth. Each bite would drown out the sounds around him and he'd smiled.

His mind returned to the matter at hand and he did his best to avoid or at least delay the expected *have you seen* or *what's happening with* questions that always accompanied dinner. "Mom, the casserole is delicious. Did you do something different?"

"No, but I'm glad you like it."

"And the carrots . . . the best ever."

"Enough about the food. *Have you seen* your brother and sister lately?"

"No, work is crazy."

"They're busy too, but somehow find time to have lunch together every week. Don't they invite you?"

Sometimes he got as far as dessert and once he had made it to the front door as he'd been about to leave, but this time the cycle of questions commenced before he even finished his main course. Dustin bit down hard on his casserole, but the crunch fell short of what he needed. He rested his knife and fork on either side of his plate. "Sometimes I go with them, but I can't always make it."

"When was the last time you did?"

"A long time ago, Mom, but the two of them have always been tight—that's their thing."

"My sister is sitting next to me in an urn, but I've got no regrets about making time for her. Maybe I could have listened to her more and I regret some of the arguments, but we were always together. Be careful . . . the way you're going, you may not be able to say the same thing."

Dustin forced a smile and moved his right arm to his thigh to steady his bopping leg.

"All right, my son, time to earn your keep. Be right back." Ilva stumbled as she navigated the mountain of old newspapers and magazines stacked next to the table and said, "Don't pass any comments."

Dustin put his hand over his heart in a mock pledge of obedience and pulled out a 2002 issue of the local paper from the bottom of the heap. "This article is seven years old. *Mother of Three Arrested in Prostitution Ring.* Another depressing story and years old to boot. Just sayin'!"

Ilva took the paper from her son's hands. "What makes it bad? The fact she got caught or that she decided to sell her body? We all do what we have to do. Never forget that." A tear ran down her right cheek and she wiped it away with her hand.

"I didn't mean to upset you."

"You didn't. Sorry if I raised my voice." She rested her hand on Dustin's shoulder but realized her mistake when his eyes started to close. Ilva slapped the top of the table with her right hand and said, "I'll get the bills."

Dustin sorted the shoebox of papers and they each got to work, proceeding without conversation until he held up one of his mother's checks to the light and said, "Give me a break, Mom, who could possibly read this? Your handwriting is terrible!"

She picked up the ledger sheet where he had logged the two payments, "And yours is so much better?" They counted, "one, two, three," and added in unison, "I guess as long as they can read the numbers, it'll be okay!"

Mother and son shared a laugh from their long-standing inside joke. He was a busy management consultant during the week, but on Sunday he was her personal bookkeeper, landscaper, and repairman of all things related to technology. Most of the time, however, they sat around the table chatting, eating, laughing, and claiming to be working on the bills. She said, "We're done, put this stuff away."

"It's time, Mom. Tell me about the family. What was Aunt Grace talking about in her letter?"

Ilva hesitated before answering. "Go upstairs to my bedroom closet and bring down the large blue box labeled *Important Papers.*"

Dustin returned a few minutes later with the box, which contained a stack of pictures and assorted documents. A worn old diary with a red cover sat on top.

"To be honest, Dustin, I don't want to read the letter from your Aunt Grace. The things I need to explain to you are in this box. No . . ." She took a deep breath. "I'm sorry. This isn't going well." Ilva glanced down at the tabletop and fiddled with her napkin. "This box is filled with records about my parents, grand-parents, and great-grandparents. There are a few documents about your father's side, though. Some of these records go back generations, but they need a little work to make sense. That's where you come in."

"Mom, I don't understand. Why is this such a big deal?"

"I guess because of the amount of time that has passed. Grace thought I made a mistake by waiting so long to give this to you."

"But why are you giving this just to me? Is it because you think I have a lot of spare time on my hands? Is this what you mean?"

"No, this isn't about you having more time on your hands. I understand you're a big-time consultant traveling all over the country—you remind me all the time." She winked. "But on Sundays, you're my baby boy and I'm telling him . . . I'm sorry."

Dustin said, "Okay, I understand that this is important to you and you're sorry, but about what I don't know. Catch your breath, Mom. If you waited al-most a half a century to let me in on whatever this is, what's another few min-utes?" He smiled.

Ilva gave her right eye one last dab with the napkin before starting. "Remember, I did what I thought was right at the time. I didn't discuss this with you years ago because you always struggled so much with your personal life and I didn't want to put any more pressure on you."

Dustin's gaze returned to the window while his mother waited for a response. His eyes followed the path of a meandering bird that hopped from tree to tree. He lowered his voice and slowed his speech. "Please don't start with that again. Why do you think my life is such a *struggle?*"

"Son, look at me. Yes . . . square in the face."

Dustin turned to his mother but refused to lock eyes.

She continued, "Let's talk about the last ten years, okay? How many times did you move? How many women did you date? What are you looking for? It's ridiculous!"

Dustin shifted in his seat. "Mom, I like coming here every Sunday, but please don't call me ridiculous. I'm better off alone. Life is simple that way. I'll be honest with you . . . I don't really understand the moving, but I'm trying to sort things out. Let's get back to the box. What's in it? Let me see."

Ilva reached inside and pulled out the tattered red journal. She pushed it across the table to her son. "This is your Aunt Rita's diary. I inserted a short note inside the pages that I wrote to you years ago that will give you some background. Start here."

"Aunt Rita's been dead for decades. Why can't you just tell me whatever it is that you want me to understand?"

"It will be easier for me if you piece things together on your own. We'll talk about what you find when you visit on Sundays. Aunt Rita's journal is the right place to begin."

"Why is that, Mom?"

"I grew up with Aunt Rita in my household and let's just say that my experience as a child was different from yours. Think of the clip from the paper, Dustin—when it comes to family, sometimes you do what you have to do. Your Aunt Grace was right, it is time for you to know. Read this and then we'll talk."

Dustin tucked the book under his arm as he made his way to his car. His weekly visits to Hicksville often triggered a mixture of emotions, some expected and others that were hard to understand. But he rarely missed a Sunday.

His mother stood by the door waiting to hear his trademark double honk. After he had pulled away, Ilva sat on the stairs, facing the front door. She hummed the melody before adding the words in between sobs:

"Are you sleeping, are you sleeping?
Brother John, Brother John.
Morning bells are ringing, morning bells are ringing,
Ding ding dong, ding ding dong."

CHAPTER 3

The Castle

DUSTIN HEADED BACK to his new apartment in Queens—his first place outside of Manhattan in several years. He stopped at a light one block away from the majestic building and admired the dozens of different terraces and balconies—some wide and expansive, others short and narrow. The best one, however, was connected to his penthouse space. Dustin called it The Castle because it had four walls with ample cutouts that served as open-air windows, reminiscent of a medieval castle.

He didn't know why he'd selected such spacious accommodations and rationalized that he'd wanted extra bedrooms for guests. Dustin laughed as he questioned himself, *But who actually stays over?* The multilevel layout with full glass windows and skylights made the apartment bright and airy. The four unusual balconies/terraces, however, were the major attractions of the space. *Maybe I'll be able to stay here for a while*, he thought as he found the perfect spot to hang the portrait.

A nail later, the antique painting faced the massive glass wall in the living room. His ancestor would have an excellent view of the almost parklike greenery across the street. Dustin moved closer to the window and took in the full scope of the heavily wooded and well-maintained cemetery on the other side of the road. His ancestor's eyes focused on an uncluttered section of grass without tombstones. Dustin turned and joked, "I hope we'll both be happy here. So sorry you can't join me outside."

He headed upstairs to The Castle with his Aunt Rita's diary in hand and pulled out his mother's note of explanation from inside the book. It was dated in 1989, when Dustin had been twenty-nine.

"Dustin,

You know a bit about your Great-Aunt Rita from our regular visits to her home when you were a child. She started journaling on a daily basis when she arrived in New York from London in 1923 (at the age of nineteen) with her mother, Julia, and her brother (my father, Bruce—twenty-one at the time). My dad got married right away to my mom (Olga) and I came along in 1924. My sister and brother followed in two-year gaps. Aunt Rita and my father never got along, but that didn't make her special. Daddy was a difficult man and he had a tough time holding down a job. By 1930, Rita and her second husband, Tito, who I loved very much, were the breadwinners in the family.

Aunt Rita stopped making entries in the journal in her early twenties but began again around 1930 and continued until 1937. I never told you so much about this period, but this will help you understand.

Mom"

Dustin looked through the cut-out windows of The Castle and admired the majestic trees that sheltered the cemetery. He remembered his visits to Aunt Rita's Long Island home on the water. Images of barbecues, dancing, drinking, and water sports raced through his mind. Aunt Rita had lived on the edge as an older woman and had been afforded great respect.

He settled into his chair as he skimmed the teenage sections of the diary and noted a distinctive change in writing style and tone as the entries resumed in the 1930s. *This is where the story starts*, he thought. The passage was entitled, "Harlem, May 1934."

Part Two

Aunt Rita
Harlem
May 1934

CHAPTER 4

The Whore and the Pimp

"You're nothing but a whore, Rita."

"And Bruce, you're nothing but a goddamn pimp who's happy to live off what I make."

Bruce stomped away from his sister and slammed the bedroom door behind him as he turned his attention to his wife, Olga. His first slap knocked her backward onto the bed. Rita ran toward the commotion, but her mother stepped between her and the door. "Olga may be little, but she can handle herself. Don't start anything with him right now."

"Mama, Bruce is in there slapping his wife and he doesn't bring a damn penny into this house. He's nothing but trouble."

"He hasn't found his way yet. Give him time."

"Time? We've been in New York for eleven years. With all of his book smarts and high language, he doesn't earn shit. Without what Tito and I make, we'd be living in the street."

"Don't exaggerate. I still have some money stashed away. As long as we live simple, we'll never be in the street."

"All I'm saying is that we can't count on Bruce."

"Your brother isn't like you. He considers the work he's offered to be beneath him." Julia paused and traced her hand on the molding on the side of the door. "Remember, he still thinks of himself as a gentleman who will one day receive an inheritance from his father's estate."

Rita's eyes widened. "Remember? How could I forget? He says that shit all the time. Daddy died a pauper four years ago. He needs to wake up and move on."

Julia Iles and her two youngest children, Bruce and Rita, had been supported in London by her estranged husband until 1921, when he'd lost his license to practice law in Trinidad and the support stopped. The family had moved to the United States and settled in Harlem in 1923. The children had grown up wealthy and privileged in Trinidad and lived comfortably in London. New York, however, proved to be a financial challenge.

Julia agreed with her daughter. "You're right—he's not above taking your money, regardless of the source."

"What? Now *you're* starting with that bullshit? There's nothing wrong with the numbers racket! It puts food on the table for lots of people in Harlem."

"What about the risks?"

"Sometimes you got to do what you got to do, especially with so many mouths to feed."

Julia put her arm around her daughter's shoulder. "I'm sorry, Rita. I just don't want anything to happen to you. I count on you. That's all."

"Okay, Mama. You and Olga better go pick up the kids from school. Remember, we're running the bank a little later today, until five thirty, so don't bring them home until then."

Julia sighed. "We know the routine. These kids have seen every movie that's out and had more ice cream than all of their friends combined, so no worries, we'll kill some time."

⊶⊷ ⊶⊷

Rita entered the office of Stephanie St. Clair, the premier numbers/policymaker in Harlem, who also went by the name of Queenie. St. Clair had established her operations in the 1920s and was the last of the original Harlem policymakers to resist a hostile takeover attempt by the notorious gangster Dutch Schultz. Direct access to the boss was rare and Rita wanted to make the most of her opportunity.

"Queenie, thanks for seeing me. Tito and I are handling everything the way you want. No reason to worry, we—"

"Wait . . . this isn't why I brought you here. Sit," Queenie said in her heavy French accent.

Rita sat on the edge of the chair and turned her head when she heard the knock on the door. St. Clair answered, "*Entrer*," and Bumpy Johnson took the seat next to Rita.

"Bumpy needs help dealing with Dutch Schultz and the police. You handle yourself well and I think you are the one to help. Let your husband handle the bank. I need you be my fixer."

"Fixer?"

"Oui, the cops arrest our runners. Mostly bullshit charges, but we bail them out and sometimes need to do more." She winked. "Understand, Rita?"

"I do, but doesn't your lawyer handle that kind of thing?"

"He also can't manage on his own and doesn't like the idea of getting his hands dirty. Not a problem for you, right?"

Rita laughed. "No shortage of soap in my house and I clean up real well at the end of the day!"

Johnson winked. "Always liked you, Rita. Happy we'll be working together."

"She's married, Bumpy. Leave her be," Queenie ordered. "Take her to the lawyer's office and work out the extra pay. *Au revoir.*"

⊷▭ ▭⊶

"Grace, over here!" Olga Iles called out as she tried to get the attention of her daughter, who was going back into the school building to find her siblings.

The schoolchildren scattered in different directions and only a handful of people remained in the courtyard. Grace peeked her head out of the doorway. "H.O. got in trouble again and Ilva stood up for him. They're both in Principal O'Neil's office."

Julia arrived and joined her daughter-in-law as they climbed the stairs of the elementary school. Grace escorted them to the office, where they found Ilva and H.O. seated at the desk with their heads down. The two women rushed in and Grandma Julia took the lead. "What did my grandchildren do? We don't have time for this." Olga sat next to H.O., angling her head so the bruising around her left eye wouldn't be visible.

The principal closed H.O.'s file and raised his head. "Yes, I'm so sorry to take you away from whatever it is that you people—"

Julia waved her index finger. "Stop right there, you won't *you people* us. Your potato-eating ancestors came to this country only a few decades before us. Why not *you people* them? Say your piece and make it quick. Believe me, you don't want me repeating any of this unpleasantness to their Aunt Rita and Uncle Tito. Now, what is it?"

The school administrator cleared his throat. "Horatio, tell them what you did."

"The teacher calls me Horatio. Every time she does, I tell her my name is H.O. The kids all laugh. I hate Horatio. They wouldn't stop laughing, so I did something."

"What did you do?" Grandma Julia asked.

H.O. lowered his head and mumbled, "I punched Johnny Sampson in the mouth."

Ilva jumped in. "I heard about the punch, so I told his teacher to stop calling him Horatio. She said that I didn't know my place and sent me here."

"Ilva forgot that she's a student who needs to show respect," O'Neil said. "In any case, the Sampson boy had to go home and his parents are furious. Punching may not be anything of significance for your family"—he paused and glanced at the shiner on Olga's left eye—"but we take this behavior seriously."

"I see," Julia muttered as she smoothed the bottom of her dress. "There is so much to discuss here. Let's start with the part my grandchildren need to hear." Julia turned to Ilva. "You did the right thing standing up for your little brother. We would have been upset if you hadn't. H.O., you were named after your great-grandfather, Horatio Iles. He was one of the wealthiest planters in the Caribbean and did many important things in his life. You are his namesake and you should be proud of your first name."

John O'Neil smirked and Julia challenged him. "Oh, you think it's impossible for my grandson to be the descendant of an affluent planter?"

"Well, aren't—"

Julia cut him off and said, "Excuse us for a moment. We need to take the children into the hallway. Please hold your thought." Grandma Julia returned alone and her family witnessed the remainder of the conversation without the benefit of sound through the office window.

Julia Iles unleashed a tirade that flowed from deep within. The principal took the brunt of the punishment for every snide comment she had received over the years about the color of her skin. People in New York didn't understand who or what she was, and while she had no desire or obligation to explain, she had a compulsion to express her anger. The three children giggled as they observed the principal's deflated body language and the outcome of the meeting became clear.

Grandma Julia burst out of the office and raised her arms. "Ice cream, anyone?"

CHAPTER 5

116th and St. Nicholas

RITA TURNED TO her husband. "Tito, let's use the third-floor apartment today. We've been up on the fifth floor for a while. One of the men will come up to help you move the bank."

"Send George," Tito answered.

Rita walked down to the lobby of the building on the corner of 116th Street and St. Nicholas Avenue. The family rented three units in this apartment house and used each for business purposes on a rotating basis. She admired the state-of-the-art mailbox system and chandelier she and her husband had purchased for the lobby. Residents understood there would be minor inconveniences in the late afternoon but were willing to tolerate them because of the favors granted by the couple. Beyond the luxurious decorations, Rita and Tito also sponsored holiday parties.

"George, go outside and check if anyone is coming in," Rita said.

George did as he was told and held the door open for one of the first-floor occupants.

"Good afternoon, Maggie," Rita said.

"Didn't see the racing form yet," Maggie responded. "But today is my day! I can feel it in my bones! I picked the lucky number for sure!"

"Do me a favor and move your lucky bones into your apartment. I need to lock the door for a few minutes."

Maggie laughed as she made her way through the lobby. Once George gave the all-clear signal, the bank moved to its new location and the runners lined up by the back door. Rita stuck her head out of the window. "Last call, fellas."

The men streamed up the stairs to deposit their slips and receipts and then returned to their waiting place in the back. George rushed into the dining room with the day's racing form. "Hot off the press!"

Tito sat at the dining room table and thumbed through the paper. The cash collections at the Belmont Racetrack totaled $89,823.19. His eyes focused on the three numbers to the left of the decimal point. The daily number was 823. He pulled out the winners, recorded their proceeds in a journal, and completed packets for each of the men who would make the payouts. At five, Bumpy Johnson arrived with his entourage to collect the take from the day's efforts.

Each of the runners reported the status of their payouts right away. If they were unable to deliver the winnings, Tito made a decision as to whether he would pull back the funds or trust the runner to complete the delivery on his own the next day. At five fifteen, one of the men still had not checked in, but at five thirty-five, George popped his head inside the front door and said, "We're all set and I'm heading out." The couple closed up shop for the day and Rita flipped up the window shade in her room. Dinnertime.

Olga held Grace and H.O. by the hand as they made their way down 116th Street. Ilva walked next to her grandmother and began to run toward the front door. Julia called out, "Wait, they're not ready for us yet." Ilva looked up and saw the window shade to her Aunt Rita's room still in the down position. A few moments later, the shade went up and the group headed upstairs.

Bruce stormed out of his room, nostrils flaring, and motioned with his right hand for his son to join him while in his left he held a belt. Grandma Julia interceded. "I spoke to the principal—if the mother of that Sampson child came over here complaining about what H.O. did, she didn't give you the full story. The boy was justified, so you can put your belt back on your pants—there's no need for any punishment."

Julia grabbed her son's hand and pulled him back toward his bedroom. Bruce complained, "Mother, his name is Horatio. Stop with this H.O. nonsense. He is my child and I'll discipline him if I want."

"No, you won't. This is my home. I let you live here because you are my son, but you don't pay for anything and complain about every single thing that puts food on our table. I won't have it anymore. Did you find work today?"

"Mother, I can't believe that you, of all people, don't appreciate what I'm going through. They talk to me like I'm nothing."

"The money is gone, Bruce. You need to accept that."

"That can't be, it just can't be."

"It's the truth—your father supported us while we lived in London, but the support stopped long before he died."

"You're wrong, Mama. He wrote to me. He promised."

"You could learn a thing or two from your sister. Your dead father can't help you. Get that through your head."

Bruce crossed his arms and straightened his posture. "You're wrong and I'm going to prove it to you one day."

"Well, that day isn't today. Time to grow up. Go out tomorrow and find some work. It doesn't matter how they talk to you as long as you get paid."

Chapter 6

The Fixer

Bumpy Johnson appeared unannounced at Rita's apartment and asked her to step into the hallway for a chat. "George got picked up with a bunch of slips. He's down at the Twenty-Eighth Precinct. That fucking asshole cop, Reardon, says Dutch Schultz paid him to cut us off. He's making a point with George and plans to keep him for a spell. This is the kind of thing we want you to take care of. Bring some money . . . you might need it."

Rita ran back inside, changed her clothes, and returned with a pocketbook filled with bills and a mink coat.

"Not a bad look, but it's not so cold outside."

"I'm not wearing this to stay warm. Let's go."

⊷⊜ ⊜⊷

Rita opened her coat as she entered the lobby of the police station. Her full-length, low-cut dress was on full display. She nodded at the sergeant at the desk. "Is Reardon here?"

"In the back."

"I'm—"

The officer winked. "No introduction necessary. Go on in."

Rita sauntered toward the back of the room, flashing smiles along the way. Several of the officers tipped their hats. One stood up, bowed, and received a loud reaction from his colleagues.

Reardon raised both of his hands. "Queenie sent you? Where's her shitbag lawyer?"

"Don't matter where he is. I'm the one you need to talk to."

"I thought you were the banker. Is this some kind of career change?" he said with a laugh.

"Is there somewhere private where we can talk? I have something for you." She pointed to her bag.

"I'll tell you this . . . I might be just as happy with what's under your coat as what's in the bag . . . what did you have in mind?"

"I'll show you once we're alone."

Reardon jumped up and called out to a group of detectives milling around the interrogation rooms. "I need Room Number Four. Don't disturb me." He softened his voice. "Right this way."

Once inside, the detective pulled out a chair for Rita, but she suggested he sit first and walked over to his side of the table. She leaned over so he could inhale her scent while she loosened his tie. "Such a hardworking man," she said. He shifted in his seat and closed his eyes. "Here's what we're going to do," she whispered. "I know you want to keep our runner overnight to make a point, but there are other points to be made."

"I . . . I . . ."

"Sshh, I'll explain. Let's make the point to Queenie that you're back on her side by accepting this little gift." Rita opened her bag, took out a stash of cash, and rifled it under his nose. "Then I want you to let George leave with me. Queenie will understand that you're back on board, and what's more, I'll owe you a personal favor. Wouldn't that be nice?"

"Yes, it would."

"So, do we have an arrangement?"

"He'll walk out the front door in a few minutes, but I won't forget about my favor."

"I didn't expect you would."

Rita walked again through the sea of desks and waved goodbye to her admirers. George followed and shook Bumpy's hand. "Thanks for getting me out. I thought for sure I'd be in for a few days."

"Thank her."

◆▬◉ ◉▬◆

Rita heard Ilva's screams as she approached the front door to the apartment.

"Daddy, stop! She didn't mean to do it! You'll hurt her!" Ilva stepped in front of her little sister, Grace, and took the impact of the belt on her leg.

"No one speaks to me like this!" Bruce swung again but lost his grip on the belt, which flew out of his hands. The buckle made a mark on the wall right next to Ilva's head. Rita walked straight toward her brother, who backed up a step. She then turned to the girls. "Go to your room. Where are your grandmother and Tito?"

"They went to pick up dessert," Ilva answered.

"Fine. We need to talk, Bruce. Girls, go now."

Rita closed the door to her brother's bedroom as the girls exited. "Bruce, let's move past our usual whore-pimp bullshit because that's not what this conversation is about."

"What do you want, Rita?"

"We're going to talk about Olga and the kids. I'm not going to sit by anymore while you hit your wife and if what I walked in on right now is you getting ready to hit the girls, know right now—that ain't ever gonna happen."

"I'll do whatever I want. Those are my kids, not yours."

"That may be true. But if you hit them, we're going to fight and let me tell you how that will play out—you'll kick my ass, but your face and arms will be all scratched up and some part of your body will have terrible bite marks. I'll be more fucked up than you, but I'll sit in the chair in the hallway and make no attempt to clean up. When Tito sees me and I point to you, he'll take you apart piece by piece. Later that night, when you're sleeping, I'll sneak up on you and do something you'll never forget. Just remember what I did to my first husband, because that's who I become when I need to. Do you understand?"

"How dare you!"

"Stop the goddamn *how dare you* speeches! I'm going to tell the girls not to mention what happened because you plan to control your temper. If you come out of this room after everyone gets back with half a smile asking for some ice cream, I'll assume you see my point. If not, I'm having a long talk with Tito to-night. Make the right choice, brother."

Bruce sat on the bed with his head down as Rita headed to the girls' room for a chat. A few minutes later the apartment door burst open and Tito shouted, "We're back!"

The three kids lined up with their bowls in the kitchen and, once they were served, a fourth bowl appeared. Tito looked up. "What will it be, Bruce, chocolate or vanilla?"

CHAPTER 7

Making It Right

TITO SCRATCHED HIS temple as he shuffled the final four illegible slips on the dining room table. Slips from another runner were also missing. He banged on the heating pipe for help, but no one came. Tito hit the pipe a second time and George appeared by the door. "Send Washington up here," Tito said. "I can't read his handwriting."

"That's because he's drunk as shit. I put him in the apartment on the third floor," George answered.

"We don't have time for this. If he's drunk and can't do his job, we'll replace him," Tito said. "Send him home, but first let him explain these numbers."

"Okay, boss, but he's mumbling that he needs to tell Rita something he's sorry about."

"Sorry about what?"

"I don't know. I'm just repeating what he said. Not sure I want to hear something I'm not supposed to. Don't want Bumpy Johnson visiting me late at night."

"All right, put Sanders by the door and we'll go down to talk to him."

Tito waved on the way out to his brother-in-law, who was sitting in his room. Bruce glanced at his pocket watch, turned the radio louder, and settled back in his chair with a book.

The door to the third-floor apartment was open and the men checked each of the rooms. The drunken man was nowhere to be found. Tito slammed the door and shouted, "When you find him, tell him he's fired. Like I said, I don't have time for this today. It's almost four o'clock." The two men hustled back upstairs. The open door was the first sign and the absence of Sanders was the second. Tito raced to the closet and reached in the hat case for the cash box. It was gone.

◦━◦ ◦━◦

"Bumpy, I don't understand what happened. George needed me on the third floor and I left Sanders as security. My brother-in-law, Bruce, was locked up in his room. Sanders said he got hit from behind when he was getting a drink in the kitchen and didn't see who did it. Bruce never left his room or heard a thing."

"This is your first day without your wife and this is how it goes? How are you going to make this right?"

"I paid the winners with my own money, but I'm not sure about the rest."

"What does that mean?"

"I need to talk to Rita when she gets home. She's been down at the court-house all day."

"I know where she's been—I'm the one who sent her there."

Tito shrugged.

"Listen, Tito. Either you're smart enough to do this on your own or you're not. We're gonna see real soon which one it is, so have your talk with Rita. In the meanwhile, I got a few more people to speak to, beginning with your brother-in-law. Boys, go tell him we're going for a walk."

⊶⊷

Rita entered the apartment with a smile on her face after another successful day navigating the New York City criminal justice system. She found her family sitting in silence, and her body hardened as she listened to the tale from her husband. She asked him, "When did they leave and where did they take him?"

"About an hour ago and they walked around the corner, so I'm assuming they're in the back of the candy shop."

"Let's go. No one fucks with my family. Not even Bumpy Johnson."

"Careful. We don't want any problems with the likes of him."

"True, but we got to protect the family. You come along but let me do the talking."

⊶⊷

Ilva opened her bedroom door a crack and called out, "Aunt Rita, I need to tell you something."

"Not a good time, Ilva. Let's talk later."

"No, you need to hear this. It's about Daddy."

"What, are you worried about your father?"

"Yeah, but that's not it. I was here."

Tito rushed over. "What? Where the hell were you?"

"I got in trouble again at school and Mama snuck me in the house after lunch. She told me to be quiet and just hide until everyone else got home. Otherwise, Daddy might give me the belt."

Rita asked, "What did you see?"

"The people who stole the money were policemen. Two of them."

Tito slapped the wall. "Ilva, why didn't you say something?"

"I didn't want to get into trouble because I was supposed to be at school, but then those men took Daddy."

Rita followed up. "Why didn't you say anything then?"

Ilva fidgeted with the pockets in her sweater and looked down at the ground. "Don't want to say."

Rita pulled her close and sighed. "You've got a bit of me in you, don't you? He hit you the other day and you liked that he might get a taste of his own medicine. Am I right?"

She nodded her head.

"And then you realized he might really get hurt, so you're telling me now. Is that it?" Rita asked.

She nodded again.

"Okay, Ilva. Your secret is safe with me, but you made a mistake here—no matter what, Bruce is your father and my brother, and we protect our own. You think about that, but don't worry. I'll bring him home before you know it."

⊷⊶ ⊷⊶

The trip around the corner was short and the couple walked in silence. Rita worried about Tito's ability to run the bank on his own. He was good as muscle and had other admirable qualities but wasn't a boss and had trouble thinking one or two moves ahead. She stormed into the store. "Where the fuck is my brother?"

The response came from the back. "Come on in and join the fun!" Bumpy

Johnson stuck his head through the sliding door and offered a smile. Rita walked over to Bruce, who sat in a chair in the center of the room with blood trickling from his lip.

"Welcome to the party. I'm getting acquainted with your brother, who seems to be kind of an odd fella. Keeps saying things like, 'How dare you!' He also thinks it is important for me to understand that he's a gentleman." Bumpy looked back at Bruce. "The thing is, I *dare* to do things because I can and nobody gives a rat's ass that you're a gentleman. Time to answer the question at hand. What did you do with the money you stole!"

"I didn't steal a thing. I stayed in my room like I always do. This is preposterous. Let me go!"

Rita walked straight up to Bumpy. Her five-foot-seven-inch height, coupled with the high heels she'd worn to impress the court officials, enabled her to tower over Johnson. Tito advanced and stood by her side. Bumpy waved and his two men stepped forward as well. He cautioned, "Mind your manners, folks; you don't want to do something that you won't be able to take back later."

Rita took a deep breath before she said her piece. "You're missing the point here. What my brother said is true. He always sits in his room with the music playing to block out the sounds of the business. One or more of the men could have been involved. George called Tito out of the apartment to help with a problem and they left Sanders by the door. When he came back, Bruce was still in his room and Sanders was knocked out cold on the floor of the kitchen. I'm going to guess that everything I just said lined up with what he told you."

Bumpy stroked his chin with his right hand and looked back and forth between the brother and sister. Rita interpreted this as a neutral response. He was not yet convinced of Bruce's innocence. She was tempted to tell him about Ilva's report of the two policemen, but that might lead to an interaction between Bumpy and Ilva. Rita thought, *There's no way I'll ever let that happen.* She continued, "We'll cover the entire bank for the day, and you should keep investigating, but move on to George and Sanders. If in the end you can't figure out what happened, the financial loss will be on me and my husband, but we'll want to replace every single person who worked in the building today. You're done now with my brother. I've got all the respect in the world for you, Bumpy, but he didn't do a thing and he's blood. You got to let him be."

Bumpy took a seat behind the small desk against the wall and rubbed his chin one last time. "Okay, there is something to what you're saying, but I'm not agreeing that this is my last conversation with this *gentleman* over here who I somehow *dare* to speak to." The men laughed. "You can take him home and I will have a few other conversations tonight. Meet me for breakfast in the morning at the diner over on 120th and we'll settle things then. Come alone."

CHAPTER 8

Blood

ALL HEADS TURNED as Rita entered the diner. Some because of her looks, others because of her walk or her insistence on wearing fur in May, but most turned because of who she'd become in the Harlem numbers racket. She worked the crowd on her way to Bumpy's table in the back. As soon as she sat, Queenie quietly entered the restaurant's seating area from the kitchen. A low buzz of whispers filled the air as the diners became both excited and somewhat concerned about the presence of this powerful threesome in their midst. Two of Queenie's men joined Bumpy's entourage and took positions by the front door.

The three colleagues exchanged nods as the waitress poured coffee and looked to Queenie for instructions. "Nothing right now," she said. "This is more of a meeting than a meal." The server excused herself and Queenie opened the conversation, "Bumpy, tell her what you found out."

"You were right, Rita. George met up with two cops last night. Looks like they got to him during holding and hatched up a plot to rob us." Johnson smirked. "We might have been better off if you hadn't done so well getting him out of jail the other night."

"So your brother is in the clear," Queenie said. "We won't need to talk to him again. Right, Bumpy?"

"Yes, Queenie. No need."

St. Clair continued, "We still need to talk about Tito. I'm not sure he's smart enough to run things on his own. Maybe yesterday would have gone different if you were there. Yes?"

Rita shrugged her shoulders.

"I understand he's the muscle and you're the brains, but he made mistakes yesterday."

Rita nodded and tried to interject.

Queenie held up her finger to shush her. "I'll split the loss with you this time because of all of the other work you're doing for me, but Tito needs to smarten up and handle things better or he's out and we'll find someone else. Understand?"

Rita nodded again. "Yes, I think that's more than fair."

"Not doing this because it's fair. This is a favor. You owe me."

Rita smiled and wondered what this would cost her in the future.

Queenie offered her final instructions. "I'm going to leave the two of you now. Stay and talk about last night—can't have bad blood between two of my most important people, so work this out. *Au revoir.*" All heads turned again as the boss headed for the door.

"How about some breakfast, Rita?" Bumpy asked.

Rita stood and picked up her pocketbook. "I'm not sure I can stay. I need to—"

"Nope, don't even try it. We are under orders to kiss and make up. You heard her."

She returned to her seat. "Let's check out the menu."

"Before we do, I want to mention how much of an odd little fish I found your brother to be. He appeared about as fucked up and guilty as anyone I ever met. It was good you came when you did. Otherwise, the *making up* part would have been so much harder." Bumpy chuckled as Rita straightened her back and stared at her associate without looking away.

"Excellent! You just defined the limit—that's always important," Bumpy said.

"I'm not following you."

"The look you just gave me is the furthest you can go questioning me or going against me in any way. So, if you ever go beyond that point to my face or behind my back with your new friend, Queenie, it will be the last thing you do." Bumpy stood and threw some bills next to his coffee cup. "The eggs are on me."

⊷▭◯ ◯▭⊶

Bruce and Rita took seats on either side of the dining room table. At ten in the morning, the rest of the family was at school or out running errands, except for Tito, who knew to stay out of sight. Bruce handed his sister a coffee mug and she bent her head to take in the aroma. "What a wonderful smell! It reminds me of mornings in Trinidad. Do you remember sitting with Daddy at the table while he drank his coffee?"

"Yes, I do. My memories from Trinidad are the best part of my life. I'm miserable here in New York. People never give me respect. None at all."

"You won't get any by shouting from the rooftops that you're the son of a gentleman or with any of your *how dare you* speeches."

Bruce let her words sink in. "It's so hard. The way they treat me. The shit jobs they offer me . . ."

"You may not like how I went about it, but I found my way, so now you need to find yours."

"You surprised me last night. After the threat you made the day before, why did you stick your neck out for me?"

"Because nothing is thicker than blood and if anyone is going to kick your ass, it will be family, not Bumpy Johnson." Rita paused and took a final sip from her mug, "I'll always look out for you, even though you continue to be the biggest *pimp* I ever met!" Brother and sister smiled and then hugged as he whispered, "Goddamn *whore*."

Part Three

Long Island
2009

CHAPTER 9

Another Sunday

"Mom, I read Aunt Rita's diary, did some additional research, and I weaved everything into a story of sorts."

"This is so exciting, Dustin!"

"I'll read it to you and then we can talk."

Ilva took her tea into the living room and made herself comfortable on the couch. Dustin turned the lights down and said, "For the proper mood." He took out his notepad and turned so the pad would be out of his mother's line of sight. Dustin told her the story of Aunt Rita, Bumpy Johnson, and the rest of the gang.

Once he was done, his mother smiled, reached for the pad, and laughed. "I was right? You didn't write a damn word!"

"What gave me away?"

"You spoke for fifteen minutes but only flipped the pages twice."

Dustin slapped his knee. "You caught me!"

"Did anyone ever tell you that you're a natural storyteller?"

"My mother may have once or twice." He winked.

"This is perfect for your brother and sister, but I lived through it and also spent a fair amount of time with the diary. Tell me, how much of the story was from what you read or researched and how much is pure bullshit you added to make it flow?" She smiled.

"I'll give you percentages: forty percent from what I read or researched and twenty percent made up. Did you like my little embellishments?"

"Yes, son, although you need to be careful not to stray too far. Your percentages only add up to sixty. Where did the rest of the story come from?"

"A dream."

Ilva coughed and took a sip of water. "I don't understand. A dream?"

"Yeah, they began over the last few weeks. Anything I read or study right before I fall asleep becomes the subject of my dreams. Odd, right?"

"Unusual for sure." She paused again. "Do these dreams upset you?"

"No, Mom. They're nothing more than pure imagination. I guess I should add the dream portion to the made-up category."

"Perhaps not," she answered.

"What do you mean by that?"

"You and I have something in common that I developed over the last thirty years or so with my excursions to Virginia Beach. I'm sure you remember me going away for those trips. I would get readings and take seminars at the institute I attended during the summer. They helped me to hone certain skills. Sometimes I sense things with touch."

"What does that have to do with my dreams?"

"Your skill relates to what you see and your visions take the form of dreams."

"I'm not sure how you came to that conclusion, but last night my dream was vivid, like I was above the action looking down."

"So, you're looking down as an observer?"

"Yeah, pretty much."

Ilva nodded and manipulated the spine of the writing pad. She turned to Dustin and then looked away.

"Mom, is something wrong?"

"No, I think we should spend more time talking about your dreams, but maybe another day. Let's finish with your Aunt Rita. What surprised you the most about her story?"

"Well, I did see her in a whole different light. I thought about the newspaper article we pulled out of the stack—the one about the mother of three who was arrested for prostitution. Not that Aunt Rita was a prostitute, but she did what she had to do to feed her family."

"I'm glad you got my point. You had no idea about all of this?"

"None whatsoever."

"I thought the stripteases she did for you and your brother when you were teenagers might have suggested a thing or two!"

"I remember those New Year's Eve dances. They were kind of weird when you think about it." Dustin laughed.

"Yes, we all thought the same thing, except for Rita. What else surprised you?"

"Some of the people she was involved with became very famous. I saw a movie about Bumpy Johnson a couple of years ago. I remember Stephanie St. Clair as well from the movie and her battle with the famous gangster, Dutch Schultz."

"I saw it also, but they got one thing wrong. In one of the opening scenes, they show another policymaker by the name of Henry Miro being dragged out of his bed to be presented to Dutch Schultz. The scene had Henry standing up to Dutch and saying he had big balls."

"I remember. It got much worse for Miro right after he made that statement."

"Indeed, it did, Dustin, but believe me . . . no one cut off Henry Miro's testicles."

"I'm afraid to ask for your source of information."

Ilva laughed. "Rita worked for Queenie until they had a falling out. In 1936, she went to provide similar services to Miro. A year later, the authorities brought the two of them up on charges and they fled to France in 1937. Rita would have never gone away with him if he had no balls!"

"Can we talk about something else? I really don't need to listen to my mother tell me a story about my Great-Aunt Rita's involvement with some man's balls. This is wrong on so many levels!" They both chuckled.

"Well, in any case, her marriage to Tito ended with her departure to France. We all missed him so much after he left, and things got tight in terms of money, but I learned more during those years about the importance of family and standing by their side, right or wrong, than in any other part of my life."

"I got it, Mom. Do what you need to do and there's nothing thicker than blood. I also learned some disturbing things about Grandpa Bruce."

"Yes, my father was a troubled man and you got the tension between him and Rita down right. They didn't like each other, but that was no reason to stop watching out for one another." Ilva looked up and to the right and fiddled with a button on her blouse before finishing her thought. "He stopped abusing my mother right after the incident in your story, but it started up again when Rita left for France. As we all got older, he didn't try to pull his shit with us, but he never stopped with my mom."

"That's why she always lived with us?"

"Yes. Once I was married and had a place for her to move to, she left him. The last forty years of her life with us in Hicksville were her happiest." Ilva patted her son on the shoulder. "You're picking things up quickly. It may be time to go back a little further, but I am worried about the dreams. Are you sure they're pleasant?"

"Yes, but the endings are abrupt. My muscles contract and I pop up in my bed. At first, the feeling is like pain, but once I'm awake, I realize it was all in my head. I don't know what to make of it."

Ilva turned away from Dustin and reached for a napkin to dab her eye. She started playing again with the spine of the writing pad.

"Are you okay, Mom?"

"Yes, I guess I was doing a little of my own daydreaming. We'll talk more about the dreams another time because they might help you to learn more about yourself. Never in the history of this family has any adult member picked up and moved as much as you. It means something, Dustin, and you need to figure out what. You can't spend the rest of your life living out of boxes. Why do you think you move so much, son?"

Dustin took time to consider his response. "Honestly, I have no idea, but I do find the question disturbing."

"I'm not trying to upset you, but if the question disturbs you, the answer might serve you."

"Nice rhyme, Mom."

She smiled.

"I have a question for you, too. Aunt Grace left me a note mentioning my *lost month* back when I was ten years old. What was that all about?"

Ilva exhaled before responding. "Why are you bringing this up after all of these years?"

Dustin tried to see his mother's eyes, but she looked off to the side. "Tell me about that time—all I can remember is changing schools when I was around ten."

Ilva clutched her glass and turned to her son. "You had some adjustment problems and we changed your school. You don't remember anything else from back then?"

"No, it was so long ago."

"As I said, you had some issues, behavior kinds of things, and we put you in a program for about five weeks to get you back on track. Nothing so interesting or exciting. Everything worked out."

"Why can't I recall anything about it?"

Ilva lowered her head, but then raised it with some energy. "Now, how would I know that? Let's shift gears because you have more work to do. Time for your next assignment and this one may take a little longer for you to complete. My grandmother Julia was the youngest of thirteen children born to Joseph Julian. His portrait, the one hanging in your apartment, was painted of him in the 1850s. His story is an interesting one. Look into this line of the family next."

"Okay, Mom. The Julians will be next."

CHAPTER 10

Daddy's Watching

DUSTIN SAT WITH his coffee in The Castle and admired his somewhat obstructed view of the foliage across the street. He opened his arms. *This may be the place that finally becomes home.* Today was the day he would begin his work on the Julians, but first he needed a little more energy. Time for his second cup.

He stopped by the portrait on the way back upstairs. "Okay, Grandpa Joe . . . your turn. Apparently, you've got a story to tell. I know you enjoy the scenery as much as I do, and today does look like a beautiful day, but I'm going to make you work." Dustin toasted the likeness with his mug.

He stood in one of the openings in The Castle and scanned the street. A statuesque woman walked at a snail's pace with a baby carriage on the sidewalk across from him. Her dark complexion contrasted well with her white blouse and slacks, but her beauty was more than skin deep. The cadence of her walk mesmerized him as she stepped in threes. *My God*, he thought, *this isn't a walk, it's a waltz!* An image of a party appeared in Dustin's mind as his total concentration on the woman's rhythm morphed into a vivid daydream.

He hovered above a party for a teenage girl and looked down at the festivities. The guests were decked out in formal clothing, but not modern styles. A waltz played in the background and a father beamed as his daughter made her grand entrance.

Dustin snapped out of his state as the woman stopped her carriage directly across from him and called out, "Hello, up there! Beautiful day!" Her voice startled him and he spilled some coffee over the side of the wall. She laughed. Dustin shrugged his shoulders and offered a toast with his somewhat empty mug.

Time to get started. He returned to the protection of his walls and summarized everything he knew about the Julians from Aunt Grace's notes:

The Julians were from Marseilles, France, and wound up in St. Croix in the Virgin Islands. Joseph Julian descended from a long line of Jewish merchants. He married Julia Stewart, an Anglican woman, and they had thirteen children over a period of twenty-three years. Ilva's grandmother, Julia, was named after her mother and became the youngest child when her sister (Rachel, born in 1871) passed away as an infant. All of the children grew up in the Anglican faith.

The family's wealth held out for a few years after Joseph and Julia passed, until one of the siblings either mismanaged or absconded with the funds. The children all went their separate ways, seeking opportunities or support elsewhere. Fifteen-year-old Julia left with one of her older sisters to Trinidad, where she became a child bride to a man by the name of Henry Mackinnon Iles. Julia became the caretaker of the portrait of her father and she subsequently traveled from Trinidad to London and finally to New York.

Dustin realized he had several leads to follow and logged into his Ancestry.com account. He established the Julian line of the family and populated the tree with all of the names and approximate dates of birth and death he could find. Hints started to appear and he found a Danish census from St. Croix that displayed the entire family. Dustin had gotten to know Julia from Aunt Rita's diary, so he paid more attention to anything he found involving her. He was also fascinated that her parents had wed months before her birth. *They waited twenty-one years to marry and only did so after their twelfth child? It doesn't make sense.*

One of the Julian children had the same name as his mother—Ilva—and Dustin wondered about the connection. The Ancestry system provided several birth and death citations, which needed to be investigated. Before reviewing those records, he went into the community tab and posted a picture of the Joseph Julian painting, along with a request for any additional information anyone might have about his background.

Information about Ilva Julian was abundant and Dustin printed everything he found for further examination. He scratched his head as he typed the name of the cemetery into the browser on his phone and clicked the link for directions. The calculated length of his trip was a one-minute walk.

He rushed across the street in search of the cemetery's administrative office and was greeted by a staff member.

"Welcome, my name is Mary Roberts. How may I be of service?"

Dustin nodded. "I'm trying to locate a plot. The name and date of death of an ancestor of mine are both listed on this paper."

The clerk checked her system and jotted the location of the plot onto Dustin's printout. She said, "The general vicinity of the plot will be easy to find, but the exact spot will be tricky."

"Why?"

"Well, it's by the gate, but your ancestor has an unmarked grave. You walked right by her when you entered the grounds. I tell you what, I'm leaving for the day and I'm parked on the street outside the gate. I'll be more than happy to help you find the location."

"Thanks. I just moved to this neighborhood. I hope everyone is as friendly as you."

"It really is no trouble at all. Give me a minute."

⊹═◉ ◉═⊹

Dustin pointed to his apartment building as it came into view.

"I love the top terrace with the walls like a rampart," Mary said. "Did they tell you that this apartment house was created out of an old factory?"

"Yes, I heard that and, by the way, the terrace you like is connected to my apartment and it has a name."

"What is it?"

"The Castle."

"A fitting name! Here we are. Ilva Julian is buried in this grassy area." She counted off ten paces from the street border and found a small plug in the ground with a numeric marking. "This spot, to be exact."

Dustin was speechless. How could it be the same section he jokingly stared at while standing by the portrait? Mary interrupted his thoughts. "Mr. Murphy, are you okay? I said this is it."

"Yes, yes, thanks so much. It is just so farfetched that this would be the spot."

"How so?"

"Look at my apartment—the living room is straight ahead." He motioned toward the building. "The entire wall is made of glass."

"Okay, hold on. I'll use the zoom lens on my camera. Let me get my phone." Mary zoomed in on Dustin's apartment. "What a lovely painting. Seems quite old."

"It was painted around 1850 or so."

"Who is it?"

He pointed to the plot. "Her father."

CHAPTER 11

Good Morning, Cousin

DUSTIN ENJOYED OBSERVING the scene from above in The Castle. He spotted a man walking with determination—*heading for the subway, I bet.* A woman with a concerned look on her face talking on her phone—*hard to say, maybe a problem with her child.* The stories flowed in his mind with unlimited possibilities. He took one last gaze across the street.

The unbelievable nature of his recent revelation gave him pause and he considered some deeper explanation of why he had moved to this particular building in Queens after spending so many years bouncing around Manhattan. His search began as it always did on Google with the phrase "luxury apartments in New York with balconies." The fact that a place in Queens popped up at the top of the results piqued his interest. All of Dustin's residences had had terraces and enough space for him to spread his arms. In this regard, the Queens duplex was overqualified, but he still could not process the overwhelming coincidence of a father and daughter being reunited in a distant land a hundred and forty years after their last interaction.

The news about Ilva Julian was groundbreaking, but Dustin liked the idea of letting his findings build up for his Sunday visit to Hicksville, so he tried his best to avoid the research topic when he spoke to his mother during the week. His list of discoveries broadened further when he woke up the next morning to the following email in response to his Ancestry.com posting:

Morning, Cousin,

I read your post about Joseph Julian. He's also my ancestor! I descend from one of the other children. You'll be pleased to learn that you have relatives all over the world. The painting is wonderful and it is so hard to believe it survived all these years.

The Julian line has been researched by a couple of other relatives I will introduce

you to. We can trace the family all the way back to Oporto, Portugal, in the late 1500s. Due to persecution, Sephardic Jews, like the Julians, moved from place to place. Their path to St. Croix went from Oporto to Amsterdam to Recife in Brazil. From there they went to Curacao, St. Domingue, and finally St. Croix. The French connection was not Marseilles, but rather St. Domingue, the wealthiest French colony in the Caribbean. The Julians departed right before the Slave Revolution in 1803 that created what is now Haiti. With your permission, I'm going to circulate your email to some other descendants and ask them to forward their information to you.
Freddi

The Ancestry cousins proved to be a motivated and efficient group. Dustin had pieced together the tale by Saturday morning. The Julians and the Stewarts had been neighbors on the same block dating back to the 1820s. Julia Virginia Stewart had been of mixed race. She had maintained a separate address from Joseph for many years after they'd begun having children. Dustin was surprised to discover the Sephardic Jewish line in his family and now learned of a mixed-race family member. He wondered why the couple had waited so long to wed.

Additional digging uncovered the fact that Jews in St. Croix had possessed full economic rights from the beginning of the 1800s but limited civil rights until 1814. Intermarriage with Christians was permitted in 1835. Slavery had remained in effect until 1848 and mixed-race individuals like Julia Virginia Stewart were not accepted by White society. The couple had begun having children around the time of the end of slavery, when St. Croix had not been ready to accept the union of a Jewish man and a multiracial woman. It might have taken twenty years and eleven children to make the couple comfortable enough to marry in 1869. Unfortunately, the death of their last child in 1873 of a contagious whooping cough had also caused the demise of both the father and the mother soon thereafter.

Dustin reviewed his discoveries and began to comprehend the enormous challenges faced by this branch of the family. If his great-great-grandmother was mixed, so were her children and grandchildren. He thought, *Perhaps this was the reason my Grandpa Bruce struggled so in New York in the 1930s?* Dustin's father was pure Irish, but his mother's family was always presented as European Caribbean, a term he could never define to anyone's satisfaction. He had so much to present to his mother on Sunday but now he had some fairly significant questions as well.

CHAPTER 12

Walls

"SUNDAY WITH A twist, Mom," Dustin suggested as he picked his mother up to spend a day in his new apartment. The beautiful seventy-degree, sunny weather made the Mets game at Citifield a popular destination—the traffic heading into Queens provided proof of that fact. Dustin was prepared with both his findings and questions as he inched along the Long Island Expressway toward Queens.

"What did you discover during the week, Dustin? Did you put your thoughts together like a story? The way you did with the diary?"

"No, but I did receive a lot of background from two cousins I found online and developed some theories from what they forwarded. By the way, they were impressed with the portrait. I sent them pictures."

"We've safeguarded that painting for a hundred and fifty years. What are your theories?"

Dustin explained his research about the Julians and the Stewarts along with his thoughts on why they'd waited so long to marry. His mother took it all in and asked, "First time I ever heard you use the phrase mixed-race. How did you feel about that?"

"Like another piece of the puzzle fell into place."

Ilva thought about his response and started to speak. "But . . ." She stopped and switched gears. "Do you think we'll be able to meet our newly found relatives?"

"Not sure—they don't live in New York."

"That's too bad. What else did you find out?"

"I have more to tell you, but let's wait until we get to my place because this you have to see to believe."

"Very mysterious, my son, but yes, let's wait. Happy to play along."

After pulling into the basement garage, mother and son settled into the elevator. "Excuse me, Mr. Big Shot, the penthouse floor—how fancy!"

Ilva paused as she approached the apartment door and pressed her hand against the wood. "Once we're inside, give me a chance to explore. Something is unique here and I want to walk around for a while by myself to take it all in. Okay?"

"Sure."

Ilva walked to the window and touched the glass and then back to the painting. "How do you like your new home, Grandpa Joe?"

Dustin laughed. "I call him the same thing!"

Ilva put her hands on the glass for a second time and went upstairs. After a few minutes, she called down to her son. "Let's sit in this marvelous terrace with the walls. Bring me a drink."

He placed his mother's beverage on a small end table next to her chair.

"This is your spot, isn't it?" she asked.

"Why, yes, Mom. It is."

"Did you figure out yet what it is about you and terraces?"

"No, not really. I just like them."

"What about this one? Can't you see why you like it so much? For such a sharp man, you can be awfully blind."

Dustin shrugged and took a sip of his drink. "Why do you say that?"

"Being up on a terrace enables you to look down on all the life taking place below. But you're not in it, you're above it and on this terrace, you're also hidden from sight by the walls. You're looking down on the world as an observer, Dustin, just like in your dreams."

Dustin forced a smile as he sat in the chair beside her with his scotch. He had broken out his Macallan 18 for the occasion of his mother's first visit to his new place and took a sip. "I'm not sure what all of this means, but I do like it up here and this definitely is my favorite terrace of all time."

"Interesting. Your massive terrace overlooking the Hudson on Forty-First Street has been overtaken as the favorite by a small ten-by-ten partially enclosed box next to a cemetery in Queens. It's the walls—you're hiding up here, son."

"Enough with the terraces and the walls. I get it. I'm isolated, disconnected, responsible for nothing. Believe me, I understand my circumstance. It's how I am, Mom. I'll think about everything you say as I always do, but let's change the topic."

"Okay, I'll stop, but why did you put Grandpa Joe where you did?"

"Somehow, I thought he would enjoy the view." He laughed and took another sip of Macallan.

"I agree. The energy downstairs is palpable. I think you may have sensed something as well. Perhaps in one of your dreams? Something to do with the cemetery. Am I right?"

"It always freaks me out when you do this. How the hell do you know?"

"Calm down and open up your mind to new possibilities; you're like me. I sense things through touch and I do believe you see things in a special way. So, what is it about this cemetery?"

"I printed out a bunch of documents about the Julian family I found online and one of them was a burial certificate related to this cemetery."

She put down her beverage. "Who's buried there?"

"Your grandmother's sister, Ilva."

"Oh my God, Auntie Ilva! I'm named after her! Take me there now. Please— right now."

⇥◦ ◦⇤

Dustin grabbed two folding chairs from his patio and headed to the elevator with his mother. She was in excellent shape and sharp for a woman of eighty-five. She questioned the need for chairs. "For my benefit," he joked, but his mother didn't laugh. She was focused and not in the mood for any foolishness. Ilva almost ran into the street before Dustin pulled her back. "This isn't Hicksville—there are lots of cars in the streets and you need to be careful."

She nodded and let the line of cars pass before making her way to the grassy clearing by the gate. Instinctively, Ilva went to the spot without benefit of any direction. She kneeled and placed her hands, palms down, on the grass and cried. "Auntie Ilva was in New York all this time! Did you say she lived around here?"

"Yes, Mom, apparently she did."

"I could have seen her and been in her life. Why did she hide like this? And why is she in an unmarked grave? So sad."

"I don't have any of those answers, Mom, but why do you think she was hiding?"

"Because of the terrible fight so long ago between her and my grandmother."

"Why did they fight?"

"Too many questions. Everything isn't a research project! I never had the chance to properly mourn her, now give me my space. You go and sit in your chair or go back to your apartment inside your walls. I need some time here. Leave me be."

Dustin didn't understand what had brought on the outburst or any part of the sensitivities involving Aunt Ilva, but he did as he was told and sat on one of the chairs, shielding his mother from passersby who might wonder if she was okay. The doorman from his building also walked across the street to ask if she'd fallen and needed help. After about thirty minutes of crying and moaning, Ilva stood up, brushed off her pants, and said, "Take me home. You should have told me. I wasn't prepared. Now take me home." Not a word was spoken during the thirty-minute ride back to the suburbs.

⇥◉ ◉⇤

Dustin returned to his apartment and hypothesized about the difficulties between the two sisters. All of his family discoveries were summed up in his notes. *She's right, everything isn't a research project.* This could be anything, but given the prominence of racial and religious themes, he thought the greater likelihood rested with these issues being involved to some extent. In any case, the answer would not be found online and would only be provided by his mother should she choose to share.

He reflected on the stories of his Aunt Rita, Grandpa Bruce, and Great-Grandmother Julia and considered his own ethnicity. He thought, *Some mysteries can be solved with science.* Within minutes, he'd made arrangements for a DNA test.

He couldn't quite shake off his mother's harsh tone and started to look at some old family photographs through a new lens. He noted the darker complexion of his mother and, even more so, Aunt Grace, compared to others in the family. *Why was I oblivious to this for all of these years? God, my brother has red hair, and my sister, well . . . actually, she could be anything. What are my roots?*

A few days later, Ilva told Dustin she had a bad cold and he shouldn't visit on Sunday. She also lacked the strength to talk over the phone. The following week, she was invited to a party. It had been a long time since the mother and son missed two consecutive Sundays. Dustin suggested that he might pop over during the week to have a quick look at the bills. His mother's response—they can wait. So they did.

CHAPTER 13

Apology Accepted

Dustin waited for his brother and sister by the front door. Patrick, who preferred the nickname Paddy, exited the elevator, followed by Charlie, who gave serious lip service to anyone who dared to call her Charlotte.

"Dustin, this building is so different," Paddy said. "The terraces are amazing. Does every unit have one?"

"I think so."

Paddy smiled. "How many do you have?"

"Four. Come inside. I'll show you around."

Paddy and Charlie entered the apartment and headed toward the glass wall overlooking the cemetery. She asked, "And how many bedrooms?"

"Three."

Dustin avoided eye contact as his big sister leaned forward. He kept his head down and started to look off to the side. His gaze settled on the portrait of Grandpa Joe. Charlie snapped her fingers. "Dustin. Dustin, over here. The question is, why do you have four terraces and three bedrooms? Is all of this just for you?"

Dustin's eyes never left Grandpa Joe, who proved to be of no help whatsoever. Thankfully, the doorbell rang after an awkward silence and Dustin excused himself. "That must be the food. Why don't the two of you head upstairs and take a look around on your own?"

⋆━◯ ◯━⋆

Paddy pulled Charlie into the master bedroom once they had climbed the stairs and closed the door. He said, "Don't drill him so much. If he can afford a place like this, what difference does it make if it's just for him?"

"After all of these years, he's still such a little weirdo. I don't understand him, never did."

"And you're never going to get a chance to if you talk to him like that. Lighten up. Agreed?"

"Yes, sir!" She saluted. "Permission to tour the apartment, sir!"

"At ease, Private."

Paddy grabbed his sister by the arm as they headed into the smaller upstairs bedroom. They both saw the entrance to The Castle at the same time. Paddy said, "My God, what is this? I've never seen anything like it. A terrace with walls?"

"Of course, only our little brother would have a terrace with walls. I'm telling you, we'll never understand him."

"Charlie, you promised, so stop." Paddy twisted his two-hundred-and-sixty-pound frame into a ridiculous version of a pirouette, which caused his sister to laugh so hard that she needed to hold onto the doorframe for support.

"Okay, I get it. Keep it light, like you!" she said.

Paddy claimed that he needed to use the bathroom and returned to the master bedroom. He headed straight for the large walk-in closet and took a quick step back as he looked down. Nothing had changed. Childhood memories of the small bedroom that he had shared with his younger brother filled his mind. Paddy waded through a fog of images and feelings and considered what he could have done differently years ago to make things better, but realized the futility of his thoughts. He closed the closet door and called out to his sister, "Let's head downstairs."

⊷▭◯ ◯▭⊶

Paddy gave his brother a subtle thumbs-up as they took their seats at the table. He had a knack for making bad situations better with his humor, even as a child. Over the years, Paddy had fine-tuned the physical aspects of his repertoire and added an impressive potbelly as a prop, which took his impromptu comedy to the next level. Everyone loved him, Dustin included.

"Sushi?" Paddy said. "Does it look like I eat a lot of raw fish?"

Dustin answered, "I did order one hot dish, chicken teriyaki."

"The chicken is mine," Paddy said as he reached for the container.

The conversation remained surface-level until Charlie made an observation. "This is a little creepy, Dustin. It's almost like he's joining us for dinner." She motioned to the portrait of their great-great-grandfather, which hung behind their chairs.

"Well, if he is, you better tell him to keep his hands off my chicken!" Paddy warned as he held up his fork in a defensive posture.

Dustin joked, "Oh, don't worry about Grandpa Joe, he's at home now that I reunited him with his daughter."

Charlie rested her glass on the table and straightened up in her chair. Dustin felt it coming and turned his head sideways toward the staircase. She asked, "Dustin, what could you possibly mean by that? I'm trying to be nice here, but you and Mom are talking about nonsensical things. She's eighty-five, Dustin. What's your excuse?"

Paddy raised his hands. "Easy. . . let's finish eating in peace." He nodded to his sister. "Give me some of your Pittsburgh roll."

"It's a Philadelphia roll, you idiot!" Charlie said as she play-punched him in the shoulder.

Paddy smirked. "Oh, pardon me for committing such a horrible sushi sin!"

Dustin spent the next thirty minutes explaining everything he'd done and found out since the initial request to investigate the family history a few weeks earlier. "Quite a story, Dustin," Paddy said. "First, I agree with Charlie. Grandpa Joe is creeping me out too. He really is staring at his daughter's gravesite, but all of this crap about what Mom thought when she sat down on Aunt Ilva's plot is a little farfetched."

"For me too," Dustin said.

"The thing is, though, I shared a room with you for seventeen years until I went into the army and I heard you at night," Paddy said. "Some of what you cried out in your sleep back then was dark and hard to understand. Sometimes I woke up and found Mom sitting next to your bed with a notepad. You were always a little different. Don't take any offense."

"I almost think I should thank you guys for not calling me a *little weirdo*."

Charlie glanced at Paddy, who raised his eyebrows. "I'm sorry about that, Dustin," she said. "I was cruel as a kid."

Paddy stared at her again.

"And some of that cruelty may have followed me into adulthood. Sorry," she added.

Dustin's eyes connected with Charlie's, and she smiled before bringing the conversation back to the topic at hand. "You explained a lot, Dustin, but why was Mom so upset?"

"I planned to accumulate my discoveries and deliver them all at once on Sunday. I thought this would be better because we could talk about them in person, but she needed advance warning about Aunt Ilva—her namesake."

"Yeah, I didn't realize she was named after someone," Paddy said.

Dustin continued, "It seems like there was a lot that she never told us. Great-Grandma Julia had a falling out with her sister, Ilva." They all turned and stared at the portrait as if they expected some commentary to emerge from the canvas. "And they never recovered from this fight. Aunt Ilva left the city and the family thought she moved far away, but she lived right around here and likely died alone because she's buried in an unmarked grave. Mom became angry with me when I asked her what they fought about."

"She'll tell us when she's ready," Charlie said.

The three siblings all contemplated Charlie's last statement, which rang true for all of them. There was no rushing Ilva Murphy. She spoke about things on her own schedule and in her own way. Charlie rose from her seat and announced, "I've got to head out for a big date." She took a step away from the table and laughed as her attempt to strike a pose resulted in a stumble. "How do I look?"

Paddy answered, "You're both the hottest and clumsiest fifty-four-year-old on the island."

"You had to work in the age, didn't you?" Charlie bit her lip as she hit Paddy in the arm—her signature move.

Dustin recalled Charlie's *how do I look* question from their childhood. Sometimes it was asked after she'd rushed down the stairs and tripped on the last step. On other occasions, she'd offered it as she jutted out her arms, knocking something off a shelf or slapping someone in the face. Dustin turned to her. "Okay, you can go in a few minutes, but I have one thing to ask both of you and then something else I thought we would do together before you leave."

Charlie chuckled and punched Paddy in the arm yet again. He overreacted and claimed injury as she responded to Dustin, "What's the question?"

"What happened to me when I was ten?"

Both siblings froze and the smiles vanished. Dustin waited for a response, but none was offered, so he broke the silence. "What is it? What happened to me back then?"

Charlie held up her finger to stop Paddy from answering. "Why did you bring this up?"

"Aunt Grace mentioned it in a letter she wrote me before she passed. I read it the other day."

Paddy jumped in. "This may not be the best time to talk about this and I'm not sure that Charlie and I are the right people to give you an answer. Ask Mom. I was twelve and Charlie was fifteen. We were so young."

Every word that Paddy offered pressed a different button for Dustin and all of them were bad. He hesitated before responding, but the moment of reflection did not prove to be constructive.

"Listen to yourselves," he said. "*Why did I bring it up? Ask Mom. We were so young.* Why are the two of you dodging my question? I want to know what happened and I will ask Mom, but the two of you should be willing to tell me what you can."

Charlie began, "Dustin, we're—"

Paddy interrupted his sister. "Sorry, he's right. We've dodged this for years. I'll tell you what I remember and Charlie can chime in whenever she likes, but as I said, Mom has the answers."

"Thank you," Dustin said.

"Your dreams became a problem. Every night you screamed stuff in your sleep. It was scary. Mom took you somewhere because of them. The two of you were gone for over a month and I remember you changing schools when you returned. You went through some bad shit back then."

"What do you mean, my dreams were scary? What kind of bad shit?"

"Hold on, this is what I can tell you," Paddy said. "Every night you woke up screaming. After a while, I made out some of the words. You repeated names and then screamed like someone was attacking you. You made me a nervous wreck."

Dustin thought back to his younger days and couldn't recall the dreams. He couldn't remember anything. "What names? What attack?"

"You called out Grace and Charlie. I don't know anything about who attacked you, but I'm sorry about what I did—I didn't understand what would happen if I told."

"Told who?"

"Dad."

Charlie finally added to the conversation. "He didn't take it well and that's why you were sent away."

"What the hell are the two of you saying?! What do you mean? Where was I sent?"

"Dustin, you really don't remember anything at all?" Charlie asked.

"Nothing."

"Okay, I was fifteen, so I understood better than Paddy and I overheard a few conversations. Dad didn't believe people could be fixed."

"Fixed? What are you saying? What happened to me during that month?" Dustin's breathing became heavy and his foot tapping quickened. He looked out the window and his mind followed his gaze to a tree across the street in the cemetery. He turned to look back at the scene from a distance but wasn't far enough away. Charlie pulled him back when she reached over to steady his leg. "Please calm down. *Fixed* was his word, not mine. We're doing our best here. The bottom line is that we have no idea where you went or what happened when you got there, but Mom went with you and said she never left your side. To be honest, you frightened me when you came back—you just seemed so far away. This is hard to talk about. Are you sure you want to rehash all of this? Why does it matter anymore?"

Dustin's leg movements slowed, as did his speech. "You said Dad didn't think people with problems could be *fixed*. What *did* he think?"

"He believed certain people should be institutionalized for their own sake and for the welfare of their family. You scared him," she said.

Dustin jumped up from the sofa and went to the window. He folded his arms and kept his back to his brother and sister. "My father wanted to stick me in an institution. Isn't that great—with a family like this, it's no wonder things turned out the way they did for me. I think both of you should go."

"I'm sorry, Dustin," Paddy said. "I feel terrible. I never should have told."

"Me too, I was older. Maybe I could have helped in some way," Charlie added. "Come back to the couch. We can't end the night like this. In our defense, we had no way of knowing that you lost your memory of this. To us, this was something bad that neither our mother or brother had any interest in discussing. Be fair, Dustin."

Dustin noted the tear running down the right side of Charlie's face. Paddy was unable to look up at all and sat with his hands folded in front of him. Dustin reconsidered as Charlie's comments began to resonate, but he remained silent, still unsure if he could forgive so quickly. *But how can I hold them accountable? Maybe she's right . . . they didn't know I'd forgotten or somehow blocked the memory.* Dustin returned to the sofa. "Okay, just tell me everything you know. Get it all out."

Charlie started. "Mom took you out of school and the two of you left, but we don't know where. The dreams stopped, but you were different when you came back. We all acted like nothing ever happened." She put her arm around her baby brother's shoulders. "Dad and Aunt Grace are dead, so the only one left who knows what happened is Mom—she was there by your side. Like we said before, you should ask her, but whether she'll answer is a whole other matter. Let's hang out some more. I'm cancelling my date." She pulled out her cell phone and sent a message to clear her schedule.

Paddy got up and rocked back and forth as he held his side. His facial expressions reminded Dustin of the kind of overacting that silent movie stars were guilty of in the early days of film. He ramped up the intensity of his rocking and fell backward over the couch with a grace that belied the limits of his girth. He crawled up from behind the large piece of furniture with a dazed expression on his face and asked, "Did anyone get the license plate number of that truck?"

Charlie doubled over in laughter and Dustin's smile gave him a much-needed break from his heavy thoughts. It wasn't Paddy's funniest effort, but after so many years, Dustin read his actions the way that others read a sentence. He extended his hand to his big brother to both help him up as well as say *apology accepted.*

CHAPTER 14

Time to Tell

"DUSTIN, DID YOU say you wanted us to do something together?" Charlie asked.

"Yeah, but honestly, after that conversation, I'm not sure how many more surprises I can take tonight."

"I don't blame you for saying that, but if it's something that involves all three of us, let's end the night with that. What do you say?"

Dustin walked back to the couch. "Okay, I had my DNA tested. My laptop is hooked up to the television. The results should be very similar for both of you, so yes, this does affect us all. Let's look at the report together."

Dustin pulled his computer onto his lap and positioned the cursor over the link for the results.

"No, wait. I think I need some popcorn and milk duds," Paddy joked.

"Forget the milk duds. Believe me," Charlie said, patting Paddy's stomach. "You don't need them. Go ahead and click."

The percentages were displayed on the large screen. Dustin had suspected as much based on his research. Paddy, in particular, was in shock. Charlie nodded her head after digesting the meaning. She broke the silence. "This is what I always thought, although I didn't think the percentage would be so high."

Paddy muttered, "But . . . my hair is red."

"Wake up, Paddy," she said. "Didn't you ever consider the possibility?"

"No. Dad was pure Irish. Murphy is an Irish name. Uncle Jackie, Aunt Joan. Everybody is a hundred percent Irish."

"Only on Dad's side of the family. We're the mixture of two very different ethnicities," Dustin said.

Paddy raised his eyebrows. "You make us sound like cake mix."

Dustin studied the screen as bits and pieces of the family story started to make more sense:

Ireland/Scotland/Wales: 75%
Benin/Togo: 16%
Mali: 6%
Ivory Coast: 3%

Paddy raised his hands, palms up. "How do we explain this red hair and fair skin?"

"The seventy-five percent category," Dustin said. "Remember, the data might vary somewhat for each of us. The Ireland/Scotland/Wales piece might be eighty percent for you."

"And maybe the twenty-five percent African DNA is thirty percent for me," Charlie said.

"Only one way to find out. I sent for a couple of extra kits, in case either of you had an interest. Here you go." Dustin tossed them each a package. "Swab some saliva and send it off."

Charlie looked at her kit. "Dustin, why do we think Mom hid this for all these years?"

The word "hid" touched a chord and Dustin wondered where his sister was going with this question. He answered, "She was passing in an all-White neighborhood and needed to keep quiet."

Charlie raised her index finger. "No, that's more *what* she did, not why she did it."

"You're right," Dustin said. "The only way we'll find out for sure is to ask."

Paddy shrugged his shoulders. "Guys, just look at me."

"What? You still don't believe it's true?" Charlie asked.

Dustin remembered a video on the topic he watched earlier that day. "Wait, let's review the numbers and think about Mom for a minute. Everyone gets fifty percent of their DNA from each of their parents, but not necessarily the same fifty percent." Dustin turned to Charlie. "If you ran your DNA, it would likely be similar to mine—all of the categories should be represented, but the mix might be different. So despite the fact it doesn't exactly work like this, Mom has to be about fifty percent Black. The blood on the Julian side came from a mixed-race mother and a White father—Grandpa Joe over here, in case you're getting lost. For Mom to be fifty percent Black, I believe the Iles side also had to be multiracial."

"Come on, why does it matter?" Paddy asked. "We are who we are and our identities at this point in our lives are pretty much developed. I don't see how it changes anything."

"That may be true," Charlie said, "but shouldn't everyone understand where they came from? I always imagined we had a Black connection, especially when I spent time with our family in the city. It was hard to miss. Every time I asked, though, Mom shut me down with her vague *European Caribbean* definition. I got tired of asking."

Dustin paused as his siblings looked to him. "And I never asked."

Paddy, always looking for a punch line, offered, "And I didn't even know the question!"

Both Dustin and Charlie forced a smile and the three siblings sat in silence as each processed their thoughts and feelings. After some time, Dustin excused himself and walked outside on the terrace. He needed to think. Charlie and Paddy didn't follow and waved goodbye from inside. Dustin considered the scope and impact of the two secrets his mother kept from him, one for almost forty years and the other his entire life. It was time for another visit to Hicksville . . . time for her to tell.

CHAPTER 15

Waiting for Answers

DUSTIN BELIEVED IN a certain sequence for success and entered any business meeting with a plan for his first few opening topics, and perhaps most importantly, the close, but he struggled to identify the best order of topics for his meeting with his mother. It had been over four weeks since his last Sunday visit and there was a lot to cover.

He decided to first clear the air regarding their last time together in Queens. He had witnessed firsthand how difficult his mother could be once she dug in on an issue or a conflict and he hoped to avoid this scenario at all costs. Finally, he added a little insurance and picked up a bouquet of yellow tulips at the corner florist. *My ninety-eight-pound, eighty-five-year-old mother is making me shake in my boots.*

"Mom. Where are you?" Dustin called out as he walked around the ground floor. He almost tripped over an empty crate and grabbed the side of the dining room table to steady himself. After checking upstairs, the only remaining place to investigate was the basement. He hadn't been down there in over a year.

He turned sideways to squeeze through the clutter protruding from the shelves on both sides of the steps and made his way down to the cellar. Once at the bottom of the staircase, he could either go right into a sea of crap consisting of papers and boxes mixed in with old furniture and clothing, or to the laundry area to the left, where there was room to walk. He went left and found the dryer running, but not his mother.

Dustin followed the small winding path through the rubbish on the other side, which led him to his mother, who lay unconscious on the floor below the window. A small amount of blood trickled from her head.

Dustin checked her breathing, which was fine, but she was out cold. He couldn't imagine an ambulance crew walking through the narrow pathway with their equipment, so he carried her upstairs and laid her on the couch in the living room. Minutes later, the ambulance arrived and EMS techs helped her to regain consciousness. She reached for Dustin's hand. "I'm sorry, it was too much to process. I needed time."

"Don't worry about that now, Mom. What happened?"

"I was trying to open the back window and fell. I can't remember anything else."

The EMS technicians strapped her on a gurney and loaded her into the ambulance. The driver walked over to Dustin. "We're taking her to Plainview Hospital on Old Country Road. Do you know where that is?"

"Sure. I grew up here."

"You're her son, right?"

"Yes, one of them."

"I used to shovel snow for her when I was a teenager. She's a nice lady. The cut on her head isn't too deep, but she might have a concussion. Her right knee seems bad and may be why she fell. We'll see you at the hospital."

⊶⊷ ⊶⊷

The three siblings met in the hospital cafeteria to discuss plans moving forward. Their mother had a mild concussion from her fall, but the bigger issue was her right knee. Her doctor had advised her to get a knee replacement years before, but she'd kept putting it off. The surgery needed to be done as soon as she was strong enough. Charlie volunteered to care for her while Dustin and Paddy took the opportunity to clear out and clean up the house in Hicksville. Dustin understood that given this turn of events, his long-overdue conversation with his mother needed to wait.

CHAPTER 16

Dancing Lights

DUSTIN WORKED WITH his nephews, Anthony and Matthew, to clear out the main floor of the house in Hicksville. Paddy's absence didn't surprise any of the men because the agenda for the day did not include either cocktails or a meal. Toward the evening, Dustin ventured upstairs to plan the next day's work and became light-headed as he walked into his childhood bedroom. His condition worsened as he moved toward the old unpainted wooden desk that sat in the corner. Dustin's heart pounded and his chest felt tight. Matthew called up the stairs, "We're heading out, see you tomorrow."

Time slowed to a crawl as Dustin spent the next few hours walking through the house, touching anything that dated back to his childhood years in the hope that something would jar his memory—nothing did. His room, however, continued to trigger the same physical response and he concluded that whatever had happened back then had taken place in his room. His memory, however, still drew nothing but blanks.

Sleep often came at unusual times during the day for Dustin—almost as if his body insisted on shutting down when it needed to recharge. The problem was the evening when the rest of the world went to sleep and Dustin's body didn't sense a need. The clock mounted on the wall of the living room read 11:45 p.m. as he spread out on the couch, closed his eyes, and started to count, extending one finger every time he reached sixty. After he went through all ten fingers, Dustin opened his eyes to see if he properly estimated the ten-minute interval. He hoped his body would tire of the game, but at 1:00 a.m., it still wanted to play. Dustin concluded that in order to rest he needed to deal with whatever had disturbed him in his old room.

He climbed the stairs and sat at the top with his back against the wall. Rays of light from a lamp on the outside of the house streamed through three square panes of glass in the top of the front door. The muscle memory in Dustin's hands took control and he began tracing figure eights on the worn carpet around the columns of light. This had been his safe place, where he could hide in plain sight as long as his father was asleep. Dustin's eyes fluttered as he heard his dad's rhythmic snore. His figure eights moved from the carpet to midair as he circled the light beams to the rhythm of the snores and conducted the orchestra. The music responded to each of his movements. He thought, *I love leading the band,* but then the snoring went off cadence and the new, erratic pattern caused the rays to dance. Try as he might, the frenetic movements mesmerized him and he lost the fight. His eyes closed as more memories returned.

Ten-year-old Dustin sat at the dinner table with his family.

"Tell me again, Dustin, how was your day?"

"T-t-told you already, Daddy. O-o-kay."

"Dustin, I want you to think and take your time. You don't have to be as smart as Charlie or a comedian like Paddy. Don't try to compete with them. You only need to do simple things like holding a basic conversation, like a normal person. You don't have to be great at anything. Hell, there's nothing special about me, but I can hold a conversation as well as a job. This is what I want for you."

Paddy started playing a rhythm on the table with his hands and spilled his soda, which drew the attention of his father. "You damn fool of a boy. You think that's funny? Well, maybe you'll find going to bed tonight at eight funny as well. Damn idiot. Clean this up."

Charlie whispered to Dustin during their father's outburst, "Tell him you had fun playing at the park and he'll leave you alone."

Francis Murphy resumed his questioning. "No one is going to touch their food until you give me a proper answer. Dustin, how was your day?"

"Francis, please let us eat. *Please.*" Ilva lowered her head.

"I don't interfere with you when you address the children and I went along with your grand plan for Dustin, but he's got to learn. Dustin, how was your day?"

"My day was f-f-f-fine. I p-p-played in the p-p-p . . ."

"Just say it! Goddamnit! Spit it out. *Park.* How hard is that? I've got one son who's an idiot and another who's a lost cause. Have it your way, Ilva. I'm taking my plate into the other room."

Dustin's eyes opened slightly, and the beams stopped dancing but increased in intensity. He closed them to stop the burning and started to drift off again, but fought the feeling. He needed to stay awake to be safe. Dustin wanted to cover his eyes with his hands but couldn't move them. His dream took him into his room, where he sat in front of his desk. Paddy was asleep to his left. Dustin tried to be quiet, but the junk inside the drawers clanked and jiggled despite his best effort. A stapler fell onto the floor. Dustin listened for movement in his parents' room, but there was none. *Thank God*, he thought as he continued searching the bottom drawer—his secret hiding place.

He felt the hard cover and recalled that he had labeled it "Math." *Right where I left it*, he thought. Dustin pumped his right arm in the air and his celebration caused him to fall off his chair. The awkward contact with the floor woke him up and he realized this was not a dream. He found himself seated on the floor of his old bedroom, clutching his childhood dream journal. He returned to the seat, turned on the desktop lamp, and opened the book. All of the pages had been removed and a note addressed to him was scribbled on the inside back cover. The poor handwriting was very familiar. It read, "Dustin, some things are better off forgotten."

CHAPTER 17

Pieces of the Past

DUSTIN PLACED THE two oversized envelopes containing family artifacts that he found during the cleanup in Hicksville on top of the table in The Castle. He began with the one labeled *Murphy's Mayo*, which related to the pub the family had owned in the mid-1950s in Washington Heights. The name was a play on words. The Murphy family hailed from County Mayo in Ireland and the bar was known for a spicy mayonnaise.

He poured the contents of the envelope onto the table. The two mementos, an ashtray and a coaster, would be put to use right away in his apartment. An article from the *Amsterdam News* (1954), entitled "Footlight and Sidelights," stated the following: *Back on the uptown beat, we stopped at Murphy's Mayo at 3872 Broadway to take a gander at the famous Grain Room so many people talk about. The spot is a cozy, intimate one, air-conditioned and is the mecca for interracial patrons in upper Manhattan. Personal proprietors Jackie and Francis Murphy lead the most gracious staff we've run into in our many years covering the amusement scene.*

Dustin remembered how his father used to brag, "Before this, you either had to go to a White or a Black club. We broke new ground!" The bar had opened a year or so before his parents had gotten married and Dustin smiled as he found a picture of both of them standing in the front doorway with a sign mounted on the wall, *Murphyburgers, 85 Cents.*

After Murphy's Mayo, Dustin's Uncle Jackie had branched out with three bars in the Bronx. Another *Amsterdam News* article (1957) memorialized the donation made by his uncle and father to the NAACP, which related to one of these bars. Dustin had never heard this story until his early thirties and he recalled his uncle holding court at a family barbecue as he'd told the tale.

"After *Murphy's Mayo,* I thought we had the formula for a successful mixed-race bar—it needed to be in a borderline neighborhood between two or more groups. I scouted out the Bronx and found a possible place on East 139th Street, close to Third Avenue, but when I tried to go inside to check it out, the door was locked. I could see people through the window, so I banged harder. A few seconds later, a man shouted through a small compartment that opened at the top of the door, 'Hold your horses, fella. I just had to check you out to make sure you weren't one of *them*.'"

"One of *them*?"

"Oh, come on, don't act like you don't understand what I'm talking about. This place is for civilized people. Do you get what I mean?"

"Sure thing, let me in."

Jackie had put both hands on his beer as he continued. "The thing is, this Irish bar only admitted Whites, preferably Irish. But the place satisfied my formula as a perfect location, so I made the owner an offer and he accepted it. I just needed to quickly change its reputation as being racist."

Dustin remembered how everybody had waited with anticipation to hear what crazy thing Uncle Jackie had done. His brilliant idea had involved the staging of an NAACP rally in this formerly racist bar on St. Patrick's Day, during which the organization received a well-publicized donation. Dustin looked at the picture of his uncle and father handing over a check to the NAACP. *Pure marketing genius*, he thought. Dustin found it interesting that no matter what side of the family, issues of race were always present.

Nevis is next, Dustin thought as he emptied the light envelope onto the table. One item wrapped in newspaper fell out—a bill of sale in 1818 for a slave by the name of John Day. Dustin scratched his head. *John Day? It sounds so familiar.*

Dustin didn't have much else to go on and began searching in Ancestry. com for *John Day*. Hundreds of records came up but none appeared relevant. The next search, *Genealogy Research Nevis,* went out to the full web. Dustin reviewed the short list of results and composed an email asking for assistance from the Nevis Historical Society. The unmistakable sound of his sister's voice called out from below, "Are you up there, Dustin? Your doorman stepped away. Buzz me in."

⋆⟽ ⟾⋆

Charlie took a seat on the terrace with her brother. "Do you mind if we talk again about your *lost month*? Mom is starting to open up about our family history but isn't ready to offer full details of what happened when you were a kid. She wants you to know that she watched out for you and she asked me to be the go-between for now."

Dustin slammed his glass on the table. "After all of this time, I still have to wait for answers? This is ridiculous."

"I think we both know that if you push her on something like this, she'll never tell you a thing."

Dustin wiped up his spill with a napkin. "Unfortunately, you're right. So, what did she tell you?"

"She said that Dad took you to a psychiatrist who recommended a home for children with emotional problems. You scared him and he just couldn't deal with your issues on a daily basis, but Mom wouldn't agree."

"Thank God for that."

Charlie nodded. "She put you in some kind of a program designed to break your connection to your terrifying dream. She wouldn't tell me what they did or where you went but she said that she sat by your side and protected you."

"So, she didn't say anything new."

"I think she wants to provide the details herself but needs time to say certain things."

"No shit."

"In any case, the program fixed your immediate problem but changed you in many ways."

"Not the first time I heard the word *fixed*."

"I'm sorry, Dustin. Mom didn't use those exact words. I didn't mean to upset you. Believe me, I'm trying here."

"I'm just frustrated."

"I understand, but Mom needs me to be the intermediary, at least for now. She also was surprised to hear your dreams are back and she's worried that you may not have told her the truth about whether they are pleasant or not."

"She keeps asking that same question. I'm learning to channel my dreams right now. They are helpful. It is the end. Waking up is kind of a thing, but nothing to worry about."

"Now who's being mysterious . . . *waking up is kind of a thing?* Is this Dustin-speak for don't ask me to explain more? I'll accept that as long as you can be satisfied for now with the little bit I just told you. Mom wants you to focus on the family stuff with her on Sunday. Okay?"

Dustin found it so hard to believe that, after all this time, he still had to wait for the full story. He smiled at his sister and thanked her for stopping by. There was no reason to be upset with her. She was just the messenger delivering an unpopular message. Ilva Murphy needed to be ready to speak and, apparently, she was not. It was that simple, but still hard to accept.

CHAPTER 18

The Talk

"THE HOUSE IS terrific, Dustin, and you were smart to ask the boys to break the news to me about the cleanup. I told you to leave it alone, didn't I?"

Ilva acknowledged Dustin's mischievous smile with a smirk.

"Yes, Mom, but sometimes following instructions isn't the right thing to do. Look at how spacious your place is now. Isn't the house better without all of the clutter?"

"This clutter, as you call it, is my property. I'm eighty-five and I want all of my important things handy, even if *others* don't like how it looks." Ilva turned her nose up as she said the word *others*.

"Fair enough, but your house also needs to be safe."

"I appreciate what you're saying, but don't think you're calling the shots around here now!"

"I would never think such a thing! Enjoy your new house, Mom."

"I will."

Dustin unpacked the Chinese food—chicken wings, chicken fried rice, and wonton soup. "Can we talk about the day in the cemetery while we eat?" he asked.

"Sure. I can only imagine what you thought."

"I had no idea. Tell me."

Ilva stirred her soup as she gathered her thoughts. "My reaction was instinctive, but I had time to think about how I should explain."

"Excellent."

"Aunt Ilva was at the house a lot and a big part of the family when I was a young girl. She often picked me up from school and took me places, lots of times without my brother and sister. I enjoyed being her favorite."

"So you were special to her and she to you."

"Yes, she was Grandma Julia's older sister. Eight years older, to be exact. I remember the argument they had—it was at the end of the school year for me. She moved away and I never laid eyes on her again."

"What did they argue about?"

"I guess it boils down to *labels*. She did something that gave us one my grandmother tried hard to avoid."

"*Labels?* What do you mean?"

"Where we are from. I didn't disclose certain things to all of you . . ."

"Mom, I'm not sure why you never told us, but let me make this easier for you. We're mixed and the combination should not be described as European Caribbean, which means nothing. You're eighty-five and I'm almost fifty. When were you going to tell me?"

"Like I said a few weeks ago, my sister and I planned to tell you together when you turned forty."

"How does the age of forty make any sense? Why would you wait so long? I had a right to know."

Ilva stiffened her back as she raised her voice. "Right to know? What the hell do you mean by that? You had a right to be loved. The right to be safe." She stopped and clutched the armrests on her chair. Her volume decreased. "And you had a right to grow up in your own home." Tears streamed down her face as she pulled her chair closer to the table and composed herself. "What I meant to say is that you had rights to all of these things, but I had the job of raising you in such a way that would give you the best chance for success. I told you what I felt served you and withheld things that didn't."

"Mom, I don't want to fight with you, but why didn't it serve me to understand my ethnicity?"

"What would you have done with this information? Made an announcement at school? Made your friends in this damn racist town uncomfortable every time anyone said or implied something that offended you? How was that going to help you in life?"

"I would have known where I came from."

"Just like how your Grandpa Bruce knew where he came from when people passed him over for jobs . . . let's be real, Dustin. Withholding this, as I did, gave you advantages in life. It really is that simple."

"You may think so, and you might be right, but you made a conscious decision to present yourself in a particular way. I never had that choice."

Ilva Murphy paused after this last remark and considered her response. "To be honest, you and your brother didn't seem so interested. Only your sister had a clue. You looked White and we raised you in an all-White neighborhood. No one ever taunted you or discriminated against you and you had all of the privileges of not only being White, but a White *man* in America. All of this was my gift to you. Are you saying you didn't benefit from what I did?"

"I'm not saying that at all, but doesn't everyone have a right to understand their background?"

"Oh, Dustin, don't go back to this talk of rights, because what I did gave you all of the rights in the world. My father's rights were limited because of his skin color and he didn't overcome this challenge the way your Aunt Rita did. I realized after all three of you were born that the discrimination could stop with my generation, but only if I didn't tell."

"So why did you plan to tell me at the age of forty?"

"Because your identity would be formed by then and you would understand the value of knowing without feeling the express need of telling."

"Know but don't tell, Mom? Really? Is this what you're saying?"

"In a way, yes."

"All right. I don't agree with you, but I understand your thinking. Let's leave it there." Dustin sat back in his chair and tapped his fingers on the table. His right leg started to bop up and down.

Ilva grabbed her son's leg. "You must be a terrible poker player. You want to continue this conversation, but you're not sure how it will end. Am I right?"

"Yes, Mom. We don't need any more fights. Let's go back to Aunt Ilva. Tell me about the rift between the two sisters and we'll circle back on the rest of the stuff on another Sunday. I may need some time to process all of this anyway. So what happened?"

"Like I said, it involved *labels*. A census taker from New York State visited and my grandma made sure the man categorized us as *White*."

"So, how does this develop into a battle with her sister?"

"A few years later, a federal census worker came around when Ilva was babysitting me and she decided to take the interview. The man labeled us *Black*. My grandma found out from a neighbor who read what the man marked on the form. She thought it set us back decades. I remember Aunt Ilva storming out screaming, 'We are what we are, Julia, and no piece of paper is gonna change that fact. You better get over it, because it is what it is.'"

"Did they make up?"

"No. The next time I saw Aunt Ilva was at the cemetery, where she was buried in an unmarked grave. It doesn't get worse than that. This is what happens when you *tell*."

Dustin cleared the plates and gave his mother some time to think. She was entrenched in her position of *knowing but not telling*, but he was pleased they had broached the topic after all of these years and he thought enough had been accomplished for the day. He returned with the shoebox of bills and they laughed as they poked fun at the bad handwriting that was as much a part of the family DNA as anything else. The Sunday conversation didn't bring closure to the race issue but marked the beginning of a long-overdue dialogue. Dustin provided the final punctuation for his visit with his trademark double honk as he pulled away.

CHAPTER 19

Another Discovery

DUSTIN PEEKED OUT through one of the openings in The Castle and winked at his Aunt Ilva as he took in the scene below. A tall woman walking her dog was being slowly overtaken by an overweight man struggling to maintain his jog. The woman looked up and waved to Dustin, who returned to the protection of his seat. He glanced at his watch, raised his tumbler of Macallan, and said, "Well, it must be five o'clock somewhere."

He began organizing his Nevis documents in an attempt to find connections and tell the story of this line of the family. He'd seen TV detectives do this kind of thing on a bulletin board and planned to use the terrace table for his project. He positioned the bill of sale for John Day in the center. *There is just something about this name,* he thought again. He then placed in a circle around the slave record copies of three pages from Aunt Rita's diary containing references to Luky from Nevis. Finally, he added the notes and certificates emailed by the researchers in Nevis.

Dustin stared at the name *Mackinnon* and noted that his grandfather (Bruce Mackinnon Iles) and his Uncle H.O. (Horatio Mackinnon Iles) shared the same middle name. He placed index cards for both of them along the perimeter and created notes regarding his three major takeaways from the Nevis narrative sent by the researchers on the island:

1. The population is virtually unchanged in two hundred and twenty years: 10,000 in 1790 and 12,000 in 2009.
2. The ethnic breakdown is also the same at ninety percent Black. The White population in the early 1800s consisted of a small number of plantation owners.

3. A wealthy Nevis planter by the name of Horatio Iles had a strong probability of being an ancestor.

After transferring his three notes to individual index cards, he placed them in the mix on the table, but he was unsure where they belonged. Dustin scrutinized his collection of evidence for possible relationships and began changing the positions of the documents. Once he moved everything with the name Mackinnon, which appeared to be a point of commonality, to the center, his arrangement felt right. He celebrated with another sip of Macallan.

A voice called up from the street and Dustin walked over to the opening to investigate. A woman stood near the gate to the cemetery and stared in his direction. He heard one of his neighbors call out from a lower terrace, "I'll be right down. Wait there." Dustin sat back down in his chair.

He surveyed his display and decided to start with the baptismal records located by the Nevis Historical Society, which named others in the family: Henry Mackinnon Iles (Dustin's great-great-grandfather), Samuel Mackinnon Iles (Henry's father), and Henry's two brothers, both with the Mackinnon middle name.

Next, he circled *Luky* and *Lucretia Mackinnon Iles* and concluded they were one and the same—another *Mackinnon*. Aunt Rita described her Aunt Luky in her diary as being eighty-five in 1913. He created an index card for her with her full name. *What is it with the name of Mackinnon? How could it also be a female middle name?* he thought. The historical society had also found Lucretia's baptismal certificate and Grace Mackinnon was listed as her mother. Now he understood. Mackinnon wasn't a middle name at all. In modern times, a hyphen might have been inserted between Mackinnon and Iles. It was a kind of double-barreled last name.

He continued his research and examined the old bill of sale for John Day dated 1818. The writing was difficult to read, but after some time, he discerned the seller's name to be Horatio Iles and the buyer, Grace Mackinnon. He pulled out his magnifying glass to read the phrase written next to her name: *free woman of color*. This was the final piece to his puzzle.

Grace Mackinnon likely had both freedom and wealth if she had bought a slave in 1818, but what scenario could cause a White plantation owner to marry a Black woman in the early 1800s? Perhaps few White women of means existed in

Nevis, making a free woman of color an acceptable choice. It might also explain the way that the Mackinnon name was used from that point forward. It seemed as if the family wanted future generations to honor the extraordinary achievement and status of their ancestor, Grace Mackinnon. Dustin realized the Mackinnon Iles surname might have ended with his Uncle H.O. (Horatio), who never had fathered any children.

Dustin appreciated the extent to which his conclusions were based on unsubstantiated assumptions, and he lacked direct proof of the marriage of Horatio Iles to Grace Mackinnon, but given how small the island was, the fact that the couple was connected through the bill of sale, and the consistent use of the names Grace and Horatio for generations, he felt he had uncovered the truth or at least a reasonable interpretation of it. *Time to celebrate another discovery.* A fresh glass of Macallan was soon by his side.

He walked out to the window again. A beautiful red bird with black feathers outlining her eyes sat on the branch of the massive oak tree above Aunt Ilva's plot. The bird was perched no more than twenty feet away from and eye level with Dustin. He stared at the creature, who appeared to relish the attention before flying off as the sun set. Dustin sat back in his chair and finished his drink.

A soft breeze wafted through the walls of The Castle and Dustin pictured the image of the statuesque red-and-black bird as he drifted off. He was on a journey and determined to uncover the remaining mysteries of his family. The results of his work would document the achievements of his ancestors and perhaps shed light on his own personal challenges. The effects of his last scotch started to kick in as another puff of air announced the return of his new red-and-black feathered friend, who resumed her perch in the tree above the gravesite. Dustin's sleep was both earned and deep. His mind started to travel, but it didn't wander. It had purpose and knew exactly where it was going because it had a story to tell.

Part Four

Nevis
1815–1845

CHAPTER 20

The Mackinnons

"Father, I'll be right down. I needed to finish this book before my tutoring session later." Grace gave herself a quick review in the mirror before heading to her father. She hesitated at the top of the staircase when she realized this would be practice for her coming-out event on Saturday night.

Bruce Mackinnon applauded as his sixteen-year-old daughter made her grand entrance. "Such an elegant and smart young lady. You'll make someone very happy in a few years. Are you excited about your celebration? I think we will call it the Montserrat Ball—a grand name for a grand event!"

"Father, I do worry about all of the expense and bother. The sugar crop isn't what it used to be. We can still cancel, I could—"

"No. Let me stop you right there. I'm not sure who the adult is and who the sixteen-year-old girl is in this conversation! It will be worth the expense for me to usher my beautiful daughter into Nevis society in such an impressive way. Come now, time for your dancing lesson. Busy days for a young girl. Start practicing your steps."

"Oh, Father, is this necessary?"

"Yes, it is. Now go on."

Grace glided along the floor to the three-fourths rhythm of a minuet, forcing a smile for the benefit of her father, one of the most respected planters in Nevis. She turned with a tasteful kick and her father beamed. Grace smiled.

⋘══ ══⋙

Bruce Mackinnon reviewed the ledgers in his study while he awaited a visit from his younger brother, Sinclair. *She's right*, he thought. The margins on this year's smaller crop were unimpressive. Bruce worried about his ability to keep everything at the Montserrat Plantation running in the fashion to which the family had become accustomed and looked up as he heard the door open.

"Bruce, how are you?"

"Doing well, Sinclair. Will you be joining us on Saturday?"

"Oh, Bruce, why do you insist on making such a spectacle of things? Everyone understands her blood. Don't you think this is throwing good money after bad?"

"I warned you before not to speak this way in my house. How dare you suggest that she isn't worthy of this celebration when you come to me so often with your hands out."

"Hands out? Now I'm the one who is insulted! I'm getting an advance on what will one day be mine and as for your daughter, she's nothing more than—"

"Stop right there! You will not speak ill of my daughter. Remember, it is my blood that runs through her veins."

"But also the blood of Luky, your slave—you seem to always forget this little, but important, detail."

"My daughter is well-read and well-bred and on her eighteenth birthday she will become a free woman of color! Her status right now is a mere detail, an inconvenience." He paused and lowered his level of animation. "Now, why did you come here today? What is your business? Are you here to repay some of the sums owed to me?"

"Why no, my brother. I didn't mean to upset you and just wanted you to understand the whispers. Actually, I'm here because I am a little short again and hoped—"

"You come in here and insult my daughter, who is also your niece, only to ask me for money? The nerve! I will extend a small sum to you as I always do, but this isn't a gift. Go take a peek at the ledger on the bookcase."

Sinclair picked up the thick book and his eyes opened wide. "What is this?"

"This book has a record of every sum given to you since father died. Your debts to him were forgiven when he passed, but your debts to me will not be similarly disposed of when I leave this Earth. I am ten years your senior, so if the natural course of events take place and I die before you, your outstanding loans plus interest will be deducted from your inheritance. The only way you can avoid this repayment is to predecease me."

"What? You can't do that!"

"I certainly can. This is all documented in my will. Now here you go." Bruce placed a sealed envelope on an empty chair. Sinclair grabbed it and stormed out of the house.

Bruce called out, "Don't bother coming Saturday night."

"Not a problem." Sinclair slammed the door.

⋆⊶ ⊷⋆

"Miss Grace, your tutor, Mr. Johannson, is here for you. He is waiting down-stairs," the head house slave, John Day, called out.

Grace made her apologies to her dance instructor and winked at the servant as she exited the room. "Is he really here?"

"No, but I could tell you were growing tired of the dancing."

"Thank you, John! What would I do without you?"

Grace put her arm around John, who was her cousin by blood. She picked up a book and walked toward the stairs, pausing by the window to survey the expan-sive grounds of Montserrat. "The days of sugarcane are long gone."

"Yes, I think you're right, Miss Grace. The land is all used up."

"I've got ideas about how Montserrat can move into something new."

"Like what?"

"I'm getting close to deciding and have narrowed the choices down, but I don't want to say until I'm sure."

John flashed a stern glare. "Fair enough, but I'll be real upset if you start tell-ing things to others before you tell me."

Grace walked over and gave him a hug. "You're like my older brother, John. I'll always tell you first and I promise you'll be free when I'm in charge. It will be my first official act!"

"Thank you, but you better tell me your ideas soon, because I think your father is planning on marrying you off. This Saturday night is the beginning of him doing that very thing."

"I'll see what I can do to slow things down." She winked at John, who chuckled.

"You're one smart girl," he said.

CHAPTER 21

The Montserrat Ball

BRUCE MACKINNON'S LONGTIME friend and wife, Horatio and Emily Iles, joined him to greet the guests at the Montserrat Ball. As the pace of new arrivals slowed, Bruce assessed the crowd and was pleased with the turnout. He evaluated at least five young men as suitable candidates for his daughter.

The parents gravitated to the right side of the room and their children to the left. The girls were all in their finest evening dresses, but Bruce was certain no one compared to Grace. At seven o'clock, John Day gave the sign that Grace was ready. The string quartet started to play as she descended the stairs. With her long flowing hair pulled up in a bun and her skin shining against her necklace, she was a sight to behold. The master of the house announced, "I give you my daughter, Grace Mackinnon!"

The applause brought a smile to Grace's face, but she didn't lose her composure or stumble in any way. She heard the conversations through the music and understood where the source of any potential trouble would be. Two boys in the back of the room were pointing and giggling and their parents came over to encourage better behavior.

Grace took her father's hand and the music stopped, but the clapping continued. John Day walked next to Grace and said, "Stay away from the two young men in the back. They're saying things."

Bruce Mackinnon raised his hand, which ended the applause. "May I have this dance? I believe we are beginning with Bach's 'Minuet in G Minor.'"

"But of course, Father, the very piece you've been practicing all week!"

The father laughed and the daughter prepared as the leader of the quartet counted, "One, two, three, and the music began."

La—lo—lo—lo—lo—li—dum—dum

La—lo—lo—lo—lo—ti—dum—dum,
Da—di—da—ta—da—du—di—da—ta—da—du—do
da—di—da—do—dum—dum

Most eyes focused on Grace, who was not only a beauty but a natural dancer, as she glided around the floor. Some, however, were impressed with the obvious effort Bruce put into his performance as he served as the straight man for his daughter's theatrical embellishments of the basic steps. Grace punctuated each bar of music with a hop and a smile. She laughed as she overheard her father whispering instructions to himself as he took each step: "Right, together, left, right, left, together. Right, together, left, right, left, together."

Bruce lost his concentration when he passed the two misbehaving young men, who doubled over as one joked, "I didn't realize *they* could dance to civilized music!" Grace acted as if she were unaware and Horatio Iles took control. He escorted the parents of the two offending boys to a separate room. Bruce excused himself and went outside for some fresh air. After a brief but firm chat, Horatio suggested an early departure was in order and the two families gathered their sons and made a hasty exit out the back door of the mansion. They were forced to endure the glare of Bruce Mackinnon, who stood a distance away with a glower that would likely take years to overcome.

The music resumed and Horatio Iles asked for the honor of being Grace's second dance partner of the evening. He was much more of a gifted dancer than his friend Bruce, which allowed Grace to truly display her skills. After the conclusion of this dance, Grace joined the younger guests and looked across the room to John Day, who stood at attention on the stairs. He bowed his head and made a fist. Grace thought, *Yes, John, I will be strong.*

A group of three young ladies approached. One of them offered, "Grace, you look so lovely in your gown. Did your father have it made for this occasion?"

"Why, yes, Camille. He did. I'm glad you like it."

"It is truly one of a kind." Camille turned to her two friends. "Girls, look at that sunburn on Esther Williams! That poor girl has no sense at all. Doesn't she know to stay in the shade on a sunny day?" She turned back to Grace to finish her thought. "Why, with our pale skin, we have to be so careful. Don't you agree, Grace?" Camille's friends giggled and thankfully Grace's father called her over before she could respond.

"Grace, it is time for your third dance, which should be with someone your own age. Let me make the announcement."

"Oh Father, please . . ."

Bruce raised his hand to get the attention of his guests. "My charming daughter will now share her next dance with a lucky young man. Who will it be? Grace will decide, but don't worry if she doesn't select you, we have several more dances left this evening! Please step forward now."

No one moved and silence took hold of the room. Bruce held Grace's hand for support and squeezed. She continued looking at John Day for encouragement. Camille and her friends offered a collective sarcastic gaze and all of the young men tried to look away. Horatio Iles made eye contact with the father of one of the young men, who then called out, "My son, Henry, would love to be so honored."

Grace saw the look on Henry's face as he stared in disbelief at his father. After another awkward pause, he stepped forward and the music commenced. They made no eye contact and the distance between them was almost inappropriately wide. Grace was mortified as she moved in a robotic fashion. All of the hops and embellishments were gone. This was a dance to be endured, not enjoyed. Grace locked eyes with John Day, who encouraged her with a pat of his right hand on his heart.

The Montserrat Ball came to a merciful end after several more dances and refreshments. Bruce Mackinnon's farewells lacked the energy of his greetings. Most of the guests saved their whispers for the privacy of their carriages as they returned home. Grace Mackinnon would never belong. She would never be an equal, no matter how powerful her father was. The Nevis elite were almost unanimous in this conclusion with the exception of the most important in their ranks, Bruce Mackinnon, who would never understand.

Grace wondered if she could have spared her father this experience. She accepted her perceived place and would never again try to be one of them. She had what she needed: money, property, intelligence, and an unsurpassed work ethic. Equality was never her goal. She would never stoop to their level.

John Day escorted Grace upstairs to her room. She hesitated as she reached the door and considered whether to indulge herself with a few private tears. In the end, she didn't cry because of what had happened, as it had been predictable.

Any tears she might shed were due to her inability to stop the party from having taken place. She turned to John. "I took the wrong approach with my father. Next time, I'll make sure that he listens."

"I'm sure you will, but before I leave, you're going to sit next to me and let those tears out. It won't help to hold onto them." John tapped his right hand on the bed as he took a seat and Grace took comfort on her cousin's broad shoulder and cried herself to sleep.

C H A P T E R 2 2

A Smaller Affair

"F ATHER, THANK YOU so much for this party. I so prefer something small like this to what we did last year." Father and daughter became lost in their thoughts as they both relived their different recollections of the previous year's celebration.

"It was lovely, but I'm sorry your Uncle Sinclair didn't join us. He will be here later to give you his birthday wishes."

"Yes, of course, Father. How are you feeling? Your color still doesn't look right."

"It hasn't been right for some time now. The doctor wants me to slow down, but if I go any slower, I won't be moving!"

Bruce's laugh transitioned into a terrible coughing fit. Grace handed him a glass of water and patted him on the back in an effort to steady him. John Day came onto the scene. "Sir, is there anything else you need to be more comfortable?"

"Yes, please fetch me a cup of tea. My brother will be here soon to discuss some business. Grace, I am going to wish you a good night and, once again, happy birthday! Seventeen is a wonderful age. Your whole life is ahead of you."

John circled back up to Grace after settling her father in the study. "Your uncle isn't here yet. Once he arrives, I'll act like I went to get you, but I'll tell your father that you're asleep. Go to the kitchen while you can. Master Mackinnon is dozing. Something important is going on tonight."

"Thanks. I'll head down right away."

⋅⊷▬◉ ◉▬⊶⋅

"Bruce, so sorry I missed the celebration. Is she still awake? I want to give her a birthday kiss!"

"I'm not sure. It is a little late. John, please go check on Grace."

"Yes, sir."

John walked up the stairs, stomping with some extra gusto to confirm his destination. He stood in front of Grace's door for a moment or two and then returned. "Sir, she retired for the night."

"Thank you. I believe that will be all for the evening. You've freshened up my tea, and as for my brother, he prefers a different kind of beverage."

Sinclair toasted John with his wineglass. "Good night. I think we're all set."

John headed for his quarters but ducked into the kitchen, which was adjacent to the study. An old pass-through between the two rooms large enough for some plates or cups had been sealed up many years ago, but sound still carried well through the former opening. Grace, already seated at the table, motioned for John to join her.

"Sinclair, I'm sick. I haven't bothered Grace with the details of my illness, but this may be the last birthday I will celebrate with my baby." He gazed out the window.

"I'm so sorry, my brother. Is there anything I can do?"

"Please do not insult me with your insincerity. I brought you here tonight to explain the terms of my will and what will happen when I die."

"Bruce, why are you being so formal? Father would have wanted everything to go to me and I'll take good care of both Montserrat and Grace."

"Oh, Sinclair, there is nothing about the way you conduct your affairs either financially or personally that would lead me to believe this will be the case, so I took matters into my own hands."

Sinclair leaned in toward his brother. "What did you do?"

"I revised my will in order to ensure an orderly transition of my affairs. As part of this, I will make one last loan to you, which is contained in this envelope." Bruce paused as he handed the sealed envelope to his brother. "It has been logged in the ledger containing descriptions of all of your debts to me and this information is recorded in the will. Upon my death, you will inherit half of all of my holdings, less your debt, which will be settled at that time."

"I always thought you were joking about the ledger. These payments aren't really loans, brother. This was just money that was due me."

"I was very clear with you regarding the nature of these transactions, even the interest rate I applied to the outstanding balances. May I continue?"

"I'm not so sure I can stop you. At least not now." Sinclair clutched the arm-rests of his chair. "Continue."

"With this last installment, your debt to me will reduce the size of your share to one-quarter—these values are all stated in my will, but should I end up living more than several months, they will be revisited over time. I prefer for Grace to buy you out, Sinclair, but it could work the other way, should you be able to raise the funds. This transaction will take place on Grace's eighteenth birthday. You will be her temporary guardian and she must be allowed to continue to live at Montserrat in a suitable manner. Are all of these terms clear?"

"Why did you do this? You were the firstborn and you inherited everything. Do you think that our father would want his property to be given over to a mu-latto? No matter what you say or think, Bruce, Grace is nothing but a goddamn half-breed."

"Watch what you say! I would be more than happy to revise this will yet again."

"Don't threaten me! I have rights here and I will seek legal advice. Remember, Grace is going to need help managing her affairs, given her age and other *chal-lenges*. You need to rethink this."

"Time for you to go and I'll ask you not to return until you change both your opinion and attitude. Good evening. Please walk yourself out."

Sinclair stormed out of the house and slammed the front door as he exited. Grace scampered upstairs and John Day saw to the master's preparations for bed. Bruce had lost several shades of color during his visit with his brother. Grace settled in for the night with a mixture of thoughts and feelings. Concern for her father was paramount, closely followed by fear of her uncle. She needed a way to deal with him because she knew full well that he was hatching his plan to deal with her.

CHAPTER 23

Changes at Montserrat

THE CHURCH OVERFLOWED with mourners for the funeral of one of the most influential men in Nevis. Bruce's brother and daughter sat next to each other in the first pew. The attendees included a broad cross section of the elite class in Nevis society. Horatio Iles and his wife, Emily, who was six months pregnant, sat behind the Mackinnons and helped with all of the arrangements, which included a small get-together following the burial at Montserrat.

Grace, dressed in black, sat in silence during the mass and rode alone with John Day back home. He took her hand as he helped her out of the carriage and said, "Everything is gonna be just fine."

"Thank you, John. I plan to spend the evening in my room after making a brief appearance in the parlor to thank the guests for their condolences. Uncle Sinclair will be the host."

The affair, which started with thirty mourners, dwindled down to just Sinclair's close friends within an hour or so. By the time the sun began to set, the tone of the gathering had switched from respectful to belligerent as the drinking increased. Grace heard the phrases *stupid Darkey, Black bitch, half-breed,* and *mongrel* repeated many times. She forced herself to fall asleep early to prepare for whatever drama the reading of the will would cause the following morning.

⌖ ⌖

"Grace, please sit. I'm going to read a summary of your father's will and final letter of instructions out loud. My comments will be brief and I want all of you to know that these documents were revised by my hand this past year. Other than the immediate family, I asked Horatio Iles to be here as he is also mentioned in the will."

Sinclair Mackinnon gave Horatio an unwelcome look. Grace, however, was thankful for his presence. The attorney began, "I will skip the pleasantries and try to present the essence of these documents. Copies will be provided to each of you to read in detail at your leisure. The letter contains information about the funeral services and burial, which, of course, have already taken place. The remaining sections are addressed to Sinclair. Your brother requires you to maintain Grace in a fitting lifestyle as her guardian until she turns eighteen and gains her freedom. Her eighteenth birthday also marks the point at which all estate matters will be settled."

The attorney paused and took a sip of water. "The will goes on to provide one piece of personal property, Bruce's prize horse, Seymour, to Horatio Iles. Mr. Mackinnon appreciated how much you admired this horse. The remainder of the property is to be divided in halves for Grace and Sinclair, with Sinclair's portion reduced by his total outstanding debt." The attorney reached into his bag and handed both Grace and Sinclair a sealed envelope. "Please open these letters in private as they contain important details and please try to find time to discuss future arrangements. It would be much better for Grace to purchase your share, Sinclair. I believe this is the best way forward for both of you and consistent with Mr. Mackinnon's intentions."

Grace opened her envelope once behind closed doors in her bedroom and started to organize her essential possessions. She could hear her uncle screaming downstairs and began to make notes while she waited for their inevitable confrontation.

⊷▄▄▄◉ ◉▄▄▄⊷

A full two hours passed before Sinclair burst into her bedroom. Grace was seated with her arms folded on her lap on the corner of the bed.

"Listen, you little bitch, there is no way this is going to stand. I'm entitled to the entire estate, and this"—he threw his papers on her lap—"is an insult. One-quarter? Impossible. My brother was not in a proper frame of mind when he did this and I am going to fight it."

"I'm sure you will do what is best for you, Uncle Sinclair."

"Don't you be sarcastic with me, you Black blood-sucking leech. Do you want to know what you are going to do?"

Grace remained silent and waited for him to answer his own question. "Fine, I'll tell you. Your father gave me guardianship over you until you turn eighteen. I believe, however, he was confused on this point. You're nothing but property and what I have over you is ownership, not guardianship. I want you out of this house and down to the block with the rest of the slaves. Your father directed me to provide you with fitting accommodations until your eighteenth birthday. In my humble opinion, there is nothing more suitable than for a slave to be with her people. Take your little pet, John Day, with you. I don't need either one of you. As a matter of fact, the mere sight of you is making me sick."

Grace had expected something along these lines after she'd become aware of her three-fourths inheritance. Her bag was packed, as were the notes she'd made over the past few hours detailing her plan of action. She and John walked out to the row of cabins that dotted the path leading up to the side of the house. Several people pointed to an empty shack at the end of the row. Grace picked up a broom and began to sweep the small sitting area out front while John cleaned the interior. A few minutes later, several of her new neighbors lent a hand, while others provided food and drink. Grace looked up at the sky and said, "Father, this may not be what you planned, but I'll be fine."

CHAPTER 24

Being Tough

JOHN DAY AND Abe, an older slave who worked in the stables, chatted about their new neighbor.

"I always knew something was going to go wrong for her," Abe said.

"Master Sinclair is a problem to be sure, but she's got a lawyer looking out for her and she's plenty smart herself. Always stays a step ahead of whatever is going to happen."

"Not so sure she stayed ahead of this, John."

"Everyone's got to be tested and she's one tough lady. Right now, she has to turn the other cheek because she's not in a position to give something back with a fight. Sometimes, being tough isn't about how much you can give, but how much you can take."

"You're speaking the truth with that, John."

"Things are going to change around here."

"Hope you're right."

⊷▬⊙ ⊙▬⊷

The slaves didn't know what to make of Grace and gave her space. Many viewed her temporary residence as an opportunity to align themselves with the new master. Others considered her new home to be proof that her promised freedom would never happen and any alignment with her might prove to hurt more than help. As she circulated among her new neighbors, her natural confidence and strength changed some minds. While her fate was uncertain, to be sure, all agreed that she was bright, determined, and a force to be reckoned with.

Grace set herself up in a chair outside her door and began sharing her plans for once she was in charge of Montserrat. Five men and women sat around and listened to her vision for the plantation.

"I want you all to understand how things are going to work when I take over."

"No offense, Miss Mackinnon, but are you sure you're taking over? You're living out here with us and we ain't running nothing!"

The group laughed and she waited for them to settle down. "Yes, I see your point, but you must understand that I will be free when I turn eighteen. I feel more comfortable here with you than I would in the house with my Uncle Sinclair. What we need to worry about is what he might do over the next few months. Now, are you ready to hear how things will work once I'm running things?"

Abe walked up with John and said, "We sure are."

"Fine. First thing, we've been working this soil too hard for too long and sugar doesn't make sense anymore. I'm taking Montserrat in a new direction, but I won't say what it is yet because I don't want any involvement from my uncle in this new business. There will be lots of work, but a different kind, and I'm going to give you credit for everything you do. John Day will keep track."

One of the younger men asked, "What does *credit* mean?"

John answered, "I'm going to keep a book with notes next to everyone's name about how hard and long they been working. This is what we're calling your credit, and this is what will make you free."

"What you mean by that? How's this gonna work?"

Grace clarified, "Let me explain. Anyone who works for one full year will be free, but then I want you to stay on as an employee, getting paid for what you do."

"I like the sound of that!"

"Me too!"

"Yeah, sounds nice!"

Abe took a deep breath. "Miss Mackinnon, I hope you gonna be able to do all these things you're saying, but you're a seventeen-year-old girl. How much of the running of Montserrat do you understand and what makes you think this new business is going to be any better than sugarcane?"

John turned to Abe. "Who do you think ran the business since the master been sick?"

Grace smiled and Abe nodded.

Over the next twenty minutes, the fifty slaves at Montserrat learned of

Grace's plans. Some wondered how a promise of freedom from another slave held any value, but the look of determination in Grace's eyes created the belief that she could back up her words with action. Grace worried about her Uncle Sinclair and asked several of the house servants to provide reports of his actions. The fact that he was running the old sugarcane business, not her new venture, provided some solace. She hoped any damage he might do would be limited to the existing crop. Grace didn't know, however, what else he had in mind.

⊷⇒ ⇐⊶

"Grace, darling. I was just checking on how you settled in. I also wanted to introduce you to my good friend, Harold. Perhaps you met him before? He is quite a popular man in Charlestown. As a matter of fact, no one in Nevis has more friends than him. Isn't that right, Harold?"

"Why yes, Sinclair. When I throw a party, there's a long line out of the door of people waiting to get in."

"Thank you for checking on me, Uncle Sinclair. I'm doing fine. Everyone is taking very good care of me. Pleasure to make your acquaintance, Harold."

"Excellent! This next part is very tricky, though, so I want you to pay attention. I told my friend here that I wanted him to meet my niece and I think we accomplished that already. I also told him he could take his pick of any of the young girls for a little entertainment. Right, Harold?"

"Yes, that's what you said and she sure is pretty." Harold licked his lips and John got up and stood next to her.

Sinclair continued, "As long as I'm in your presence, Harold understands he cannot touch you, but after I leave, you might be his entertainment. He suggested it might be fun to hold one of his parties right here in your little place. How do you think we should set up the line? Maybe your friend John Day will help? You'll be much too busy to manage it on your own. After a while, you'll hardly even be able to say, 'Next.'" The two friends broke into uncontrolled laughter.

John advanced toward Sinclair and Harold wrestled him to the ground. He didn't resist because the penalty for taking a step toward a White man was reason enough to receive the most serious of punishments.

Sinclair barked orders. "Harold, pick him up and walk him to the barn." He then turned to John and said, "How dare you try to attack a White man? We'll teach you a lesson soon enough." Grace tried to move to her cousin's side, but her uncle threw her against the wall and called out the front door, "Abe, come in here."

Within minutes, Abe and Harold had marched John Day toward the barn and tied him to a spare wagon wheel, spreading his limbs as wide as possible while securing them tightly with rope. Abe consoled his friend. "They got you on the wheel, but your back is facing out, not your front, so they ain't gonna break you—you'll live, but it'll be the whipping of your life. Remember what you said before—being tough is more about how much you can take. Show me how tough you are, my friend."

Sinclair called the slaves out to see the spectacle and pushed Grace toward John. She fell in the dirt and refused to stand. Sinclair slapped her in the face and dragged her to a chair placed close to her cousin. "Best seat in the house. Abe, tie her to the chair. I want her to see his face as he learns how to behave." Sinclair turned to the crowd, "Take this as a warning. Anyone who tries to help this woman will get the same treatment."

Grace shouted, "You bastard! How can you be this cruel!"

"This is what happens when things get turned upside down, little Gracie. Slaves aren't supposed to inherit plantations—they should do as they're told or suffer the consequences. Tonight, you'll learn that I can take anything I want away from you, including John Day. Tomorrow night, Harold and his first group of friends will join you for a party and it won't even be against the law. It may not make me popular with certain people, but popularity is not my concern." He laughed and signaled to his friend, who wielded the whip.

Whap!

Sinclair directed, "Again."

Whap!

"Keep going until you get enough exercise. You'll have a different kind to-morrow night." Sinclair walked back to the house, laughing.

⊶⊷

John looked at Grace's face but then turned away, unsure if he could continue to put on a brave front. The first few lashes brought on a kind of pain he'd never experienced in his life. He wished he knew how many more blows from the whip he would need to endure, but his sentence was up to the whims of the master's friend. John screamed as the whip struck the back of his head. Harold laughed.

The blow to the head caused John to shift his face back toward Grace, while his mind left his body. His eyes drifted upward and he focused on the platform on top of the roof. The entire plantation could be seen from that vantage point. He'd been up there many times and he tried to go there again, climbing the steps of the ladder one at a time. He got to the third rung and fell backward but regrouped and started again. Finally, he made it to the top. John walked to the railing and looked across the way at the whipping from above, no longer in it. *Got to stay above it. Learn from this, Grace, pay attention. You'll need to know how to do this. Look down from above. You can do it. Be tough.*

The punishment ended when Harold collapsed from exertion. He sat on the ground smiling as he admired his work. John's flesh was striped with blood and he was barely conscious. Abe and Grace rushed him back inside and tended to him as best they could. After some time, John asked for water and gave one instruction. "Grace, write a letter to your father's friend, Horatio Iles, and give it to Abe." John grabbed Abe's hand. "I need your help. Please take the letter to Mr. Iles or we'll all be tending to Grace tomorrow night."

CHAPTER 25

Charlestown

ABE ARRIVED EARLY in the morning with directions to take John Day to the doctor in Charlestown. He shrugged as he explained, "I'm supposed to pick up some things while he gets treated and then bring him back. The man's crazy. One minute he's the devil and the next, he's doing something that shows some heart."

Grace asked, "Did anyone overhear anything in the house about this? Maybe he's got some other plan."

"I checked with the folks in the kitchen. No one knows for sure, but it could be what he says. This also gives me a chance to drop off your letter. Mr. Iles's plantation is between Montserrat and Charlestown. I'll say I had a problem with the wagon and had to stop if anybody asks me."

"Okay, here it is. You can give it to either Mr. or Mrs. Iles, both are friends. Let's wake John up. We can spread him out in the back."

Grace waved as Abe headed out. The wagon made slow progress toward Charleston and Abe glanced at the paper with drawings of the three items to be picked up at the market. He thought, *At least he doesn't understand I can read.* The two men passed Fort Charles as they approached the town from the south and pulled up to the doctor's office.

"John, you wait here. Let me check on the doctor. Be right back."

The voice came from behind. "No, Abe, don't worry about the doctor or the supplies. You can go on back to Montserrat. Tell Mr. Sinclair that you delivered John Day to his friend, Harold. Also tell him the line tonight will be three friends long." He laughed and slapped John Day on the back. "How does that sound, John! Aw, did I hurt you? Poor little fella. Come on now." Harold pulled him out of the wagon. John cooperated. "That's right, no need to put up a fuss. Time to serve someone new. You'll be auctioned with other slaves. If not for this mess on your back, you might fetch a nice price. Now come on."

John Day walked off with his head down to an open-air shed and joined the nine other slaves who sat expressionless as they contemplated their fate, which would be decided later that day.

⊷⊷⊷ ⊶⊶⊶

"Mr. Iles, so sorry to disturb you and the Mrs., but Abe from over at Montserrat just arrived with an envelope and wonders if he could have a word."

"Emily, I'll be right back."

"No, bring him in. The Mackinnons are my friends as well."

"As you wish, but I don't want you to become too excited. You are due to give birth in a few short weeks."

"Oh Horatio, you fuss over me far too much. Please ask him to come into the parlor."

Abe entered with his head down and body trembling.

"Abe is your name, am I right?" Horatio Iles asked.

"Yes, sir."

"Please try to relax. I'm a friend of Miss Grace Mackinnon. Why are you here?"

Abe gave the note to Horatio, who handed it to his wife. "Thank you, Abe. My wife will read it. Anything else?"

"Yes, sir. John Day asked me to tell you he's gonna be auctioned in Charleston."

"Let's take this slow. How did you get this envelope and how did you hear about John Day?"

"Sir, Master Mackinnon will have my hide for this. Please read the letter. It came from Miss Grace. They whipped John last night something awful and then said I should take him to the doctor this morning, but it was a trick. Master Sinclair's friend took him for the auction later today. They're going do some terrible things to Miss Grace tonight. She needs your help."

"I understand, Abe. Sinclair Mackinnon will never know you were here. Emily, what does it say?"

Emily put the paper down on the table. "It is bad, Horatio. She was forced to move out of the house by her uncle and she's worried that he won't let her be for the next few months leading up to her freedom. He's threatening to bring men over every night to have their way with her."

"I thought he'd do something, but not this. My God, he's her uncle. What kind of man is he? Abe, you run on now and head back to Montserrat and leave this with me."

⊷▭ ▭⊶

Sinclair Mackinnon headed for the stables as soon as the wagon pulled onto the property. Abe spotted the master approaching and turned to Sam, another stable hand. "They took John Day to put him up for sale. I need for Miss Grace to get that message. Go behind the wall over there and listen. Pass along anything else of interest. Understand?"

"Yes, but I don't want no problems."

"Understood. Now do what I say."

⊷▭ ▭⊶

The master asked, "Abe, what happened in town?"

"Your friend, Harold, took John Day. Said he had your permission."

"He did. Do you understand why I didn't tell you?"

"No, sir, I don't."

"All of you think that little bitch is going to be your savior and I want every slave on this property to learn that this is what will happen if they side with her. I knew I couldn't trust John. Can I trust you, Abe?"

"Yes, sir. I do my work and mind my own business."

"Just to make sure this is the case, you're going to stay in the main house until we leave for the auction. I don't want word of this getting back to Grace. Follow me."

⊷▭ ▭⊶

Sam heard everything, including the warning, and felt as if he were frozen in place. *Not sure if I should tell her, but Miss Grace says she's gonna help us. Maybe she needs to know?* "Don't want no trouble with her either." He realized that he had spoken his last thought out loud when Grace entered the stable and asked, "Would 'her' be me?"

"Well, yes, but I'm not sure if I can tell you something. Master Sinclair said I couldn't."

"No one will ever find out that you are the one who told me, whatever it is you are going to say. I'm fighting for all of us here, Sam. Please tell me whatever it is."

"Okay, Miss Grace. They took John Day in town to be sold this afternoon. Master Sinclair said he didn't want you to know. Abe said I should tell you everything."

"You did well, Sam, real well. Thank you. I won't forget."

CHAPTER 26

The Auction

THE TEN SLAVES about to be sold milled around the shed with a variety of attitudes and strategies. A family of four had no concern other than staying together. The father planned to brag about his productivity as a worker, the wife her prowess in the kitchen, and the young pre-teenage boys intended to demonstrate their value with a series of drills involving jumping and flexibility. A young man in his twenties practiced his limp. An older woman asked, "Why you limping? You walked fine a while ago."

Several of the men smirked and John Day explained, "A young man in top physical condition will sell for a high amount, so he'll need to work for many years for the master to earn back his money. If he's lucky enough to be bought by someone who will let him pay for his freedom, the price will be too much. So being sold high means you're never gonna be free."

"That's right," the twenty-year-old said as he turned to John. "The way you look right now, you may not sell at all and if you do, it won't be for much."

"I don't think my master cares what he gets for me. He's selling me to make a point. Here they come."

Several potential buyers stopped by early to examine the merchandise. Each slave had a small placard mounted around their neck with a number. John was number five and was preceded by the family, who was one through four. The father liked the look of the couple who began browsing and motioned to his boys, who started to jump in place. The couple walked right past them toward the twenty-year-old, who stood at attention, but then fell to the side. "Sorry, sir. I'm lame in my right foot."

Sinclair Mackinnon stood outside Grace's door. "Come on now, you're coming with me into town. Follow me back to the house, clean up, and put on one of your nice dresses. I need to show you something and then I'm going to suggest a solution to all of your problems. Now, doesn't that sound good? Let's go."

Grace did as she was told and walked to the house to prepare. She selected her black funeral dress out of respect for her father's recent passing. No words were exchanged in the back of the carriage as they rode the short distance to Charlestown. About halfway to their destination, Sinclair glared. "Don't you want to know where we're going?"

She took a deep breath. "No, it isn't my place to ask. As you pointed out, I'm nothing but a slave. You'll tell me where we are going and why we are going there when you wish to do so."

"Wish to do so? You watch your tone with me! I'm not beyond giving your back a little taste of the leather as well. Be careful."

Grace turned and resumed her examination of the scenery. The carriage passed Fort Charles and came to a halt at the marketplace. John Day was up next for auction and walked up the two steps, hunched over in pain, to take his place at the top of the blocks. The auctioneer did his best to call the crowd to order. Sinclair told Abe, "Turn back to Montserrat. She's seen what she needed to see."

Sinclair turned to Grace. "Understand that I can take anything away from you, even your precious John Day. I want you to be aware he's being sold, but I won't give you the courtesy of knowing who his new owner will be. You'll know what I want you to know and do what I want you to do. As I said last night, my plans for you begin this evening if you do not sign these papers. In return, you will be spared from humiliation and receive a small sum of money that you can use to get started on some other island, because you're leaving Nevis. I'm not offering you any great financial gain, but freedom and a new start isn't so bad. I promise you that if you reject this offer, the next several months will be pure agony. I'm warning you, don't test me."

Sinclair laughed and reached over to wipe away a tear streaming down the side of Grace's face. She pushed his hand away and said, "Permission to speak freely."

Sinclair slapped his thigh in celebration of the extreme formality of his niece's reaction. "Of course, my dear."

"You are wrong about the upcoming months. Have you read the letter of instructions and the will?"

"Of course, my fool of a brother gave you three-fourths of the estate."

"Uncle, it is so much more than that. There are details about how you should maintain a fitting lifestyle for me during your period of guardianship, or as you like to say, *ownership*. One of the provisions involves weekly visits from the attorney. The first such visit is today. If you deny him access or if he doesn't like what he sees upon arrival, he has the authority to appoint a new guardian and invalidate your inheritance. I will not complain about living in the slave quarters because I do not wish to be in the house with you, but I will be quite vocal about any other abuses of your authority. What you did last night and today with John Day are your first two infractions. So let me use your words, dear uncle, *I'm warning you, don't test me.*"

Sinclair slapped Grace in the face and screamed, "You insolent little bitch!" She didn't flinch and returned to her stern glare. Minutes later, uncle and niece were greeted by the lawyer as they entered Montserrat.

⊶⊷

Grace retired to her shack as the attorney met with Sinclair in the house. During the time of their meeting, Abe spread the word of how Miss Grace stood up to the master. All fifty slaves walked by and offered a greeting, a nod, or a simple good afternoon. The lawyer found his way outside as well and assured Grace her uncle understood that no threats or misdeeds could change the predetermined outcome of the disposition of the Mackinnon estate.

Grace waved to Horatio Iles, who waited outside the gates of the plantation. She touched her hand to her heart and assumed he was there to ensure that the visit by the attorney took place and went well. Horatio's concerned look blossomed into a smile as the attorney acknowledged him. Horatio tipped his hat to Grace and departed.

Over the next few weeks, the deal to transfer Sinclair's portion of the estate was negotiated with the attorney as intermediary and the document was signed, but post-dated to Grace's birthday. Sinclair moved out of Montserrat and purchased passage for himself on a boat to a neighboring island. Grace Mackinnon lived with the slaves until her birthday, winning over the hearts and minds of everyone on the block. By the time she assumed control of Montserrat, she was nothing short of their savior.

CHAPTER 27

Emancipation

AN ENTOURAGE OF fifteen escorted Grace back to the mansion on her birthday. She went up to her room and selected an outfit for the event that would change the course of her life. The attorney arrived with his associate, followed by Horatio Iles, who entered with a small group. The full Montserrat community crowded around the front steps to the house and greeted both parties with enthusiasm. The lawyers organized the documents while Horatio took time to settle his group in the parlor. Grace, outfitted in a multicolored dress, took her seat at the head of the table. The three men nodded as she sat.

Grace offered condolences to Horatio. "I'm so sorry about your wife. She was so young."

"Thank you, but she'll always be in my heart and she left me a son to remember her by. His name is Alex."

"A fine name for a fine young man."

"He is with me today and you can say hello to him when we're done."

"I'm looking forward to it. Thank you for all of your help during these last few challenging months."

The lawyer cleared his throat. "Now that the difficult business with your uncle is over, we can focus on the documents that transfer your father's property to you and make you a free woman."

The associate took over and clarified. "We will need for you to sign or make your mark in three sections. For example, here—"

The senior attorney interrupted. "She can read and write better than all of us. Limit your explanations to the bare minimum."

Grace signed her name for the first time quickly, reflective of her impatience in waiting for this moment. Her second signature became more pensive as she considered all of the opportunities that would now open to her, and her third was one to savor as she added a little flourish to the last "n" in Mackinnon.

Grace stood to thank her guests, but the assistant remarked, "Almost done . . . one more document to execute." She returned to her seat. Horatio reached over and scribbled something on the paper. The associate objected, "Sir, it is inappropriate for you to adjust a legal instrument in this fashion."

Horatio held his hand up and smiled. "Gentleman, I wonder if you would allow me some privacy with Grace. I've not yet explained this final document to her and would like to do so without an audience."

"Mr. Iles, again, this is—"

The senior attorney interjected. "Our work here is done. Good luck, Grace. I'll see you soon, Horatio." The two men scooped up their papers and made their way to their waiting carriage.

"Mr. Iles, what just happened?" Grace asked.

"Let me explain. When I received your letter months ago regarding your difficulties with your uncle and then heard about the auction of John Day, I followed up on both issues. Your lawyer assured me that he resolved the immediate threats to your welfare and I made it my job to track down John to check on his condition. Thankfully, an acquaintance of mine, who lives across the narrows in St. Kitts, purchased him. After some negotiating, I repurchased and returned him to Nevis. He has been on my property for the past two weeks. This is a bill of sale for you to purchase him from me so he may again be by your side. I wrote *Free Woman of Color* next to the line for your signature, which seemed fitting given the nature of the meeting."

"Oh, my God! Thank you, Mr. Iles!" Grace scanned the bill of sale and then protested, "But this amount is much too low!"

"Yes, it is. I only listed a token amount so the transaction will not be questioned, but I want something in exchange."

Grace stiffened her back.

"All I ask is that we form a partnership of sorts. I agree with you—the day of sugarcane is over, and I know from my conversations with your father that you have ideas about what we should turn our attentions to next. The first of us to do so will have the advantage, but I would imagine that there will be enough benefits for the first two of us as well." He winked. "So what I am asking for is access to your thoughts and youthful energy. In return, I assisted with John Day and, at your request, I will act on your behalf should anyone else in Nevis look to deter you in any way based on either your former or current status."

Grace extended her hand. "I believe we have an understanding, Mr. Iles."

"You're an adult, Grace. Time to call me Horatio. Now let's get John in here so the two of you can get reacquainted. And remember, I want you to meet my son, Alex."

John and Grace hugged long and then short. Smiles morphed into laughter and ended with tears. The cousins were reunited, this time for good. They walked out to the porch, where Grace waved her freedom papers in her left hand and the bill of sale in her right. The entire slave population of Montserrat cheered and walked the cousins to the block for a feast. Grace sat with John at the head of a long wooden table, which had been fashioned out of an oak tree. She laughed with her neighbors into the night and celebrated because success for one meant success for all.

CHAPTER 28

Years Later

THE COLLABORATION BETWEEN Grace and Horatio became more than a loose arrangement. She shared her ideas and the two met with some frequency to plan and execute business strategies. Given the beautiful weather and scenic shores of Nevis, tourism was a natural fit. The move away from farming was gradual as Montserrat transitioned into a resort. A portion of the Iles estate became a sister property with access to the beach. Many of the slaves who toiled in the fields worked at the Montserrat Hotel for years to come. John Day became the first slave to be emancipated and acted as one of the primary managers of the facility. He wore the scars on his back as badges of pride and a reminder of the cruelty created by the institution of slavery.

Grace also became close with Horatio's son, Alex, and spent holidays and other special events with the Iles family. In time, she moved into Horatio's home. After leaving her bedroom door open for months, hoping Horatio would wish to express his affection, she climbed into bed with him one night and that's where she slept from that point forward. By the time Horatio was forty-six and Grace twenty-nine, they made it official with a small, private wedding ceremony at Montserrat. Horatio wanted a grand social affair, but Grace never quite recovered from the spectacle of her sixteenth birthday party and never over-celebrated or over-invited guests for any occasion. By the time of her marriage in 1829, her reputation as a shrewd businesswoman proved to be all the protection she'd need from the whispers.

Soon after the couple had married, Grace began having children. The first, a girl, was named after Grace's mother, Luky. Two years later, a son, Samuel, joined the family. This increased the family size to five going into the early 1830s. The idea of the double-barreled name of Mackinnon Iles was suggested by Horatio during Grace's first pregnancy.

"Grace, your father was right about many things."

"Of course, Horatio, but he could also be blind when it came to me."

"Maybe not as much as you think. He always said that you would do great things in your life. Look at this resort that you've built. Yes, I give you full credit. You've achieved much more than even your father could have imagined."

"Don't you think that you played a role as well?"

"Thank you for saying that, but we both know where the ideas and energy came from."

Grace smiled as she gazed out on her property, which had become the finest resort in the Eastern Caribbean. Horatio joined her by the window and the couple took time to appreciate their accomplishments.

"Grace, the fact of the matter is that the Mackinnon and Iles families are among the most established in Nevis and our union has led to many important things." He gazed into his wife's eyes and took her hand.

"Well, yes," Grace said as she placed his hand on her belly. "Many wonderful things to be sure." The couple smiled as they felt a kick.

Horatio continued, "I want our children to have a daily reminder that they are the result of this wonderful union and I have an idea. You were the driving force behind all of this and I don't want your legacy to be forgotten."

"Oh, Horatio, I've got so many other things to worry about before I ever consider my legacy!" Grace laughed.

"I'm serious—this is important to consider right now because our children will provide an opportunity."

"I really don't understand what you're saying. What is this opportunity?"

"Our children should have both of our surnames. I know it is unusual, but if you give birth to the girl that you continue to hope for, her first name will come from your mother, Lucretia, and her full name should be Lucretia Mackinnon Iles."

Grace repeated the name to herself silently several times and then shortened it as she said it out loud. "Luky Mackinnon Iles. I love it!"

Luky would prove to be the only female who was given the double-barreled name, but all males for the next hundred years were named in this manner. Grace's son, Samuel Mackinnon Iles, fathered Henry Mackinnon Iles, who then brought Bruce Mackinnon Iles into the world when he relocated to Trinidad.

Bruce wound up in New York and continued the naming tradition with his son, H.O., who died childless in 2003, marking the end of Mackinnon Iles line.

Horatio Iles passed away at the age of fifty-one, months before slavery was abolished in 1834. Grace lost her husband, but John Day and her children, including her stepchild, Alex, gave her the support she needed to move Nevis's premier family forward. Alex was devoted to his stepmother and later in life joked that his success as a politician was achieved without benefit of the famous double-barreled surname, of which he was unfairly deprived.

A day didn't go by without John and Grace getting together in some way. Their connection stood the test of time and they looked after each other's interests for the rest of their lives. John maintained records tracking the work of each of the slaves at Montserrat and Grace kept her word. After one year, seventy-five percent were emancipated and after another six months, the remainder were free as well. More than half stayed on as employees.

Grace Mackinnon Iles, a woman born before her time, found her way to freedom, success, and love without ever compromising her beliefs or principles. She gave each of her children the following advice: "Your father was a White man and a rich one at that. Your mother is mixed, which in the eyes of the world makes her colored. You're the child of this union, so you're also mixed. Always remember . . . don't ever try to hide it. This island is too small. Everyone knows everyone else's business. This means that you need to look ahead and avoid putting yourself in situations where you can be embarrassed. You can always count on some Whites to throw your blood in your face, no matter how much you accomplish in life—expect the worst and prepare accordingly, but remember, never try to hide it."

Grace followed this approach until the day she died at the age of forty-five. Her death devastated John Day, who passed one week later. She never saw her stepson, Alex, assume his seat on the Executive Committee of Nevis, one of the highest positions in government, a few years later in 1852. Grace also never witnessed the migration of the family when her daughter, Luky, accompanied her grandson Henry as he left for Trinidad to pursue a career in law. Grace lived her life like she signed her name, by adding a little extra flourish to that final "n."

Part Five

Long Island
2009

CHAPTER 29

Daydreams

ILVA STOOD AND gave her son a kiss on the cheek. "Dustin, this story about the Mackinnons answers so many questions. No one had any idea about the generation before my grandfather, Henry Mackinnon Iles, in Trinidad. We knew he came from Nevis and there was also something about a famous politician back then, but nothing more."

"Some researchers did the legwork for me and I just pieced it together," Dustin said.

"I hadn't realized all the men in the family had Mackinnon inserted before Iles. My brother didn't even want to use the name Horatio, so there was no way he would use Mackinnon."

"Yes, he was Horatio Mackinnon Iles and his great-great-grandparents were Grace Mackinnon and Horatio Iles."

"Something we never knew. I wish your Aunt Grace were here for all of this. It also explains why there are so many Graces in the family."

"What about Horatio Iles? Did you have any idea about him?"

"No. We thought my grandmother Julia made up the story about the rich planter from Nevis so my brother would feel better about his name. We always thought H.O. was named after Horatio Nelson, the famous Navy captain who spent time in Nevis."

"I must say, I am enjoying this project, Mom." Dustin smiled as he considered the value his research added to the family's understanding of their story. He wondered what other mysteries and discoveries awaited him. "So what's next, Mom? Where do we go from here?"

Ilva slumped her shoulders. "Wait, Dustin. First, tell me about some of the details, like Grace's sixteenth birthday party and cruel Uncle Sinclair—things you couldn't have determined from your detective work. Where did all of this come from? Are the dreams continuing?"

Dustin's smile dropped from his face and he turned his gaze from his mother to the world beyond the window. The touch of his mother's hand on his own pulled him back inside.

"Dustin, please stay with me. I just want to know about the dreams. Tell me as much or as little as you want."

"Okay, Mom. I figured out how to direct them. If I immerse myself in something right before I go to sleep, there's a strong possibility I'll dream about that thing. This is what happened here. I woke up on my terrace and scribbled on a notepad for about a half an hour."

"Here's a suggestion for you—always hold onto those notes because then, later on, you'll be able to distinguish that part of the story from what you add to make it flow so well."

Dustin straightened up in his chair and his right leg started to bop. "I kept a journal of dreams when I was a kid. Whatever happened to that book, Mom?"

"Let me hold your hand." Ilva grabbed her son's right hand and laughed. "You are such a bad liar, Dustin! You must have found the book when you cleaned up. Ask your question."

"Why did you tear out the pages and leave me that note?"

"I did that a long time ago, because I thought reading about your old dreams could trigger something that we didn't want."

"I guess I understand, but why do you want me to keep a journal now? Aren't both the dreams and my imagination nothing more than two parts of the same thing? The only hard facts in the story are the connections made through the John Day bill of sale and my other digging about Grace Mackinnon and Horatio Iles. Everything else is from my head—you've always known that your youngest son has an imagination." He laughed.

"I told you this before—your dreams aren't the same as your imagination." Ilva turned toward the window and admired the willow tree in the yard as she organized her thoughts. Dustin's chuckle had morphed into a stare as his eyes locked onto the teenage portrait of his mother. Ilva touched him on the shoulder and started to hum, but before she began singing the words, she shifted gears and snapped both of her fingers several times. "Son, are you with me? We need to talk about something."

"Yes, Mom. I'm here."

Mother and son had replayed the same scene many times, so Dustin understood that certain body language combined with a handful of leading questions offered in a particular tone meant that an uncomfortable discussion about his challenges and shortcomings was imminent. He wasn't in the mood.

"Mom, you're about to explain how I'm troubled. Please don't start with this again. I know already—I move too much, no woman is good enough, I'm not connected to anything, and I'm responsible for no one. I get it, I'm a goddamn messed-up mystery. Please let this go and stop rehashing it every time I see you."

It was Dustin's turn to wander out the window. His eyes traveled along the largest branch on the willow tree and inched along its length toward the main trunk. Ilva waited for his attention to return inside. Once he focused again on the young teenage portrait of his mother, Ilva touched him on the shoulder and started to hum the melody before singing the words, "Are you sleeping, are you sleeping? Brother John, Brother John . . ."

Dustin's eyes closed and Ilva left to start dinner. She returned several minutes later and pulled her chair closer to her son before touching him again on the shoulder. "I'm sorry, Dustin. I wasn't going to rehash anything. I wanted to talk about your dreams because I found them fascinating years ago. Sometimes I sat by your bed with a pencil and paper. They went both ways."

"What do you mean, both ways?"

"Some were from the past and some went forward. I'll tell you right now, the future wasn't all made up. There was always at least a kernel of truth in those visions. Don't dismiss them as nonsense. What parts of the story came from the dream, Dustin?"

"I had images of the party when Grace was sixteen and picked up on her sense of ridicule, as well as visions of her both in the mansion and the slave quarters. One of the themes was also prominent."

"Which one?"

"Don't ever try to hide it . . . Nevis is too small."

"Well, this is where she and I differ. Nevis is a world away from New York and this city is one of the largest in the world. You can hide whatever you want in New York. Grace Mackinnon's rule was for a different time and place."

"I'm not so sure. This may be what you did, but I don't think it will work for me."

"I'm warning you—don't start with all of this *I had a right to know* crap. I did what I had to do to enable all three of you to be where you are today. Maybe you can scream it out loud now because you no longer need to create your path in life . . . the very path that I gave you."

Dustin didn't want the evening to deteriorate, so he resisted the urge to escalate the tension. He said, "Mom, I thank you for what you gave me, but when you talk about this in such a way that it seems like you view it as a scandal or a burden, it bothers me. Some of our ancestors were amazing people who did important things. What's wrong in celebrating them?"

"You're right about that—we do come from good stock, but the world isn't ready. I would like to think things have changed, but the more I watch the news on television, the more I appreciate that things haven't evolved enough for us to be shouting anything from the rooftops." Ilva clapped her hands together and then slapped them on the tabletop. "Enough. Let's see if your poor handwriting has improved. On to the bills!"

Ilva's suggestion to switch gears lightened the mood for the rest of the visit. Tuna fish casserole with crushed potato chips followed their brief bill-paying session. Dustin's mind started to wander and then a spinning sensation took control as his eyes moved to his mother's portrait. The spinning eventually subsided and Dustin found himself still in the dining room, but his mother was young and they weren't alone. It was 1970 and Dustin was eating the same exact casserole at the same table. Paddy gargled his soda and Charlie chuckled as some of the drink shot from his nose. Everyone laughed, except for Dustin, which Paddy took as a challenge. Charlie, frustrated with Dustin's nonresponse, said, "Paddy, don't waste your time on the little weirdo."

Ilva took hold of his hand. "Dustin, where did you go, what happened?"

"Sorry, Mom. I have a lot on my mind." He stood and started packing up his things. "I need to head out. I'll see you next Sunday."

"But you didn't finish your meal. What's wrong?"

"Sorry, I'm not feeling well. I think something hit me all of a sudden. Got to go."

Dustin scrambled away from the table and headed straight for his car. His mother barely had arrived at her customary spot by the door before he provided his signature double honk. The remnants of his daydream were slowly replaced by an overarching question as Dustin headed back home. *What was wrong with me when I was a child?*

CHAPTER 30

What Are You?

DUSTIN ARRIVED LAST at the Mexican restaurant and stood at the door for a few moments as he heard the applause emanating from the back of the dining area. Paddy, who was already three drinks and two appetizers into his evening, had just performed a comedy routine for the server and surrounding customers. Dustin made his way to the table and told the Mackinnon-Iles story while they awaited their dinners. The food arrived as he finished the tale and Charlie held her question until the waitress walked away. "How do you come up with all of this? What's real and what's made up?"

Dustin was tired of answering this question and worried that weaving facts, dreams, and imaginary tidbits together was proving to be more of a distraction than anything else. He exhaled and took a sip of his scotch. "I had a talk with Mom about this—it seems like what I'm doing might be a problem for everyone, including me, so I'll stop embellishing the stories. The John Day record is legit. The discovery of our ancestors Horatio Iles and Grace Mackinnon is verified. You can forget the rest of what I said."

Paddy tried to take control. "Calm down . . . I know you better than anyone. Remember, I slept five feet away from you for seventeen years. You were different back then because you were going through something. I don't say that to upset you, but that's the truth."

Dustin played with the guacamole on his plate. He alternated between building a pile and creating shapes. Paddy and Charlie exchanged glances and tried not to stare at their upset younger brother. Dustin shrugged his shoulders. "I'm sorry. You're right, we were all kids and you did apologize." He tapped his spoon on his tumbler and made a toast. "To us." The three siblings touched glasses, which cleared the air, and Dustin asked, "Tell me what you remember about what I did at night, Paddy."

"The drama began when you were about nine years old. This is when Dad started using the word *normal*. First, your dreams weren't *normal*—then it was you. Around that time, your dreams became dark."

Charlie asked, "What do you mean by dark?"

"Dustin wrote stuff down in the book by his bed when he woke up." Paddy turned to his brother. "I read your note about Aunt Rita. Never told you, but I did tell Mom."

Dustin lowered his head as he remembered.

Charlie put her fork down and planted both of her fists on the tabletop. "Where the hell was I when all of this was going on? What note about Aunt Rita?"

Paddy lowered his voice. "He knew she was going to die and she did the next day. Dustin, your dreams can be like visions and they aren't total bullshit. You're bringing the past to life, but I'm not sure what all of this means in the present."

Charlie's fists opened momentarily to grasp the napkin and then clenched again. "Paddy, what do you mean by that?"

"What do we do with this revelation about being mixed-race? What does it change? If someone asks me, 'What are you?' Am I supposed to answer in a different way than I did before?"

All three siblings returned to rearranging the food on their plates. Food shuffling while avoiding or contemplating the answer to a question was a longtime Murphy family tradition. Charlie was the first to respond. "I'm not sure, but what did you say before?"

Paddy raised both hands. "I always went with the obvious."

Charlie turned to Paddy. "Why are you making me work so hard in this conversation? What's your obvious answer?"

Paddy stood and shouted, "What am I?" He punctuated his question with a twirl, which almost knocked his glass to the floor, and then answered his own question. "I'm a big fat fuck!"

Charlie's fists opened as she laughed and the people at the surrounding tables provided their second round of applause of the evening, but Dustin only offered a smile as he couldn't move his mind out of the past. He recalled the vision of his Aunt Rita lying on her hospital bed as Charlie and Paddy continued their conversation.

"When you think about it, why do people ask this question?" Charlie asked. "Why do they need to put everyone they meet in a category? Did you ever ask Mom that question, Paddy?"

"Yes, she stares you down and says, 'I'm American.' The stare tells you to stop asking stupid shit and her response points out the issue with the question."

Charlie nodded. "Yeah, I understand. People are trying to determine ethnicity in an indirect way. So they ask, *What are you?* This kind of implies nationality, like how Mom responds. I get this question sometimes because I'm darker."

"People assume I'm a White Irishman," Paddy said. "How about you, Dustin?"

Dustin's mind was years away as he recalled his dream about Aunt Rita. He remembered somehow understanding her thoughts as she'd taken stock of her life. Whether she had considered things she'd done or wanted to do, Aunt Rita had felt no regrets and wouldn't have changed a thing if she could've done it all over again. *That's the way to live a life.* He snapped out of his daydream when he heard his name. "Sorry, Paddy, my mind wandered for a minute. We're talking about the *what are you* question, right?" Paddy and Charlie nodded. "For the most part, only people who don't look White get asked this question—it actually is pretty inappropriate to ask someone you just met. Perhaps the best thing to do is ask another question in response."

"Like what?" Charlie asked.

"How about, *Why do you ask?* This will force the person to understand the awkwardness of what they're asking."

Charlie took a sip of her drink and tilted her head sideways. "Good point, but you never said how you answer the question, Dustin."

"I used to say that I'm an Irish Trinidadian because I thought it sounded interesting."

Charlie's eyes connected with Dustin's. "And how did you explain Trinidadian?"

Dustin smirked. "I used Mom's meaningless European Caribbean explanation, which never made sense to anyone."

"It shouldn't have made sense to you," Charlie said.

Paddy added, "You can respond however you want, but I'm sticking with my *fat fuck* answer."

Dustin straightened his back and cleared his throat. "I know you're keeping things light, Paddy, but let's think about this for a second. We laughed at your an-swer because—I hate to say it—by any reasonable standard, you are a *fat fuck* and, oddly enough, it is somewhat acceptable for me to make that observation because I too could eat a little more salad. We've all seen Black comics make Black jokes, heavy comedians make fat jokes, and it's all okay because they own it. But for us, we grew up White, embracing the White world, and just because our mother thought it was time for us to understand a few things and I did some research, we don't own any part of the Black experience. So where does this leave us? Are we White, Black, mixed, or what?"

The three siblings again turned their attention to their plates. Dustin lined up his beans in orderly rows on either side of a river of sauce while his brother and sister focused on finding something of interest in the remains of their salad. Again, Charlie broke the silence. "I guess we'll always live some-where in the middle and this may be the only thing we can own—we can't cross certain lines. So, if you ever decide to do stand-up, Paddy, take that advice to heart."

"For sure," Paddy said.

The server overheard *stand-up* as she approached the table. "I knew you were a comic! Have I seen you on TV?"

"I doubt it. I haven't been on the tube for the last two years." Paddy winked. "Could you bring me another sangria, please?"

"Paddy, you lied to that woman," Charlie whispered.

"How so? Was I wrong? Have I been on television in the past two years?"

"Come on, your answer was vague and you let her assume," Dustin said.

"We may have done it unwittingly, but isn't this what we've done our whole lives?" Charlie asked. Her comment lingered as they continued to pick at their food. Paddy protected his black beans inside a fort made from his remaining pieces of lettuce. Three tortilla chips lurked outside the gates. The waitress came back with the bartender before the chips made their move. "A complementary round for the celebrity and his party. Enjoy!"

The barkeep turned to Paddy. "I think I saw you at Caroline's a few years ago. You were really *on* that night."

"Thanks, I may have been a few drinks into my evening. Sometimes it helps." Paddy smiled and took a sip of his sangria.

Charlie waited for the bartender to walk away. "You're terrible. Are you saying none of *that* was a lie?"

Paddy laughed. "Total truth. I was at Caroline's two years ago. I had several drinks and was *on* as I enjoyed the show. The cocktails did help that night!"

Dustin shook his head. "Smooth, Paddy, very smooth."

On the ride back home, Dustin considered both his regular Sunday visit with his mother, as well as dinner with his siblings. Each discovery hinted at an underlying truth that would either free him from the ghost of his childhood or push him back to a dark place long forgotten. He was determined to deal with whatever his ghost proved to be. The discovery part, however, depended on his mother to open up, and this would not happen without a tremendous amount of patience and finesse—two things currently in short supply.

CHAPTER 31

Two Meatballs

THE RICH AROMA from the large pot of sauce wafted through the kitchen, thickening as it traveled. It brought back childhood memories of wading through the heavy aromatic air of his mother's kitchen in the hope of getting an early sample. The coast was clear and Dustin removed the lid from the pot. Anthony's voice came from above. "Uncle Dustin, no cheating. Wait for dinner."

Dustin turned to his nephew, who was on the staircase. "Really? We have enough food for ten people."

"You have a point . . . go ahead and knock yourself out. Here's Matt now."

Matthew offered his brother and uncle a fist pound. "Hey, just came from a video shoot. Did we already go over the fact that the food may be a bit too much?"

The three men laughed. "I'll bring the dinner out now," Anthony said. "We want to talk to you about something, Uncle Dustin. We think you need a different viewpoint on all of this stuff with the family history."

The three men filled their plates with linguini while Anthony added his homemade sauce and meatballs as the topping. They weren't in the habit of saying grace, but their momentary pause as their senses were primed by the sight and smell of the food accomplished the same objective. After the first few mouthfuls, Dustin asked, "So what different viewpoint should I consider?"

Anthony dabbed his mouth with his napkin before he responded. "We started to tell you when we worked on the house in Hicksville, but I'm not sure you understood. This whole mixed thing is new for you, but not us." Anthony motioned to his brother and then back at himself. "You could learn a thing or two from us on the topic."

"Feel free to school me, but first, I have to ask you—are there beans inside these meatballs?"

Anthony nodded. "Yes, I didn't want to tell you until you tasted them."

Both Dustin and Matthew took another nibble, and Matt proclaimed, "Damn, I think you found a new taste sensation! Let me have some more. Do you think we have enough?" He smirked at the mountain of unserved food still in the bowl.

The chatter slowed as the consumption increased. Anthony placed his fork next to his plate, gazed out the windowed walls, and said, "What's with the red birds?"

"Yeah, check out the cool black outline around their eyes," Matthew added.

"I spotted one over there the other day and now I see three at times," Dustin said. "Must be something about the greenery or the trees or someone is feeding them. In any case, I don't need anything else to investigate at this point. So, what are your thoughts on all of the family discoveries?"

Anthony led the way. "We have a different take. Both Matt and I felt like we didn't fit in growing up. Remember, we grew up in White Floral Park, which was surrounded by two Black and Puerto Rican/Central American areas. There was a division by neighborhood and some people believed we lived in the wrong part."

"I never thought about that," Dustin said.

"Neither did our father," Matthew added. "Welcome to the middle. We've been here for a long time, but it's different for us as compared to you . . . and different still for Grandma."

"How so?" Dustin asked.

"Well, with you, the difference is the appearance," Anthony said. "You look White, pure and simple. Both Matt and I look more Puerto Rican and first impressions create the reality of a situation. People only think we're mixed when they meet our Dad, which means that we encounter a lot of first impression issues you could never understand."

"Like what?" Dustin asked.

"Being spied on by a clerk in a store," Anthony answered.

"Being looked down on before someone says hello," Matthew added.

Dustin placed his fork next to his plate and sat back in his chair. "Why do you think it's different in another way for your grandmother?"

Matthew looked to his older brother, who held up his hand as he finished chewing a sizable mouthful of pasta. "Okay, Anthony, I'll take this one. Grandma probably could blend in on either side, but given how she hid things from her kids, I wonder if she did other things to avoid the issue altogether."

"You mean that she might have tried to *pass* at a young age?" Dustin asked.

Matthew answered, "We don't know if this was something she did early on or maybe it started when all of you moved to Hicksville, which, from what we understand, was even more White than Floral Park."

"But getting back to us," Anthony said. "I'm sure we can all agree it is understandable for people to dislike Matt after they meet him, but fair is fair—to think bad things about him even before he opens his mouth? Come on now, that's not right!"

The three men chuckled.

"Do you remember when I was deep into my basketball days and had the long braids?" Matthew asked.

"Yeah, it was a look," Dustin said.

"I focused on my differences, trying to find out where I belonged, or at least thumbing my nose at the group that didn't accept me. Kind of making a statement. I'm not sure it helped in any way, but it was part of my process in finding myself. Do you get that, Uncle Dustin?"

Dustin smiled. "Yes, I think I do. Thanks."

Anthony threw the first meatball at his brother. "Why don't you get *this*, Matthew?" Matthew returned fire.

Dustin stepped away from the table, laughing. "The two of you go from being deep and profound to absolute idiots in a heartbeat."

Anthony laughed. "Yeah, we've got skills!"

Dustin retreated to The Castle as his nephews cleaned up their mess. Three of the masked red birds sat quietly above Ilva's plot and offered a knowing stare. The dinner conversation had provided a different perspective and one significant takeaway. Dustin realized that his privilege was due primarily to his clear first impression.

CHAPTER 32

Three Vignettes

DUSTIN WENT ABOUT his typical evening routine. Glasses on the nightstand and phone next to the bed. Music created the best environment for him to enter into a deep, dream-filled slumber, so he selected smooth jazz and started shuffling songs from an online station. Dustin needed answers and, for him, many of them came with sleep. The first song featured a saxophone trading solos with a piano, but not in competition, but rather in concert with each other. The piano posed a question and the saxophone provided the answer, and the two master musicians displayed a sense of cooperation as their improvised interaction continued. After several bars, however, their melodic gymnastics moved into the background and Dustin's mind concentrated on the pulsing bass line. First, he heard it, then he felt it, and by the time he saw it, his eyes were closed.

Two themes kept circulating in his mind: Grace Mackinnon's *never try to hide it* and his nephews' *the power of first impressions*. The bass line became the path and he traveled upward until he reached an altitude that seemed right—high enough to provide separation, but close enough to see down below. After a brief trip, he arrived.

Three vignettes appeared from the past: the interview for his first management job that set the trajectory for his career, an airport security desk, and a traffic checkpoint with a line of cars. He started to descend. The year was 1982 and Dustin was fresh out of college and looking for his start in business. He *earned his bones* in his initial job and made all the contacts that would lead to the successful management consulting practice he enjoyed for many years.

Dustin studied his competition, a sharp-looking Black man, perhaps a few years his senior, and a young woman about his age. The hiring manager walked to the reception desk and called out, "Mr. Murphy." Dustin followed him back to his office.

"Good morning. May I please have a copy of your resume?"

"Yes, sir." Dustin passed the document to the interviewer and glanced at it himself. *Wait, this isn't where I went to school. I attended a neighborhood two-year community college and then got my bachelor's degree at another local school.* This Dustin Murphy graduated from Fisk University, a well-known Southern institution. Dustin reviewed his impressive list of collegiate accomplishments, including his involvement with Greek life. He even had excellent internship experiences tied to his field of study. Dustin realized this new resume was much stronger than the original.

"Mr. Murphy, your background confuses me. How does someone like you, from Hicksville, wind up at Fisk and become such a well-connected member of the community?"

Theme #1: never try to hide it.

"I'm not sure I understand the question. What do you mean by someone like me? Someone from Long Island?"

"Well, not exactly, but I guess I'm saying that you don't fit the typical profile of someone who attends Fisk."

Theme #2: the power of first impressions.

"Oh. I understand." *Someone White like me from a White area like Hicksville.* "I always heard great things about Fisk and as a mixed-race person proud of his Black heritage, a historically Black college proved to be an excellent choice. I was quite involved while pursuing my degree."

"Yes, *very* involved. I'm afraid, though, that I have some bad news for you. This is a courtesy meeting, because we filled the job a few hours ago. We're finishing up the interviews in order to build our bullpen. You know, people on standby should we need someone in the future. I want to thank you . . ."

Dustin raised his finger and headed back into the sky. He couldn't believe what he had seen. Initially, the interviewer had loved him and they had kept a lively and easy banter going throughout the meeting. He wondered, *If I didn't land this job with this stronger resume, it was the admission of my connection to the Black community that denied me the position, but my physical appearance got me through the door. Without this job, what would have happened with my career?*

Dustin pointed down again, but this time to an airline security desk in 2001. He remembered this scene, right after 9/11, when all airports had tightened their security protocols. He had shown up at the small airport in Oklahoma especially early in anticipation of the new security measures.

Dustin took it all in. On the left side, two mature White men waiting in an orderly line to see a check-in attendant. To the right, a mass of people waiting in a disorganized fashion to have their bags inspected. Dustin decided to go to the left and recalled what had happened the first time this scene played out. Within minutes he was checked in and directed to the gates. He decided to ask about all of the craziness on the right side of the check-in area, and the airline employee said, "Oh, you didn't go there first?" Dustin shrugged and realized he had made a terrible blunder. The agent took a long gaze at forty-year-old Dustin and said, "Ah, no worries. You don't look like a terrorist."

Theme #2: the power of first impressions.

The scene began to replay itself as Dustin entered the more orderly left side, but with a Black businessman, similar age and dress, following behind him. They settled into the line behind the two older gentlemen, and the agent instructed, "I hope both of you went through the bag search on the other side. If not, head there now."

There was one more vignette to relive and Dustin pointed down to a line of police checking vehicles in Bayside, Queens, on a Friday night in 1995. He'd been out with a few of his friends and they had each consumed a small amount of alcohol, but they were all in good enough shape to drive. Dustin remembered what had happened the first time with this traffic stop. The policeman came up to the driver's-side window and asked Dustin if he had anything to drink. Dustin answered, "Yes, but very little and over a long period of time." The officer asked him to clarify. "Two light beers over three hours." He was told to drive on.

The scene rewound and Dustin was now in the back seat and one of his friends, a Black man about the same age, sat in the driver's seat. The same policeman walked toward the driver's side but stopped when Dustin's friend rolled down the window. He called back to his partner, "Joe, give me a hand." The two officers approached the car and asked for all the windows to be rolled down. They started with the driver. "Have you been drinking?" The friend said, "Yes, but very little over a long period of time." The lead officer said, "I'm going to need you to step out of the vehicle, sir, and submit to a sobriety test." Dustin returned to his vantage point in the sky.

A jolt of energy ran through his body, tensing his muscles. Dustin popped up in bed and out of his dream. He pulled his pad and pen onto his lap, but there was nothing to write despite all that he had learned. Rather than providing new information to be recorded, his dream provided the gift of perspective. Dustin's skin color always enabled him to *pass*. He asked himself, *But is it passing if you are unaware of your ethnicity?*

He thought about his lost job opportunity, which was classic racism without the name-calling. The position had come down to three candidates: Dustin, an older Black man, and a woman. If he hadn't been hired because of the late realization of his background, what chance did the Black candidate have? Could it also be that in order to justify hiring a White man, having the two runners-up consist of a woman and a Black man had created the perfect cover? *Was I really the best person for this job, the one that set me up for life?*

Dustin had gotten through the first fifty years of his life oblivious to so much. He was torn by the sense that his advantages in life translated into disadvantages for others and wondered if he had deserved his business success. He got himself organized enough to go downstairs for coffee and opened the mail as he sat at his kitchen table. The envelope with poor handwriting stood out.

Dustin,

I never claimed to be a perfect mother and I waited too long to explain about your race and your lost month, as we've been calling it. My sister pushed me to tell you sooner, but I wouldn't listen. This note may seem odd, but I needed to tell you something without seeing your face when I said it—not sure I'm making sense. The first thing is the race issue. I cannot speak about it anymore and I trust you will safeguard this sensitive information.

As for what happened years ago, I thought I could use Charlie as a go-between, but I don't think this will work, because I'm not ready to talk about this either and I'm not sure I ever will be. I made a decision back then to do something to keep you with the family and you're still dealing with the fallout from this after all of this time. I want you to understand that I was by your side and always watched out for you, but I see now that I made mistakes.

Your time away as a child was traumatic and I don't think reliving the trauma will help you to move forward with your life. I also think there is a good chance that it

will take you many years to forgive me for what I did. I'm eighty-five years old and cannot leave this world without the forgiveness of my baby boy. I believe it will be easier for you to accept my inability to continue these two important dialogues, rather than deal with the reality of what happened. I'll understand if you stay away for a while, but I want to return to our routine soon. Sundays are my favorite day of the week.
Mom

Dustin walked out to The Castle and thought about his mother's message and request for forgiveness. He had done the work asked of him and solved some family mysteries along the way. In doing so, however, he had raised more questions than provided answers. He thought, *What should I do with this newfound knowledge? Maybe she's right. Why do I need to relive whatever happened forty years ago?* His eyes focused on the red birds and they returned his glare. Someone passed by on the street below, noticed him, and waved. Dustin went back inside.

Maybe I've taken this as far as I can. Dustin placed his box of family research on the top shelf in his bedroom closet and concluded that it was time to get back to both his business and his regular routine. He turned to Grandpa Joe and said, "It looks like all the excitement and discovery is over—just the two of us now. Oh, sorry, Aunt Ilva. It's the three of us." He turned his head toward the grassy area as he said her name and his eyes headed up to the red birds. They were gone.

Part Six

Long Island
2017

CHAPTER 33

Déjà Vu

DUSTIN WOKE UP covered in sweat on the floor of his bedroom closet. "The basement again! Damn it!" He threw on some clothes and headed for his car, but he couldn't call the police. How could he explain the source of his information was a dream, the first of this type in many years? The last flurry had taken place during the time he'd conducted the research on his family history about eight years earlier. He neared the turnoff from the expressway. *I wonder if I should move her?* he thought. *I made a mistake the last time.*

He pulled up to the house and rushed in. The front door was unlocked and the door to the cellar ajar. Dustin navigated around the junk that had reaccumulated. His mother's leg stuck out from behind a stack of newspapers. She was crumpled almost in a pile, no visible blood, but unconscious.

He didn't dare move her and called for an ambulance. The same attendant from the last incident was the lead EMS agent. "Mr. Murphy, this is like déjà vu. This is where she fell eight years ago, right? Does she still live by herself?"

"No, I mean, yes, she does. Please check her out."

The two attendants revived Ilva and placed her on a gurney. She took Dustin's hand. "I'm glad you're here. She needs you."

He offered a quizzical glance as he grabbed hold of his mother's hand.

Dustin followed the ambulance to the hospital in his car, making calls along the way. Within the hour, all three children were gathered around their mother's bed in the ER. "Thank you for being here," Ilva said. "Bruce, please lean down. I'm having trouble speaking in a loud voice."

Paddy touched the palm of his hand to his chest. "Do you mean me?"

"Yes, of course, Bruce, please bend down."

Paddy lowered his ear to his mother's mouth. She whispered, "I'm so proud of what you did for Grace. It took real courage and love." Paddy turned back to his sister and shrugged.

Ilva also wanted to speak to her. "Grace, my dear. Please come closer."

Charlie bent down and her mother said, "Your father loves you, but"—she motioned to Dustin—"now you must count on him."

Charlie smiled and gave her mother a kiss on the temple, "Of course, Mom."

Ilva found being referred to as *Mom* to be funny and started laughing. "You people and your games! Don't worry. I've known for some time." She looked at Dustin. "He showed me the way."

The doctor popped her head through the curtain. "The nurse needs to check out your mother again, so can I ask all of you to please step outside? We can use this time to go over a few details about care moving forward." Once in the hallway, the doctor closed the door to the room before continuing. "Your mother survived her fall very well, although we are still running some tests to rule out complications. The fact that she lost consciousness for so long is a concern. She's ninety-three and lives alone, so can I assume she was more fully functioning before the fall?"

Charlie nodded. "Yes, she was, Doctor. She drove as recently as last month."

"Well, I suggest you take some time to rethink both the driving and the living arrangements. Your mother may or may not regain more of her lucidity. It seems clear that she needs some help, but don't worry—there is ample time to work things out. We'll keep her here for a couple of days to run more tests and for observation. Rehab will follow before she can go home. Right now, she's unsteady on her feet. Understand?"

"Yes, thank you, Doctor," Dustin said.

The doctor continued, "Your mother is fortunate to have the three of you working together. Arrangements for the rehab facility need to be made with the social worker, who you can find in the offices at the end of this hallway. Admitting also has some questions regarding insurance, and then, of course, there is the most important job of all."

"Which is?" Paddy asked.

The doctor laughed. "What all of you are here to do! Keep your mother company and try to make her laugh." The doctor turned to Paddy. "I think that might be your job. Paddy, is it?"

"Yes, Paddy Murphy, at your service." He curtsied and bumped into a tray of food in the process.

The doctor broke out in a hysterical laugh. "I heard your little routine with the staff earlier. I think she would benefit from some of your humor. You definitely brightened my day."

Charlie waited until the doctor was out of earshot. "Jesus, Paddy, you're flirting with the nurses and now the doctor?"

He chuckled. "I'll go back with Mom."

⋆──◯ ◯──⋆

Paddy stepped out from behind the curtain as Dustin and Charlie returned to the room and ushered them back out to the hallway. "Let me talk to the two of you for a minute."

"What's on your mind?" Dustin asked.

"When I went back inside, I started making some jokes and Mom showed no interest. Since I killed it with the young girl in the bed next to her, I knew it wasn't the quality of the material or my delivery."

"Duly noted," Dustin said. "So what did you want to tell us?"

"Well, after she listened for a few minutes, she told me, in so many words, to stop all of the bullshit."

"Actually, those were likely her exact words," Charlie pointed out.

"You're right. Can't put anything past you," Paddy joked.

Charlie stuck her tongue out and punched Paddy in the shoulder.

Dustin grew impatient. "So what happened? What do you want to tell us?"

"All right, I'm getting there. She called me Bruce again and, since she was so clear, I corrected her and said, 'I'm not your father. He's Grandpa Bruce to me. I'm your son, Paddy.' Then she sat up in her bed and said, 'Stop the shit. Yes, you're Paddy, but I mean who you really are.' This is when it got a little weird." Paddy waited a moment to organize his next thought. Charlie put her arm on his shoulder. "Don't leave us hanging. Who did she say you *really* are?"

"She said that I'm Bruce Mackinnon and you're my daughter, Grace."

"And Dustin?"

"He's the one that you count on more than anyone else in the world. She said you're going to be tested and this is the person who never lets you down."

Charlie stared at her brother. "Who would that be?"

"John Day."

CHAPTER 34

Back in the City

THESE TRIPS ARE killing me, Dustin thought as he entered the Midtown Tunnel, ninety minutes into his drive from the rehab center. The traffic crawled through the tube and he glanced down at his watch. *It could take me another half-hour to go crosstown.* He had stayed in Queens for three years and, since his return to Manhattan, he was now on his second apartment. He pulled up into his garage and collapsed onto the bed the moment he set foot inside.

His work had morphed in the last few years from traveling and speaking to more of the written word. His last nonfiction title had added enough to his savings to enable him to slow down at the age of fifty-seven. He needed to publish the follow-up to his successful book within the next few months to take advantage of his initial momentum, but his mother's fall had set him back from his schedule. He took his laptop onto the terrace and dug in for what he hoped would be a productive session.

The text messages started slowly at first and increased in frequency to the point that he silenced his phone. *She won't stop.* After the vibrations had become as annoying as the bells, he typed the same message one last time: I'M SORRY I LET YOU DOWN. I'M NOT READY TO COMMIT. TOO MUCH GOING ON. He knew the procedure well to block a number, which, for him, marked the true end to most of his relationships.

Two thousand words later, Dustin wanted a break and headed over to his favorite restaurant, a Spanish tapas place called Meson Sevilla. His outdoor table was waiting for him, as was a glass of Macallan. The waiter said, "We upgraded you to an 18 on us, courtesy of the manager. We missed you."

"Thanks, I love you guys." He paused and took a long sip of his scotch. "I'm spending a lot of time on the Island. My mother is having some problems."

"You sound like a good son."

"Thanks, I do what I can."

Dustin enjoyed his little alfresco cut-out next to the steps leading down to the restaurant. The oversized menu facing the street blocked the view of him from the sidewalk, but he had a clear line of sight and enjoyed the variety of people who passed by.

She appeared two-thirds into his first scotch. "Blocked me, didn't you?"

"Yes, I figured after my five I'm sorrys and your sixty-two fuck yous, we pretty much covered it."

She chuckled. "Yeah, I think you're right. Sorry about all the texting, but you infuriate me. You just won't talk. It is clear, though, that you're going through something because you cry out at night. Who's Grace?"

"Not from this world, Josy."

"What the hell does that mean? If you started taking up with someone else, you could just tell me. I can't keep wasting my time. I'm no spring chicken."

"I'm ten years older than you, so what does that make me?"

"That's not the point. I just mean to say that there is something about you that I'm drawn to, but you're too much of a mystery and I don't know if I have the time to figure you out."

"I've been trying for the last fifty-seven years and I'm still working on it. Don't feel bad."

"See, that's the thing. You talk like you're not worth anything. Not worth my trouble or time, but I know that's not true. I snooped around a little bit in your apartment. Don't be mad at me. I found the picture book labeled Long Island Gaels and spent some time with it."

Dustin put his glass down and furrowed his brow. "My God, where are you going with this? My nephews were in that program when they were teenagers. The Gaels send talented kids to basketball tournaments all over and I help a little bit. Nothing more to it."

"I disagree. I learned something about you when I flipped through the pages. I did see your nephews' pictures in the beginning of the book, but you continued to save pictures of all the other kids every year for almost twenty years. You wrote down their names and made notes about who went on to play college ball. You even clipped a few newspaper articles about a handful of kids who made it big."

"So what's so mysterious about that?"

"I saw the letter they sent you last year."

"So now you're reading my mail?"

"I told you not to get mad at me—it just kind of fell out of the book. They wanted to honor you last year but you declined their offer and told them it was important to you to remain anonymous. Why, Dustin? You got to know them through pictures and newspaper articles. Why can't they get to know you?"

"I'm not doing it for recognition. The Gaels are a great organization and I was happy to help back then and I'll continue to do so for as long as I can. Not such a big deal. Really."

"You downplay everything that has to do with you. I hope you get that. You matter, Dustin. You'll always matter to me."

"Thanks, Josy. I appreciate that."

"I want you to do me one favor. This is why I came down here tonight."

"What is it?"

"Unblock me. I won't do any more bulk texting, I promise, but I want to be able to reach you if I ever need to talk. Somehow, it's important to me. You're just one of those people. A real shitty boyfriend to be sure, but someone who matters to me. Will you do this for me? Will you unblock me?"

Dustin handed her his phone and allowed her to unblock her own number. She stood up, kissed him on the cheek, and left. Thirty seconds later, she texted, GOODBYE, I HOPE YOU FIND YOUR WAY. He responded with a heart emoji and a smile. It was the best end to a relationship he'd had in ten years.

⊷▬◉ ◉▬⊷

Dustin indulged himself and lit a fine Cuban cigar out on his terrace. He loved the view of the Hudson River and the shoreline of New Jersey off to the right, but also enjoyed the ornate green masonry work of the Greek Orthodox church, which was next door. It featured a large cross that was angled perfectly with the center of his personal outdoor space. While this was a turnoff to some, Dustin sat outside early in the morning or very late at night to participate in his own personal mass. He asked God to nurse his mother back to physical and mental health and for only the best things in life for the rest of his family. His last request, however, related to him. "Lord, if you can help me find my way, my purpose, and where I belong, I will be grateful. I can't say I'm doing so well on my own, but only if you have time, Lord. First, make sure everybody else is okay. Amen."

CHAPTER 35

Home Again

"We'll be home soon, Mom. Do you remember when you were in rehab for your knee and the boys and I worked on the house?"

"You worked on the house?"

"Yes, years ago. Remember how Anthony, Matthew, and I cleared things out for you so you would have more space?"

"Anthony and Matthew are such good boys. How are they?"

"They're just fine—you saw them the other day in the rehab center."

"Yes, they brought a computer and showed me pictures of their new house. They set it up just like mine."

Dustin forced a smile. "How are you feeling?"

"Okay. Still a little unsteady on my feet and I'm always falling asleep. My dreams don't have a good on/off switch, so sometimes they continue when I'm awake. Do I sound crazy?"

"I wouldn't use that word, but I might say you sound confused. But no worries, Mom, we're all here to help."

"Once I'm home, I'll be fine on my own."

"How are you going to clean up the house, cook your meals, and manage day-to-day? You need help."

"Don't you tell me what I need. We've gone over this before. What I need is independence and privacy."

Dustin parked the car and walked around to open his mother's door. She struggled to both get out of the vehicle and set the walker on a straight path to the house. He helped her and after she was seated in her favorite chair in the den, he asked, "Are you sure you don't need any help?"

"Well, maybe a little, now that you mention it." She smiled. "Why are we here? This looks like the place the boys had on their computer when they came to the rehab center the other day. I thought you were taking me home?"

"Yes, Mom. You are home. Don't you recognize everything?"

Ilva stomped her foot on the floor. "Don't try to fool me, Dustin. Did Charlie put you up to this? This isn't my house. Look over there!" She pointed to an empty space next to her favorite chair. "My reading pile should be there. So where is it?"

"We cleaned up a little. That's all."

"Don't try to fool me, Dustin. I know that Charlie is behind this. She's always trying to be the boss. Enough with the games. Take me home. I'm tired and I want to go to sleep."

"Mom, it's only six."

"But everyone is waiting for me—you understand that better than anyone."

"Where are your dreams taking you?"

"To interesting places—I spend time with old friends and relatives. I love dreaming."

"I get that, but going to sleep at six? Can you hang in there for another couple of hours?"

"Okay, Dustin, I'll try." Ilva scanned the room and then scratched her head. "Maybe this is my house. I just don't know, but I trust you and it's so easy to read your face—you gave me a look like I was a crazy person when I said it wasn't my house."

"I'm sorry, Mom. You always did tell me that I have a bad poker face."

She smiled and took his hand. "I need to tell you something else, but I need for you to take me seriously. I've been thinking about this for a long time. Does it seem like I'm making sense right now?"

"Yes, it does."

"Look at me, because I want to say this the right way. When you discovered what you did about the Mackinnons, John Day, and Horatio Iles, you opened things up for me again. At the same time, things shut down for you because I told you I couldn't handle any more tough conversations. That was a failure on my part and I'm sorry."

"Mom, you don't need to bring all of this up again. I put it behind me."

"Maybe you shouldn't have because you stopped dreaming. And the dreams, Dustin, are what make you special. I should have told you that a long time ago."

"Let's not worry about me. We need to get you settled in. I—"

"No, this is important and I want you to hear me out. You need to start think-ing about your sister before you go to sleep at night because she needs help and your dreams will point you in the right direction. She's going to need you very soon and you have to promise me that you'll help. Do you promise?"

"Yes, I do. Scout's honor." He raised his right hand to his heart.

"Good, the two of you have been together many times. Do the right thing. I'm counting on you."

Ilva held out until eight and she was in a deep sleep by nine. Dustin was in the ad-jacent room watching television, but his mother's screaming and laughing became so loud he pulled a chair next to the bedroom door and started taking notes. The time period was clear—1930s New York. Ilva was reliving the scene where her father tried to beat Grace with a belt, but she dodged his blows. Aunt Rita came to the rescue.

The talk became muted and Dustin suspected something new had begun. He wrote what she said: "I won't do it, Aunt Rita. Let Bumpy Johnson find someone else to babysit his girlfriend's kid. Why do I have to do it?"

The volume decreased and the words became gestures, sighs, and waves. Three coughs provided the segue, leading to laughter and then clapping. Young Ilva turned to her mother in the theatre. "Can we go home now? Mama? I'm tired. No more movies. Do you think they're done yet?"

Dustin listened as his mother relived these scenes from her past as a young, vibrant girl. He understood why she so enjoyed her dreams as he looked at her walker and all of her medications lined up on the dresser.

A few minutes after Dustin had retired to the den, he heard the crash. His mother had fallen out of bed and lay on the floor moaning. He tried to open the door, but her body was in the way. "Stop. You're hurting me," she cried out.

"Move away from the door, so I can open it."

"Is that you, John? Don't worry about me, help Grace. She's going to need you soon."

"Mom, it's Dustin, try to move your body a little bit."

Dustin pushed the door open and lifted his mother back onto the bed. Once she was settled, he returned to his chair in the hallway and reviewed the notes he'd taken throughout the night, which included the names of people, places, and things from years ago. His mother's days had become nothing more than hours that needed to be passed, whereas her evenings were filled with laughter, tears, and action that could be enjoyed or provide challenge. Her cycle of life had taken a turn with this latest fall and Dustin understood she may have just rounded her final bend.

CHAPTER 36

Traveling Together

ANTHONY AND MATTHEW had a keen sense about when they were needed and Dustin, still exhausted from the night before, appreciated the help. Anthony cooked, claiming to have perfected his bean meatball recipe, and Matthew brought a six-pack of hard apple cider. Dustin couldn't keep his eyes open.

Ilva, sitting nearby, asked, "Is it time for bed?"

Matthew summarized things well. "This is one of the most boring parties I've ever been to! Grandma, I'm going to walk you into your room now."

As he left, Anthony gave the instructions, "Uncle Dustin, go upstairs. We'll clean up and take the first two three-hour shifts. This means you can have a solid six hours of rest. Now, go on."

Matthew took the first shift and retired to the den, where he could watch a little TV and be close to his sleeping grandmother. The screaming and laughing started after an hour or so, but Matthew ignored the sounds until he heard a crash. Both he and his brother ran into the room and found the lamp from the nightstand on the floor, but nothing else was disturbed in any way. Both boys decided to stay up and pulled two chairs by the bedroom door.

Ilva sat in a light rain, almost a mist, and kept rising but falling back. She wanted to be with all of her old friends and family. They were waiting for her, but every time she rose, she fell right back down to her bed. After three attempts, she felt the mattress jiggle and understood without any words being exchanged. He apologized for being late and they both elevated above the clouds. The skyline changed from day to night so fast it became steady gray, but as they neared their destination, they could once again distinguish the passing of each day. After some time, they descended for a look. The Montserrat Plantation peaked through the opening. Grace and John Day sat at a table in the slave quarters having dinner. Ilva called out, "Stay with her, John Day, we're all counting on you."

⋯⊷ ⊶⋯

Dustin also started to travel. It had been a long time. His last vision of his mother's fall had been abrupt and hadn't required flight. He flew at a high speed and moved on his own, but not by himself and not in the lead. Dustin followed and took direction without exchanging any words. He had a deep connection with his guide and caught a glimpse of one of her red feathers. The clouds thinned somewhat when they slowed down. He looked into the crowd and spotted Charlie. People were running away from something, but she fought through the mob and moved toward the source of the excitement. The lights dimmed as she made progress and Dustin couldn't make out anything else. He needed to move closer. Charlie was in trouble, but why? *What's happening?* He turned his nose down to dive into the scene, but his companion wouldn't let him go. "Why are you stopping me?" he said, using words for the first time. She answered, "Not now, only when the time comes . . . stay with her, John Day, we're all counting on you."

⋯⊷ ⊶⋯

Dustin felt the jolt, popped up in his bed, and ran downstairs to check on his mother. He'd slept for five hours with only the last portion somewhat unsettled. He found his two nephews asleep on chairs outside their grandmother's bedroom and pulled the yellow pad from Matthew's grip. He read his note, "Stay with her, John Day, we're all counting on you."

Anthony stayed with his uncle for a few minutes. "Uncle Dustin, what do you make of this?"

"Your grandma gave me the same message. Aunt Charlie was in some kind of trouble, but I couldn't move closer."

"What about the time when Grandma fell?"

"That was abrupt with no flying to speak of."

"Okay, I think we're getting somewhere now. When you saw Montserrat in the older dream, did you travel longer than you did to the scene with Aunt Charlie?"

"Yes."

"So, this is what I think. The length of the trip represents how far into the past or the future you're going. The vision about Grandma's fall was brief because it was almost present tense. The trip to Montserrat took longer because you traveled back to the early 1800s and the trek to Aunt Charlie's was short because it is in the near future."

"You make some sense, but why couldn't I get closer to the problem with my sister?"

"Maybe you're allowed to study the past up close to understand and learn, but you're only permitted a glance of the future—just enough to know something is coming, kind of a warning."

"Yes, you may be right—pretty sharp analysis for the middle of the night."

"Clearly the bean meatballs are making all the difference for me."

"Yeah, must be the meatballs. Get some rest, wise guy."

⊷⊨⊙ ⊙⊨⊶

Dustin sat in a chair across from his mother. When he opened his eyes, he found her seated on the side of her bed in her robe. "I'm supposed to be watching you!" he said. "Give me a second." He walked to the bathroom and splashed some water on his face.

Ilva stopped him before he returned to his seat. "Bring the small wooden index-card box on the bookcase to me."

He handed her the box.

She took some time to sort through the cards until she found the one with three short sentences written on the front. "Take this and read it several times before you go to bed tonight. It is time for you to remember."

Dustin scanned the card and a chill ran up his spine, but he made his way out of his childhood home as the aide relieved him. He stuffed the card in his pocket and didn't think he needed to go to sleep to remember. The memories flooded back. *How did I block them for so long?*

Chapter 37

The Lost Month

Dustin closed the blinds on his windows to make the room as dark as possible but didn't bother with music or any of his other bedtime rituals. He repeated the lines on the card five times: "I'm alone and must only worry about me. I'm not connected to anyone and I'm not responsible for anyone. My dreams are to be ignored."

Dustin's eyes closed and the clouds came into view. First, he needed to rise in order to travel, but he understood what awaited him and hesitated. His guide arrived and hovered above his bed. Dustin stared at the black feathers around her eyes, but this time she didn't want the attention. He pointed up and started to ascend.

Dustin made quick work of almost fifty years of sunrises and sunsets before he saw his ten-year-old self lying on a bed in a small motel room on Long Island. Young Dustin stared at the ceiling fan and focused his eyes on the turning blades, imagining he was in a helicopter that would lift him up and outside of the room. The little man with the heavy beard would be there soon and Dustin wanted to be up and away before it all began. *Oh no, the smell. He's here. I need more time. Not far away enough.* He closed his eyes tight. Seeing the man made it harder to rise up and away and, with his eyes closed, he couldn't focus on the blades of the fan to make his escape.

The man patted Dustin on the head and the first tear streamed down the young boy's cheeks. Dustin heard the click of the suitcase and the clanking of the equipment and took a deep breath. *I did it.* He was above and looking down.

The man consulted with Ilva and took a step back as she pointed and spoke. Her words were loud but also mangled and nonsensical. The man didn't respond and started to pack up. Dustin smiled from above, but his mother grabbed the man's hand and lowered her tone. He unpacked again and set up the equipment on the dresser. Dustin was given two small pills to make him sleepy, but he needed to stay awake . . . he hated what the man did every time he dreamed. Dustin fought to stay awake but always lost the battle.

Ilva recited the phrases on the card in an endless loop: "I'm alone and must only worry about me. I'm not connected to anyone and I'm not responsible for anyone. My dreams are to be ignored."

Once Dustin was asleep, the man prepared Dustin's temple with grease and attached two metal plates with a belt secured by a buckle. Now Dustin smelled like the man.

"Mr. Hilbert, are you sure this therapy won't do any lasting damage to my boy?" Ilva asked.

"Mrs. Murphy, I told you before, there are no guarantees. Do you want his nocturnal behaviors to stop? This is how we can do it. If you want to go to a specialized hospital for them to perform the same procedure, feel free, but they're not going to let him go home and your husband will get what he's been asking for. You'll end up visiting your son every weekend in an institution. Is that what you want?"

"No, but it seems so cruel."

"It may be, but it's also effective. Let me do my work. Sit back."

Dustin screamed and grabbed his side. "No, stop. Grace, no, Charlie. Leave her alone. Aaggh."

The man barked at Ilva, "Put in the mouthpiece and let go of his hand." As soon as she did, he flipped a switch. A jolt of electricity ran through Dustin's body and he strained to handle the stress. He popped up in the bed, crying, and his mother took hold of his hand. The man turned to Ilva. "I'll go outside for a smoke. Let me know when he's ready again."

Ilva consoled her son, who continued crying in her arms. "Please stop him, Mama. I won't dream anymore. I'm sorry. I won't sleep. I'll be good. I promise."

"Sssh. Everything will be okay. Just lie back down. Soon we'll be home. I'll always be by your side." Ilva wiped the tears from her eyes as she retrieved a small framed portrait from the dresser. "Dustin, this is a picture of the portrait of me as a child that hangs in our house. Look at me in this picture. I was a bit older than you back then, but I got through my troubles and you'll get through yours. Imagine that you're in our house in Hicksville, Dustin. Look at the portrait. It hangs on the wall. Everything is okay. Everything is fine." She rested his head on the pillow and touched him softly on the right shoulder as she hummed the melody and then sang the song:

"Are you sleeping, are you sleeping?
Brother John, Brother John.
Morning bells are ringing, morning bells are ringing,
Ding ding dong, ding ding dong."

The man finished his smoke and twenty minutes later Dustin screamed and grimaced as he clutched his side. Ilva learned precisely when to release her grip on her son's hand as the next jolt coursed through his body.

Dustin took two jolts every other night for two weeks. By the third week, the electric shock treatment had stopped and the hypnosis began. A different man came during the day and reinforced the suggestion that he was disconnected from the world. By the fifth week, the visits from strange men had ended and mother and son were alone in their room.

"Dustin, let's go to the park around the corner. You can take some shots on the basketball court. What do you say?"

He lowered his head and kept looking out the window. When someone walked by, he ducked in order to remain undetected.

"How about some ice cream? We passed a parlor a few blocks away."

Still no response. Ilva wiped a tear from her eye and started to tidy up. When she reached for the container of sleeping pills, he ran into the closet, closed the door, and pleaded, "No more, Mommy. Please, no more."

Dustin and his mother spent several more days in the motel room before returning home. They would never speak of what happened and he learned to block it from his memory. Paddy found him curled up most mornings on the closet floor and assured him that everything was okay, but it wasn't and never would be. Paddy knew it, Charlie suspected it, and Ilva felt it deep in her bones.

Dustin got up from his bed and opened the blinds. He stared at the oversized light green cross on the Greek Orthodox church. Tears flowed down his cheek.

◦─◉ ◉─◦

Paddy and Charlie waited for their younger brother in Paddy's home. Dustin insisted on the meeting and asked that it be just the three of them. From the tone of his text and his refusal to speak on the phone, they understood that something bad had happened. Paddy didn't joke and Charlie withheld her playful punches. Whatever was going to happen was long overdue. They braced themselves.

"I found out about my lost month." Dustin handed the card to his sister. He gave them a moment as he paced back and forth.

"Dustin, take a seat," Paddy said. "Whatever this is, we'll figure it out."

"I was programmed with this message while attached to electric shock equipment. Every time I dreamed, they flipped the switch and the jolt woke me. I started to associate the pain of the jolt with dreaming, which discouraged the dreams as well as sleep in general. The messages they forced into my head added another layer of protection, because they determined my dreams involved saving someone important to me. I was programmed like a cheap computer." He slumped on the couch.

Brother and sister sat on either side of him and Charlie took hold of one of his hands. "We didn't know, Dustin," she said. "We're as surprised as you."

Dustin squeezed his sister's hand. "We were all kids. I don't blame either one of you for what happened. It's just a lot to process."

The three siblings sat on the couch, unsure of what else to say or do. Despite their combined hundred and fifty-plus years on this Earth, no past experiences could guide them. What had happened to Dustin was unthinkable. Their eyes were drawn to Paddy's antique clock, which sat on the shelf mounted on the wall across from them. The advancing second hand pounded like a bass drum as it marched forward. The minutes would eventually arrive and in due time, the hours, but for that to happen, they needed to get through the next few seconds first. They planned to do that together.

CHAPTER 38

The Castle Calls

DUSTIN VISITED GREAT-AUNT Ilva's gravesite for the first time in many years and admired his old apartment from across the street. The doorman, Benny, waved as he stepped onto the sidewalk and Dustin shouted, "How's the best doorman in Queens doing?"

"Fine, Mr. Murphy."

He walked to the entrance and shook Benny's hand. "We miss you in the building," Benny said. "I thought of you the other day when the penthouse apartment became available again."

"You mean my old place is empty?"

"It sure is. The super isn't here right now, but they're handling the rentals through an agency. Are you thinking of moving back?"

"I did like it here, but I came today to visit my relative's plot."

"Yeah, I remember your mother sitting on the grass and crying. Is she doing okay?"

"We're not so sure, Benny, but thanks for asking. Can I tour my old apartment?"

"I'll be happy to give you my passkey, and here . . ." Benny went to his storage closet. "Take my folding chair, in case you want to sit out on one of the terraces like you used to."

"You noticed?"

"Everyone did. It was kind of your thing."

"That it was, Benny. I might hang out for a bit. Will that be okay?"

"My shift is over soon. As long as I get my keys back by two, it's fine."

Dustin stopped halfway to the elevators and called back. "I think I am interested in coming back. Can you do me a favor and call the agent and ask him to meet me upstairs?"

Benny smiled. "Will do."

Dustin experienced a sense of it in the lobby and it grew as he chatted with the doorman, but now that he was inside his old place, he felt the undeniable feeling of home. He smiled as he opened the photos on his phone and scrolled to a picture of Grandpa Joe's portrait. "What do you think, Grandpa? Is this home?"

He walked toward the main terrace off the living room and held his phone up so his grandfather could say hello to his daughter. "You missed her, right?" he asked and headed upstairs. The place was in decent shape, and with a coat of paint, it would be perfect. He entered The Castle and unfolded his chair. *It feels good to be back.*

A text arrived from Matthew: *ARE YOU ON THE ISLAND TODAY? UP FOR LUNCH?*

> Dustin: *YEP, IN QUEENS. I'LL BE HERE FOR A LITTLE OVER AN HOUR. GUESS WHERE?* Dustin texted a video of the view from The Castle.
>
> Matt: *GOT IT! I HOPE YOU'RE MOVING BACK. I'LL PICK UP SANDWICHES AND BE THERE IN A FEW.*
>
> Dustin: *SOUNDS LIKE A PLAN.*

He was back in his element, but it was different somehow. He stared at a beautiful woman with a familiar face who passed by with a carriage. Her walk had a distinctive rhythm that Dustin tried to decipher. She waved and Dustin didn't retreat or hide in any way. He waved back and she called up, "I thought you moved."

"I did, but I'm thinking of coming back."

"Look, my second grandson. Two years old." She held the child up in the air. "My first, the one I used to walk with in this carriage, is now eight."

"Hard to believe you're a grandmother!"

"Oh my! The Man in The Castle is flirting with me!"

He laughed. "You actually called me that?"

"The whole neighborhood did. As far as I know, I'm the first person you ever spoke to."

"Well, I guess that makes you special."

The woman motioned with her arm as she walked away. Dustin followed her path. She headed for a private house across from the cemetery and waved again as she made an exaggerated knock on the door. Dustin continued to look out onto the street for the next few minutes and acknowledged or engaged several familiar faces.

⊷▬◯ ◯▬⊶

Matthew and the rental agent arrived at about the same time and Dustin agreed to terms. He would move back in at the beginning of October. "Are you sure you can move so fast?" the agent asked.

"My Uncle Dustin is a professional at moving," Matthew said. "He can be out in an hour. Right?"

"I do have a fair amount of experience when it comes to moving." Dustin winked at his nephew.

The two men sat down to eat their lunch. "How've you been, Matt? How's my mother this week?"

"She's okay, but she misses you on Sundays. We've all missed you for the last few weeks."

"I needed time to figure things out." Dustin waved to the mailman down below.

"Holy shit, I never saw you speak to someone from up here. Maybe this place will be good for you. I know about what happened when you were ten, but don't worry, we don't have to talk about it."

"Thanks."

"Grandma wanted me to tell you that she understands why you're staying away, but you still need to protect Aunt Charlie. She said you would know what that means."

"Yeah, I think I do, Matthew."

"My dad and Aunt Charlie also want to make sure you're okay, so I told them

I would reach out to you today. They're going to some Mexican restaurant and said you would remember. Tomorrow night at six. Join them if you can."

"I'll try."

Steering dreams was more of an art than a science and Dustin failed in his last few attempts. The threat to Charlie was in the near future and he needed to determine its true nature. Dustin scrolled through the photos and posts on Charlie's Facebook page but worried that they were all too superficial. His most vivid dreams came when he was relaxed and immersed in the family research, so he pulled out his box of materials and turned to some scotch for relaxation. Dustin settled into his favorite chair and flipped through the pages of Aunt Rita's diary and then focused on the John Day bill of sale, tracing his fingers over the phrase *free woman of color*. His eyes started to close and he sank deeper into his chair.

Dustin elevated above the clouds quickly and the trip was both in the forward direction and very brief. The red bird that had guided him the last time was waiting for him at the spot. She motioned down with her bill as Charlie fought against a tide of people running away from something. Dustin pointed downward and tried to move closer, but the image went dark just as Charlie broke through the crowd. A sense of danger took hold of Dustin's body, but he didn't pop up with a jolt. The electricity was gone. Dustin awoke focused, refreshed, and ready.

CHAPTER 39

Helping Charlie

THE WAITRESS GREETED Paddy. "Hi, remember me? It's been a long time."

He beamed. "How could I ever forget! How've you been?"

"Doing okay. I'm the manager now. Could I talk to you for a second?"

"Sure." Paddy turned to his sister. "Excuse me, my fans are calling."

Charlie couldn't discern the words but watched the body language. At first, the manager pointed her finger into Paddy's chest and he held his heart, feigning an attack. She laughed as he tripped, almost knocking over a customer's glass. The woman resumed her finger pointing and handed him a ripped-out page from a newspaper. Paddy came back to the table laughing.

Charlie raised both of her hands. "What the hell? We can't even come here for dinner without all of this drama? What did you do to the poor woman?"

"You're never going to believe this. She remembered me from years ago and said that when I was here last, she never laughed so much in her whole life, but she doubted my story when she compared the autograph I gave her to the one I gave the bartender. Apparently, I signed two different names." He laughed.

"You used to be an excellent liar. Better work on your game."

"You can say that again! She Googled the names I gave her and one of them is a Russian cosmonaut and the other a French scientist. Apparently, neither one of them has ever played Caroline's. Do you get my drift?"

"I do! Did she rat you out to the whole restaurant? Do we need to leave?"

"No. She said I'm one of the funniest people she's ever met and that, if I go to this open mic night at this spot she told me about, I will legitimize my story somewhat and she'll keep my secret."

"Terrific idea. I always thought you should have tried stand-up at least once."

Paddy showed his sister the ad for the club. "I could never do something like this, Charlie. I'm not a professional. I just fool around for family. It's nice, though, that she remembered me."

"Don't sell yourself short. You make people laugh wherever you go. Is this woman family? Think about that, Paddy. Why not give it a try? We'll get everyone to go and support you."

"I appreciate that, but I'm too old to start something new like this. Let's get some drinks and maybe order some appetizers. I'm not at all sure that Dustin is coming tonight."

⊷▭◦ ◦▭⊷

Dustin arrived about twenty minutes after his siblings and picked up his scotch before walking over to the table. Charlie and Paddy didn't know what to expect and waited for their little brother to open. "Listen, before we say anything else, I want you to know that I'm taking control of my life. I'm going to focus on the future, not the past."

Paddy gave him a high five and Charlie hugged him. "And I'm guessing this is all you want to say on this topic," she said.

"You understand me well. I do think we need to talk about something else, though, that *you* don't want to speak about, Charlie."

"You better not be talking about all of this trouble I'm in and how I need to be saved by John Day, are you? Because—please don't take this the wrong way—I think you have a real strong imagination. Mom is the same way."

Paddy stepped in to back up Dustin. "Remember how he knew that Aunt Rita was going to die and that Mom fell? His dreams aren't bullshit. Dustin, tell her about the note on the pad."

Dustin spent the next few minutes describing the events of his night with the boys in Hicksville as well as Anthony's theories. Charlie reached out and grabbed Dustin's hand. "Listen to yourself. I'm not Grace Mackinnon and you're not John Day. Let's start with that. Yes, take a minute and think about this simple truth, because once you process that properly, you'll be open to understanding what really happened here."

Dustin pulled his hand away. "Which is?"

"Do you remember when we were kids and used to get in trouble and run upstairs to our rooms?" Charlie asked. "Mom yelled at us from downstairs in the kitchen and even if we put a pillow over our heads, we could hear every single word. There was simply no escaping her wrath. So, if you were sleeping upstairs and she screamed something downstairs, isn't it quite possible you just overheard what she said and incorporated the same line in your dream? Doesn't this make more sense than any of these other theories?"

Dustin thought before he attempted to respond to his sister's logical interpretation of events, but Paddy interrupted. "I'll say it again and this is not me being funny. I'm dead serious. Aunt Rita's death and Mom's fall—who knows what else he's dreamed that we're not aware of? You didn't share a bedroom with him like I did. His visions are real and when they get dark, they are scary." Paddy looked at his brother and back at his sister. "We're not going to let you dismiss this, Charlie. We're keeping an eye on you."

Charlie smirked. "Oh, my two brothers are worried about their big sister! If you two morons want to follow me around to make sure I'm okay, please understand that my job doesn't always take me to glamorous places. Two days from now, I'm in Texas. Not exactly Paris, am I right? And I make a quick stop in New Orleans—maybe that's not so bad—before taking some time off in Virginia. Either one of you want to tag along . . . be my guest."

"Why are you vacationing in Virginia?" Paddy asked.

"I'll tell you, but I don't want to listen to any crap about how dangerous it is."

Paddy pulled his chair closer to the table. "Oh jeez, what the hell are you up to, Charlie? I thought you got all of that out of your system. I've picked you up twice from a police station, but the last time was over twenty years ago. I'm not looking to do it a third time. Who or what are you protesting against now?"

"You make me sound like I'm some kind of nut. I haven't been part of a demonstration in a while. Lately, I've limited myself to expressing my views on Facebook and I got involved in discussions about the removal of a Confederate statue from a park in Virginia. A friend of mine lives in the next town over and she said I could tag along with her. There will be lots of police, but the whole thing should be very safe and I want to be part of it."

Dustin thought about the scene with the crowd and imagined it could have been at this demonstration. "You're not going alone."

"Let's say that I let you and Paddy follow me around from meeting to meeting, which by the way will be weird, and stalk me while I visit with my friend—who takes care of Mom?"

The brothers looked at each other but had no answers. The reality was that they had been dividing the nights up between them with assistance from a few other family members. Charlie did more than anyone, so when she went away, there were lots of holes to plug. The server came back and motioned to Paddy. "The bartender loved your set on Conan O'Brien the other night and sent over these drinks."

Paddy didn't know how to respond and held up his glass to the barkeep, who offered a thumbs-up in return. The manager slapped him on the back. "You're not the only one with jokes! These are from me." She turned to Charlie and Dustin. "You better make sure your brother does an open mic night. He's a natural."

⋅─▬◯ ◯▬─⋅

Dustin took the train back into the city and stopped by his spot on Forty-Sixth Street for a nightcap. He had a lot on his mind and enjoyed sitting among the animated patrons who cheered for the Real Madrid soccer team. He used the word *soccer* twice and was told that from this point forward, the sport was to be referred to as *fútbol.*

He felt the tap on his shoulder. "Hey, your doorman told me I would find you here."

Dustin turned and fist-pounded his nephew, Anthony. "What's going on? Pull up a chair."

"Who's playing in the soccer game?" Anthony asked.

The bartender jumped in. "I would have liked you, young man, but there is just too much wrong with that statement."

"Rolando, this is my nephew, Anthony. Go easy."

Rolando laughed. "Okay, but first understand this sport is played with the feet and is called fútbol. Second, there is no such thing as a soccer game—it is called a match—and third, no one asks who's playing when it is a Real Madrid match. That should be known and understood deep in your bones."

"Go easy, like my uncle said. No offense intended. Give me a Coors Light."

Rolando pounded his fist. "Will this never end! We don't drink Coors Light in Madrid, Anthony."

Anthony jabbed his uncle in the side. "Should we tell him this is New York?" Dustin laughed.

The bartender returned with a poured glass of San Miguel beer and a smile. "This is as light as it gets in Spain. Enjoy."

"To what do I owe the honor of your visit?" Dustin asked.

"My father called me about all of the stuff going on with Grandma and what might happen to Aunt Charlie. Matthew and I have an idea."

"What's that?"

"We're going to give more help with Grandma and move in for the foreseeable future, which will free you up. How does that sound?"

"Are you sure you can take the time from work?"

"I have to be there certain nights before the aide leaves at six. I can do that and Matthew can work from anywhere with his video production."

"It does sound like a plan. Cheers! Now what is this game called again?"

"It's a match, not a game, and it is called . . ." Anthony performed his best drum roll on the bar top before he shouted, "Fútbol!"

The entire bar lifted their glasses as the bartender joked, "These New Yorkers *can* learn when they want to! Salud!"

Part Seven

New York to Virginia
August 6–11, 2017

CHAPTER 40

Right by Your Side

DESPITE HAVING BEEN her brother for fifty-seven years, Dustin needed to under-stand his sister better in order to protect her. He decided to start with her online presence and spent time at the gate at JFK researching her social media accounts. Her LinkedIn page was fully developed with all relevant professional background and contact information, but nothing of a personal nature. On Instagram, her presence was also impressive, with active postings of dozens of pictures with short captions. It seemed as if wherever she went, she took a picture of the outside or the inside and posted it with a short phrase. She had over a thousand followers, so people clearly had interest in what she did.

His last stop was Facebook. Dustin took note of many of the same pictures from Instagram with more complete descriptions. Several of the postings, how-ever, had a definite political bent. He laughed as he read the conversations initi-ated by his sister and the dozens of comments posted by a variety of people. The banter was sarcastic and occasionally caustic but always ended well. She enjoyed stirring the pot but had an effective way of bringing a discussion to closure with a *let's agree to disagree* type of message. Her Facebook followers were even more numerous than Instagram and numbered over two thousand.

Facebook chronicled her life well with photos organized in folders and Dustin marveled at her robust list of friends and family. He flipped over to his own account and noted his three pictures and four posts. They might have grown up in the same household, but they couldn't have taken two more different paths in life. He thought, *I'm happy for you, Sis.*

Just as he prepared to shut down his detective work, a post appeared from his sister with the caption, "Taking a trip with my little brother. Houston, NOLA, and a little time off in Virginia. Back in NY in six days." She added a picture of the two of them. Dustin guessed that he was about eight and she thirteen. Immediately, twenty people commented and he noted that a few of those friends who exchanged sharp words with her over the last political topic wished her a great trip.

⊷⊷⊷ ⊶⊶⊶

Dustin waited by the check-in kiosk with a carry-on bag that contained all of his essentials. It was getting late and they would need to clear security soon in order to make their flight to Houston. Charlie rushed through the crowd with a massive jingling suitcase that clanked as she rolled it toward the ticket counter. She waved.

"What's in the bag?" Dustin called out.

"Anything and everything I could need."

He laughed.

"I'm so happy I amuse you, little brother. Remember, I agreed that you could come along, but this is my business trip, so I set some ground rules for you to follow."

"Do tell."

Charlie reached into her carry-on, which was as badly organized as her suitcase, and pulled out a ratty yellow legal pad. She ripped off the top sheet and read it to her brother, "Rule #1: We'll have separate rooms at each stop. Rule #2: Stay out of the way during the day when I'm working. Rule #3: Vanish if I have a date." She winked. "One gentleman in New Orleans is particularly attentive."

"Got it," he said.

"Repeat the rules back to me."

He grabbed the yellow sheet from her. "Rule #1: We will either be in the same room or have adjoining rooms. Rule #2: I will escort you to each of your appointments and you can explain me however you like. Rule #3: Your NOLA boyfriend will get the creeps, because I will always be in the vicinity. How did I do?"

"Perfect."

After getting to the hotel, they spent the evening in the tavern eating dinner and having cocktails. Charlie explained every detail of her life and devoted twenty minutes to her mysterious man from New Orleans. Dustin didn't say much but nodded a lot. After four glasses of wine, Charlie shifted the conversation. "You told us some serious shit the other day about what was done to you, Dustin. I'm here for you if you want to talk."

"Thanks, but I don't think so. I'm glad I remembered, though, because it explains a lot."

"Why am I not surprised that Dustin Murphy doesn't want to talk. Shocking, I tell you!"

"This trip is about keeping you safe. It isn't about me. Let's finish up. I've got work to do tomorrow."

"You've got work to do?"

"Remember, explain me however you want, but wherever you go, I'll be right by your side."

⊷⊷ ⊶⊶

Charlie snuck out of their adjoining room while Dustin finished up in the shower, but he didn't rush. After all, he had the license plate number of her rented car, the location of her iPhone plotted on his phone, and a copy of her schedule for the day. While it was unfortunate that she resisted his involvement in her daily activities, he would be able to hook up with her whenever he wanted.

Dustin arrived at her first appointment in a taxi and found his sister's car parked outside the building and her iPhone location somewhere inside. He pulled out his newspaper and sat on the hood of the car. An hour later, he raised his head as she called out, "Don't be mad at me. You were taking a long time in the bathroom and I was late for my first appointment. I knew you would catch up."

"Quite a likely story! This isn't starting well."

"You're my little brother, not my father. I'm here, you're here, and we're both okay. Come on. We need to go."

Charlie drove as they traveled down the major downtown thoroughfare. She pulled her mirror down to reapply her lipstick at the traffic light. The light turned green and the cars behind her honked. "Okay, okay," she said and narrowly missed an elderly woman who had wandered into the intersection.

"Charlie, maybe I should drive. You have a lot going on."

"What are you trying to say?"

"Not trying to say anything. I'm suggesting that you and I, as well as the entire city of Houston, might be safer if I drove."

"Wiseass! We're here. You can drive to the next location."

Charlie hopped out of the car, tripped on the curb, and fell forward onto the pavement. She popped right up and brushed off her blouse and pants. "Do I look okay?"

"Like you always say, you're the hottest sixty-two-year-old in New York. Houston should love you."

Dustin marveled at his accident-prone sister and returned to his perch on the hood of the car until she returned. The brother and sister continued this routine until the last appointment ended at three.

⊷▬◉ ◉▬⊶

The next leg of the trip consisted of a five-hour drive to New Orleans. They decided to stop for food about halfway and pulled off the highway into a small town in Louisiana called Crowley. They settled in at a diner for some lunch and couldn't help but overhear the conversation in the neighboring booth.

A fiftyish White man held court. "It ain't right, I tell ya. They can't take down our flags or our statues. This is all part of our history and our culture. Taking them down won't mean that they never existed. You can't erase history!"

"I agree. My family has been in this state for almost two hundred years. I'm proud of them and I'm proud of my flag."

Charlie whispered to Dustin, "Are you hearing this?"

"Yes, but this isn't Facebook. Don't offer your opinion. This is real life and we don't want any problems, only lunch."

Charlie smirked. "Yep, and we're done. Let me ask for the check. I can expense it."

The siblings headed for the exit but Charlie turned as they neared the door. She called back, "Sorry to interrupt, but I couldn't help but overhear your conversation and I got a little confused. I know I'm from New York, but isn't *this* your flag?" She motioned to the American flag hanging on the wall.

The group offered a variety of comments in return.

"What are you trying to say, lady?"

"You calling us stupid?"

"Why are you sticking your New York neck in our Louisiana business?"

Dustin grabbed her arm and pulled her to the car. "You sure like to be the center of attention, don't you? Remember, this is real life. This is not you sitting behind your laptop in your kitchen. Be more careful."

"Yes, Daddy."

⊷▭⊙ ⊙▭⊶

Dustin smiled as they entered the New Orleans city limits. There was something about a big city that led him to believe his sister and her views would be better tolerated. Their adjoining rooms in the Royal Sonesta had been Dustin's idea. He loved the music scene in NOLA and the jazz club at this hotel, in particular. Dustin hoped he'd be able to catch a show but needed to follow his sister's agenda. She spent the early evening preparing for her special date.

Charlie emerged from her room at about seven and twirled for her little brother.

"Wow, this is one lucky guy," he said.

"I can't wait to see George. He's an old friend from college. This is what we're going to do. I reserved two tables in your favorite jazz club downstairs for eight o'clock. Your table is right by the stage and mine is in the back. You can be in the same room but leave us alone. Got it?"

"Got it."

"God, you always say that, but I'm not sure you ever mean it."

"Nice to see you're catching on."

CHAPTER 41

NOLA

DUSTIN WANTED TO become lost in the NOLA vibe, like he had on many previous trips to the city, but he needed to stay alert to any possible threat against Charlie. He sat at a table that was both close to the band as well as the bar. With a simple wave to the bartender, a fresh Macallan would arrive at his side. He guessed that if he made the effort, he had a strong chance of spending some time with the attractive brunette sitting alone and to his right. This was not the night, however, to either overdo his scotch intake or invest in any substantial flirting. He was here to keep an eye on his sister, who sat with her date in the back of the room.

The band fascinated Dustin. Never before had he seen a tuba play the bass line in an indoor jazz club. It was both different and special. Dustin raised his glass to the talented brass player as the first set of music came to an end. His sister handed a note to the waiter, who in turn, gave it to the bandleader. A few seconds later, the leader announced, "We received a message telling us about a very talented piano player sitting right up front next to the band. Not sure who sent this, but we'd like to give Mr. Dustin Murphy a NOLA welcome. Stand up and take a bow, Dustin."

Dustin squirmed in his seat and waved with his right hand and the band-members chuckled. "Come on, Dustin, please stand, and everyone else who plays some piano should stand as well." Three more people stood. "Now let's have all the drummers, bass players, and guitarists join them. Are there any singers with us tonight?" Thirty people out of the fifty in the audience were now on their feet with Dustin. The band leader turned to him and said, "NOLA is chock-full of talented musicians like you, and Wednesday is the night we invite people to sit in. You're welcome to join us later on, and, again, welcome to NOLA. One, two, three, four . . ."

The band started to play and the crowd returned to their seats. The comment about piano playing put the woman next to Dustin over the top and she motioned for him to come over and join her. At the same time, the waitress arrived with a bill. "But I didn't ask for the check," Dustin told her.

"Yes, sir, this is for that couple in the back. The woman said she was your sister." Dustin glanced back at Charlie's table and she was nowhere to be found. "She's got to stop doing this," he muttered as he peeled off a fifty-dollar bill from his billfold and activated the tracking device on his phone.

Dustin started to head down Bourbon Street but realized he was moving away from the signal. *She might be back in the room.* He headed upstairs to check, but no Charlie. The tracking signal, however, was still strong. He called her but got no answer. Dustin continued wandering around, but as he walked down the stairs from the fourth floor toward the lobby, the signal became strongest toward the back wall of each level. Once he was on the ground floor, the front desk clerk called out to him, "Mr. Murphy, your sister left her phone for you. She said you wanted to borrow it. She also left this note." The clerk handed Dustin the folded piece of paper that read: SORRY, DUSTIN, YOU'RE CRAMPING MY STYLE. I'LL BE OKAY WITH GEORGE. SEE YOU LATER. DON'T WORRY.

Dustin slammed his fist down on the desk. "Damn it!"

"Is everything okay, Mr. Murphy?"

"I'm not sure. Which way did they walk?"

"They made a right when they exited the hotel. They spoke about dinner, I think."

"Thanks."

Dustin walked down Bourbon Street, checking each of the restaurants along the way. After he had finished his first pass, he heard Charlie shouting his name, "Dustin, over here. Over here!"

The apology was brief but heartfelt, and George said goodnight after being introduced. Once they were alone, Charlie explained what had happened. "We decided to cut through one of the side streets and this scary guy ran up to us and demanded money. He didn't hit us or anything, but I was so afraid. He got spooked when a policeman passed by, but it shook me up so much and we came back."

"You're okay? The man didn't hurt you?"

"I'm fine but I realized how fast things can change. I was happy and laughing in one moment and then scared shitless the next. I didn't like the feeling."

"Nobody does. I'm happy you're okay, but you do need to stop running away from me."

⊷▰⊙ ⊙▰⊶

Dustin stretched out on the couch in Charlie's room while she sat on the floor by the coffee table instigating another debate on Facebook. He saw the post on his phone and realized that she still had the conversation from earlier that day in the diner on her mind. She read a piece online about the statue of Robert E. Lee near the University of Virginia campus, which was at the center of the controversy in the upcoming rally. Virginia was their next stop and Charlie was prepping herself for the protest. She took the position that the statues of Southern generals and soldiers were both inappropriate symbols of intimidation and fear, like the Confederate flag. Dustin liked the post and shared it with his four friends. He joked, "Read your post, Charlie, and thought I would help you go viral. Sent it to all four of my avid followers."

She giggled. "Check the post again, Dustin." It had already been shared over one hundred times. Charlie got a flood of friend requests, which she accepted as soon as they were received. She started reading the comments with her brother by her side.

"Charlie, a few of these comments are scary and a couple are threatening. Some of these new friends are bad news and I think you should unfriend them right away."

"No, I never do that. I explain my viewpoints to people and we always find the middle ground."

"These aren't your high school friends from Hicksville or your business associates from the last twenty years. Some of these people are dangerous. Unfriend them."

Charlie reluctantly agreed and investigated how she would accomplish the unfriending process as another comment appeared, "Watch your back, you New York bitch. We're gonna find you at the Royal Sonesta. You're in our neck of the woods now."

"Charlie, how do they know you're here? Did you write that in one of your posts?"

"No. I don't understand. Why would someone say something like that to me?"

"You need to be careful. You're expressing a Northern point of view in the South and while many Southerners might agree with you, those who don't think you're sticking your nose where it doesn't belong. Look down below at your *Check-Ins* on the site. You announced to the world that you arrived at the Royal Sonesta earlier today. No more *Check-Ins*. I'm sleeping on your couch tonight. Everything will be fine. We head out tomorrow."

⊷▦ ▦⊶

Dustin drifted off to sleep while Charlie finished working on her laptop. About an hour later, he was down deep and the transition was almost immediate. He went into a dream state after about twenty minutes and Charlie pulled a chair up next to the couch with a pad. She had never witnessed one of his dreams. The expression on Dustin's face was stern and he extended his arms but put them down right away. The first few sounds were unintelligible, and then he started to mumble, not sentences, but single words: house, mailbox, chimney. The severe expression returned and then he repeated the line: "No, stop. Grace, no, Charlie. Leave her alone. Aaggh." Dustin clutched his side in pain before opening his eyes.

"Are you okay?"

"Um, yes, I mean yeah, I'm fine, but I understand more now." Dustin tried to shake off his dream and took a sip of the water on the end table.

"What do you mean?"

He traced his fingers along the edge of the water glass. "Give me a second."

"Dustin, tell me. What did you see?"

Dustin turned to his sister. "Okay, but just know you'll be fine. Three men are involved and it won't happen as part of your daily routine. Also, it will be soon—there was no traveling to speak of. I was there right away. It's about to happen."

"Oh my God! What does soon mean? How long do I need to live under this damn cloud?"

"Soon is all I can say, Charlie, but like I said, you're going to be okay."

"How about you?"

Dustin paused. "I think I'll be fine as well."

"What kind of answer is that? I'll be okay and maybe you will be as well? I'm putting you at risk. This is too much. You should go back."

"Charlie, we don't know how this works. Go back to where? Why would we think 'back' is any safer than anywhere else? All we can do is look after each other and be careful, so no more ditching me, and—I mean it—stop picking fights on Facebook. We do what we can to minimize the risks and stay together. This is all we can do."

"I'm not so sure, Dustin. Why me? Why would anyone want to attack me?"

"Who knows? It could be a random act."

"You said some other things as well." She read from her pad, "House, mailbox, chimney."

"I remember. I was much closer this time in my dream, so I saw the outline of the three men, but the biggest clue of all was what was in the background—a single house surrounded by trees with a very prominent chimney and a red mailbox. Whatever happens with these men takes place in front of that house. We need to keep an eye out for it."

"This is so crazy. I don't even know what to say anymore."

"Honestly, Charlie, neither do I."

CHAPTER 42

Middle Ground

"Hey, why didn't you wake me up? I thought I was going to help with the driving," Charlie said.

Dustin shrugged his shoulders. "You were tired, so I kept going."

"Okay, tell me when you want a break."

Charlie started checking email on her phone and wound up on Facebook. "If you think I'm a troublemaker on social media, wait until you meet my friend, Barbara. She posted a comment about the Unite the Right rally in Charlottesville, and people are yelling and screaming on both sides."

"What does she say about it?"

"She's worried the protest will go well beyond its stated purpose of trying to prevent the removal of the statue of General Lee."

"How so?"

"Lots of White supremacy groups like the neo-Nazis and the KKK will be there in force and they'll be pushing their overall agendas."

"The statue issue is a heated enough debate without groups like that joining in. It's been a hot topic ever since the church shooting in Charleston two years ago."

"God, that was so sad. It's hard to believe two years have passed already, but you're right, that's when all the talk about statues and Confederate flags ratcheted up a few notches."

"I've been following it, Charlie. One side claims these things are part of the culture while the other says they're symbols of hate and intimidation."

Charlie logged out of Facebook and rested her phone on her lap. "Listen up, Dustin. Don't try to play both sides. I won't have it—I'm telling you right now."

Dustin realized he had pressed a button and flashed a reassuring smile to his sister before he explained. "Don't worry, Charlie, I'm not trying to find the middle ground here. The *part of the culture* argument only holds up if the statues are in museums, where additional context can be provided—without that context, they only serve to intimidate many and inappropriately inspire racism in some."

Charlie relaxed her shoulders and picked up her phone as she said, "I'm happy to see we're together on this, because people can't have it both ways. There's no middle ground."

Dustin pulled off the highway when a diner came into view and turned to his sister after parking the car. "You know, Charlie, I'm also a little worried about you."

"How so?"

"Well, you shouldn't dismiss the large group of people who tend to be in the middle on big issues."

"Listen, Dustin. I don't have time for people who want to have it both ways and, frankly, I don't think it's your place to lecture me on who I should or shouldn't dismiss."

"Hold on, I'm just pointing out that lots of things change a little at a time, until they get to a tipping point, when the final change can be massive and permanent. Many people who bring about those little early changes are definitely *in the middle*. They need people like you to keep pushing, but don't discount them because you don't want them to start going backward. That's all I'm saying. Do you get me?"

"Well, when you put it like that, I do. All of these protests are really geared to sway the people in the middle; there is no swaying the extremists. The tipping point, as you call it, comes when the middle swings."

"Exactly, but we have to try to prevent that middle group from moving backward."

"That's why the far right is so dangerous. They seem to be focused on making things return to the way they were years ago. It scares me."

"Me too. Let's get something to eat."

⋆⊶◉ ◉⊷⋆

The brother and sister entered the diner and took note of the Confederate flag on the wall behind the register, flanked by framed portraits of two famous Southern generals, Robert E. Lee and Stonewall Jackson. Charlie leaned over to Dustin. "Is this 2017 or 1862?"

"This isn't a place for you to join any conversations, Charlie. Let's just eat a hamburger and hit the road. Okay?"

"Absolutely. You'll get no trouble from me."

The waitress winked at Dustin as she approached the table. "How can I help you folks today? Are you still on breakfast or looking for some lunch? This is kind of an in-between time."

"Me and my sister have been on the road for the last five hours. We're ready for lunch."

The waitress took a greater interest in Dustin once Charlie was identified as his sister. She shifted her body so that she faced him. "So where are you from, honey?"

Charlie interrupted. "Dustin, please order me the cheeseburger and a diet soda. I'm going to use the restroom."

Dustin nodded and said, "We're from New York."

"Don't get many New Yorkers around here. Must be exciting up your way. I would love to visit sometime. Could you show me around?"

He glanced at her name badge. "Sure thing, Wanda. We'll have two cheeseburgers and two diet sodas."

"Okay, handsome, I'll be right back with your food and if you decide to stay in town tonight to break up your trip, I'm off at six."

"Thank you, but I think we need to head out."

Dustin closed his eyes for a moment, which enabled him to focus on the sounds coming from the surrounding tables. At eleven in the morning, the diner was about one-third filled. The men to his right were deep in discussion about the upcoming rally. One of them offered, "Our former grand wizard, David Duke, will be there. He's going to lead the way. Charlottesville will be the turning point, boys. We're taking our country back!"

CHAPTER 43

Waynesboro

"I WARNED YOU, Dustin. I travel lots of places for both business and pleasure and I may have spoiled you in NOLA. Waynesboro is a whole different kind of a place." She laughed. "But while there are no skyscrapers, there are some excellent restaurants and bars. Give it a chance, it'll grow on you."

"I'm sure it will. Let's check in. Remember, you agreed to stay in the same room. We'll ask for a room with two double beds."

"Yes, sir."

Charlie headed for the restroom while Dustin handled the room registration. He fell in line behind two young men in their twenties. The clerk looked at the IDs spread out on the desk. "Atticus and Waylon Willard. Welcome, gentlemen. Are you here for the rally?"

Atticus answered, "Why else would two brothers from Arkansas be up this way?"

"I'm only asking so I can place you in the right part of the lodge. We have two wings and we are trying to keep like-minded people together."

Waylon slapped his hand on the counter. "I like that! We need to be with the rest of the folks who are fed up and want things to go back to the way they were in simpler times."

The clerk understood. "I think you'll be very comfortable in our West Wing. I have a room with two double beds. Will that work?"

Atticus nodded.

The clerk finished the check-in and the Willard brothers were on their way. Dustin couldn't believe what he'd just overheard and decided not to make things so easy for the clerk. He stepped up to the counter.

"Good morning, sir. Are you checking in?"

"Yes, I am. Dustin and Charlotte Murphy. We need a room with two beds."

"May I see your license and credit card?"

Dustin handed over the documents and smiled.

"Welcome to the Wave Creek Lodge. We haven't had so many New York guests over the years. Are you here for the rally?"

"No. My sister's friend lives across the road. We're visiting. Heading back home in a couple of days."

The clerk took a breath before he explained. "Most of the folks checking in today are here for the rally over in Charlottesville. We have these two different wings, the East and the West, and we're trying not to put people who don't agree with each other close by. Everyone might get along a little better that way."

"So, you're asking me to declare my political views before you assign a room?" Dustin asked.

"It sounds weird when you say it like that, but, yes, I guess that is what I'm doing."

Dustin shrugged. "You seem like a nice fellow who is just following some questionable instructions from his boss, so I'll answer, but your question is wrong in so many ways. Let's just say we're not interested in Uniting the Right."

"Thank you. You'll be in Room 121 in the East Wing. Two keys?"

"Yes, please."

⊷▭ ▭⊶

"The room isn't so bad, but not much of a view," Dustin said as he opened the back curtains to reveal the side of a massive truck parked directly across from their window.

"Maybe so, but if you look out of the front window," Charlie said, pointing, "you can see my friend's house. The one on the corner with the swings in the back. You'll literally be able to keep an eye on me when I'm over there."

"I thought we were staying together. Don't go back on your word now. Whatever is going to happen is happening soon. I had another—"

"I know . . . another dream. I heard you repeat the same things and then clutch your side."

"I think it will be either tomorrow or on the way back to New York. Very soon."

"I'm not going back on my word. We can go out to dinner with Barbara and you can drive us back to her house, but then I need to talk to her about some personal stuff she's going through, so you'll leave us there. If you want to sit out in front of the room and stare at her house the whole time I'm inside, feel free. I'll text you when I'm ready to come back and you can even escort me. How's that for cooperation?"

"Actually, not bad at all."

⇥▬◯ ◯▬⇤

The restaurant tried to use the same basic approach as the motel but lacked the space to separate the various factions. The competing sides were well behaved, however, and Barbara pointed out who was who at each of the tables. "All right, I'm gonna give you the rundown. About half of the people in this restaurant are from out of town and almost all of them are here for the protest. The men in the corner are mostly Klan. The people next to them are skinheads, part of the neo-Nazi movement—they're all bad news for sure. I don't know the other people, but from the amount of smiling and backslapping we're seeing, I imagine they are from other splinter groups. Now, the cluster of people in the middle were on the news the other day and are connected to the ACLU, which believe it or not, represented the far right in their effort to have this rally at their originally requested location. Everyone between us and the ACLU folks are locals who aren't looking for trouble. Some may agree with the far right, but they don't say anything publicly. But most of them think like we do. We're tired of the hate and all of the White supremacy bullshit."

"Thanks for the explanation, Barbara. Do you think most of these people will be at the demonstration?"

"I'm guessing all of these out-of-towners and a number of the locals. We're real close to Charlottesville. I hope that both of you will come along with me. I'm leaving at about eleven thirty."

"Yes, we plan to go but do you think it will be safe?" Charlie asked.

"The buildup to this event has been months in the making, so I'm assuming the police presence will be strong. Staying in the designated areas should be fine."

"I hope you're right," Charlie answered.

"Okay, let's go back to my place to discuss the remnants of my love life. Dustin, are you sure you don't want to join us? It's a thrilling story, but with a real sad ending."

"Poor baby." Charlie took hold of Barbara's right hand and squeezed.

"As exciting as it sounds, I think the two of you need some private time," Dustin answered. "I'll stay back in the room."

CHAPTER 44

The Flamingo

DUSTIN SAT IN his chair in front of his motel room and remembered the suggestions planted in his mind in a similar room when he was ten years old . . . *you're not connected to anyone or responsible for anyone.* Those instructions charted the course of his life for so many years. *If it was all nothing but old programming, why was it so hard to break the code?*

His phone vibrated and he read the incoming text.

Charlie: I CAN'T BELIEVE THAT YOU'RE ACTUALLY SITTING OUTSIDE THE ROOM STARING AT BARBARA'S HOUSE. THIS IS OVER THE TOP. FINISHING UP SOON.
Dustin: OKAY, DO YOU WANT ME TO COME OVER NOW?
Charlie: NO, BARBARA WILL WALK ME AND YOU CAN WATCH. OKAY, DADDY?

Dustin looked up as Charlie and Barbara headed toward the road. Both women waved but then stopped as Barbara noticed several of her neighbors entering The Flamingo, a bar across from the lodge. Charlie made a drinking motion with one hand and then held up one finger. Dustin glanced at his phone and read the text.

Charlie: JUST ONE DRINK. COME IF YOU WANT, BUT I'M GUESSING NO MACCALAN.

Dustin waved and settled back in his chair.

⊶≡◉ ◉≡⊷

The pub didn't fill up often, but Waynesboro was one of the more popular places to host out-of-town visitors for the rally. There were three other small motels in close proximity. Barbara's neighbors, who were all in their forties, ordered a round of shots to start their evening with a bang, and whiskeys were waiting for the two friends as they slid onto their stools.

Charlie also asked for a beer, which she considered to be her one drink. The group finished two more rounds of shots and became the loudest contingent in the place. A Blake Shelton song came on the jukebox and three of the women started to gyrate and scream on an improvised dance floor. Charlie turned to her friend. "I think your neighbors are a little too wild for us. Let's leave."

Dustin continued to sit in front of his motel room and noted that his sister was thirty minutes into her first drink.

A bunch of men approached and steered the dancing women back toward the bar. Charlie recognized them as part of the Klan from the restaurant earlier that evening. Barbara's friends appeared to be acquainted as well and didn't seem to mind their political orientation. The men nodded to the bartender, who poured another round of shots. Barbara and Charlie moved their stools away and one of the women said, "Come on back. Both of you gals are single and these handsome men are buying. What could be better than that!"

Barbara turned toward her neighbors. "No, you go ahead. My friend and I will be heading out soon."

Across the street, Dustin checked the time again. His sister had been inside for fifty minutes. He began a slow walk toward the bar.

One of the Klansmen, a thirtysomething heavily tatted man with a full beard, walked over and put his arm around Charlie. "What's the rush? I don't mind an older woman, especially one as hot as you! You could teach me a thing or two." He turned to his friends, who laughed at his line.

Charlie pushed his arm away. "We're not interested in your booze or your company and stay the hell away from me unless you want me to teach you how to pick your balls up off the floor."

The men erupted in laughter.

"Oh yeah, and how is little old you gonna do that to me? I think you just want to fight some, probably like it rough."

"Listen, buddy. I'm not from around here. I'm a New Yorker and I've got no interest in whatever it is that you're selling. Back the fuck off!"

The man reached for Charlie again and she slapped him in the face. He returned the slap with one of his own and screamed, "I got me a fighter!"

"Listen, you KKK trash, I told you to fuck off!"

"KKK trash? Careful what you say, honey. I'm warning you right now. We don't need no New York bullshit down here. I'll do whatever the fuck I want with you. You're in my world. This ain't New York, you stupid bitch."

"I'm warning you. Stay away from me!"

"Or what?"

Dustin ran toward the commotion and arrived in time to step between his sister and the man. "Or you'll need to deal with me. I'm her brother and we're leaving."

"Not so fast, old man. I'll deal with you as well . . . maybe in a different way, though." He winked at Charlie. "You New Yorkers think you can come down here and call us KKK trash? We're gonna teach you a thing or two . . ."

The bouncer interrupted. "I got the police on speed dial, fellas. These folks said they want to leave and that's exactly what you're going to let them do, and you won't follow them either. I'm going to buy you a round of drinks while they go."

The bartender turned to Barbara. "Take your friends out of here. These fellas didn't mean nothing by what they did and your friend did slap him first, so go on."

"Really? I slapped him first? That's your summary of what happened?" Charlie protested. Dustin grabbed his sister by the arm and ushered her out of the bar. Barbara followed. After escorting Barbara home, Dustin and Charlie hustled back to their room.

⊷▭◉ ◉▭⊶

Atticus and Waylon Willard observed the confrontation from the other side of the bar and remembered Dustin from the check-in line earlier that day. Atticus peered through the window and kept his eye on the motel across the street. He directed his younger brother, "I want you to go and buy us another round of beers plus one extra. Stay up by the bar and I'll be right over. We need to start making some friends."

Waylon did as he was told and his older brother joined him and grabbed the extra beer. "Follow me."

Atticus walked over to the Klansman who had the confrontation with Charlie and slid the beer in front of him. "This is for you, my friend. Me and my brother saw what happened and we like how you handled yourself. Just wanted to let you know."

"Like how I handled myself? You ain't seen nothing yet . . . this was just a little fun is all, but thanks for the beer. My name is Merl Miller."

Atticus shook his hand. "I'm Atticus Willard and this is my little brother, Waylon. We're up from Arkansas for the rally."

Merl turned to his friends. "You hear this? These boys came up all the way from Arkansas. We got people from all over. Welcome to Waynesboro!"

Atticus leaned in and whispered to his new friend, "I kept an eye out for you. Those two New Yorkers are in the room straight across from the bar on the corner. Thought you might like to know."

"Thank you, my friend."

⊷⊨⊙ ⊙⊨⊶

Dustin and Charlie entered the room tired, frustrated, and somewhat afraid. He opened a beer from the refrigerator and sat by the window with the curtain partially open. He trained his eyes on The Flamingo. Dustin hoped to see the Klansmen drive away. Charlie planned to soak away her troubles in a hot bath or, at the very least, gather her thoughts.

Dustin thought back to his programming at the age of ten . . . *you're not connected to anyone* . . . and wondered if it was true after all. Maybe the smelly little man in the motel had his number. Perhaps, he wasn't any good to anyone. Why did he think that he had all of the answers? These dreams might be pure nonsense and nothing more than a total waste of his sister's time. He planned to tell Charlie when she finished her bath.

⊷⊨⊙ ⊙⊨⊶

Charlie was lost in her own thoughts and wondered when she'd become such a magnet for trouble. Her instincts used to keep her out of danger, but lately every move she made led to some problem. Who was she to drag her brother into her mess? He could have been hurt in that bar. Hasn't he been through enough? He should go back to New York for his own welfare. *My problems are my own, not my little brother's.* She planned to tell him as soon as she got out of the bathroom.

⊷═◉ ◉═⊶

Charlie walked into the living area with her hair in a towel. Dustin was already in bed as the Klansmen had left without incident ten minutes earlier. Brother and sister stared at each other and each took a deep breath before they spoke.

"Good night, Dustin."

"Sleep well, Charlie."

Part Eight

Waynesboro/Charlottesville
August 12, 2017

CHAPTER 45

The Opposing Sides

THE MUCH ANTICIPATED Unite the Right rally in Charlottesville was the logical conclusion to a steady buildup of momentum over the summer, highlighted by a KKK event in July. The first unofficial activity had taken place the night before, Friday, August 11, when a band of White nationalists marched with tiki torches onto the University of Virginia campus. They headed toward the lawn, chanting "White Lives Matter" and "You Will Not Replace Us." The march ended at the statue of Thomas Jefferson, which was guarded by about thirty counterprotesters who encircled the structure. After a brief standoff, the two groups had an all-out brawl. The protesters used their tiki torches as weapons and the counterprotesters defended themselves with pepper spray. The state police broke up the hostilities, but many suffered minor injuries.

By the end of the night, the sides were delineated, but the initial reason for the protest, the opposition to the removal of a statue of Robert E. Lee from Emancipation Park, had morphed into a demonstration in support of White supremacy. The major organizations of protesters included members of the alt-right, neo-Confederates, neo-fascists, White nationalists, neo-Nazis, and Klansmen. Richard Spencer, chairman of the National Policy Institute, and David Duke, former Ku Klux Klan imperial wizard, led the list of well-known far-right figures in attendance. The weapons brandished by the protesters served to intimidate as well as enforce their right to protest and express their world view.

The counterprotesters banded together in their opposition to White supremacy but differed in other material ways. These groups included many Charlottesville residents, a number of faith-based and civil rights organizations, Black Lives Matter, and Anti-Racist Action, along with members of the Antifa (anti-fascist) movement. The counterprotesters differed greatly in the degree to which they would permit their words to escalate into physical action. Many, like

Barbara, were shocked at the number within their ranks who appeared to be ready to engage in actual battle. Some carried signs that read "Punch a Nazi in the Face," and reasoned that the time to sit back and take the abuse was over. Today they would fight back and argue that the punch of the abuser was not the same as that of the abused. Fighting back was their right and, perhaps, their duty.

The protest itself was scheduled to start at noon, but each side assembled early in the morning—the protesters in McIntire Park and the counterprotesters across town at St. Paul's Memorial Church. Both sides planned to begin a slow march toward Emancipation Park at about ten in the morning and expected the authorities would not allow the rally to run its allotted time from noon to five. The initial march, therefore, held an even greater importance.

⊷⊶

Charlie shouted through the bathroom door, "Barbara sent us a text—she left first thing this morning for Charlottesville."

"Why so early?"

"The word is that the authorities are going to stand by until things get out of control and then end the rally early. She also didn't want to pressure us to go after what happened last night."

Dustin grabbed his phone and noted the early reports of violence and the inadequate police presence. He showed the screen to Charlie as he left the bathroom. "It doesn't seem safe, Charlie. The police weren't ready and it's not starting well."

Charlie sat on the bed as she read the reports. "I think you're right." She walked to the window and stared at Barbara's house across the way. "Let's pack up and head back home. This isn't what I thought."

Dustin nodded and waited for Charlie to relax her shoulders and smile. "I think that's the smart move."

Brother and sister began to organize their things and each became lost in their thoughts. Both understood that they made the smart decision, but this didn't necessarily mean it was the right decision. They still needed to be alert and ready for whatever the day would bring.

⊷⊶

The Willard brothers arrived at McIntire Park at about nine and immediately felt a connection with the protesters, but they didn't belong to any of the established organizations. Atticus slapped his brother, Waylon, on the back. "This is the best thing we've done in a long time. These folks really get it."

Atticus concurred. "All we want is what's due us, like Papa always said. We need to bring back the days when White males got their rightful due. These people understand that and they're willing to fight for it."

"Sure are. We got more firepower here than I remember in the service. Today's gonna be a great day!"

A man with a bulletproof vest and some large white boards walked over. "You boys got any signs to carry when we start walking?"

"Nah, we don't. Are you offering?" Waylon asked.

"Yeah, I can give you a choice of four: *You Shall Not Replace Us*, *White Lives Matter*, *Blood and Soil*, or *Russia is Our Friend.*"

Waylon scratched his head. "What does *Blood and Soil* mean?"

"It's a Nazi phrase, *Blut and Boden*, which means that who we are is based on the blood in our veins and where we come from."

Waylon smiled. "I like that, give me a *Blood and Soil*. Brother, why don't you take a *White Lives Matter*?"

The Willards took a step back to appreciate the magnitude and strength of their brotherhood. They didn't understand all of the different factions but realized they were all united on the issues that mattered—the things, people, and policies that had held them down all of these years. Atticus rested his sign by his side and placed his arm around his brother's shoulders. "Papa would have been so proud of us!" Waylon beamed.

⋅─═◎ ◎═─⋅

The scene at St. Paul's Memorial Church was also busy with preparations. The largely religious contingent joined hands and began to sing:

> "This little light of mine,
> I'm gonna let it shine,
> This little light of mine,

> I'm gonna let it shine,
> This little light of mine,
> Yes, I'm gonna let it shine,
> Let it shine, let it shine, let it shine."

Others worked on the preparation of placards with messages like *Black Lives Matter* and *Punch a Nazi in the Face*. Barbara was on the scene at the church but struggled to relate to some of her fellow counterprotesters. She asked a man who she thought was an organizer, "Excuse me, who are the folks out front with the guns? What's going on here?"

"The protesters are almost all armed," he said. "They do that to intimidate us, so we fight fire with fire. You better at least take some of this." He handed Barbara some pepper spray. "We're going to be marching soon. Be ready."

"Won't the police protect us? Aren't we making a mistake with all of this firepower?" Barbara asked.

"Didn't you hear about the brawl last night on the UVA campus? The police presence was shit last night and it will be shit again today. Got to go."

Barbara moved back from the front of the group. The deeper she retreated, the better she felt. Many of her Charlottesville and Waynesboro neighbors were by her side and, other than having pepper spray, very few were armed. This was the group she had expected to encounter and this is where she would stay. She felt a kind of dread in the air as most who surrounded her recognized that the police presence was woefully inadequate. While they didn't share a sense of connection with the more aggressive elements on their side of the divide, some were thankful for their presence. Barbara wasn't sure.

◦━◉ ◉━◦

The protesters left McIntire Park at ten, many of them brandishing automatic weapons and carrying either Confederate or Nazi flags. The Willards held their *Blood and Soil* and *White Lives Matter* signs high and looked with pride at their fellow protesters. The volume of their chanting, *We Will Not Be Replaced*, increased as the counterprotesters could be seen in the distance. Law enforcement stayed on the sides of the streets and seemed ready to intervene but were understaffed for a crowd-control operation of this scope.

The counterprotesters abandoned their hymns in favor of their own chant of *Black Lives Matter,* which then morphed into *Punch a Nazi in the Face* as the battle-ready members of Antifa took the lead about a block away from the confrontation. Barbara felt lost in the middle of the pack because as much as she believed in the cause, nothing about what would likely transpire could be considered safe. She held onto her pepper spray for dear life and continued to chant *Black Lives Matter,* although the much louder *Punch a Nazi in the Face* drowned her out.

The two contingents were now about a hundred feet apart and the chants ramped up in volume on both sides. The Willard brothers gave each other a fist bump as they experienced the feeling yet again. Waylon first felt it as a young man before a football game and Atticus experienced it while deployed in Afghanistan. The sense of impending battle provided a sorely missed rush. Atticus turned to Waylon. "Are you ready, little brother?"

"Been ready my whole life!"

Objects flew before fists connected or pepper was sprayed. Within minutes an all-out melee broke out in the street. One protester used a Confederate flag as a weapon but was peppered in the face after delivering his blow. Atticus Willard called out to his brother, "Two o'clock, tall guy with a baseball cap." He wound up and fired his water bottle like a fastball toward his target, striking the man directly in the face. Atticus raised his hands in triumph. "Your turn, Waylon."

Waylon identified his target. "Straight ahead, yellow shirt." The bottle missed its mark but hit a woman in the back, making her double over in pain. Waylon was embarrassed by his inaccuracy and started firing water bottles in rapid succession. Atticus joined in the fun. One of the counterprotesters ran at Waylon using his "Punch a Nazi in the Face" sign as a weapon and Atticus tackled him to the ground, pummeling him into submission. The two brothers shared another fist bump.

Barbara sought refuge and spotted a pickup truck off to the side of the road. She ran toward it. After crouching down behind the vehicle, she curled into a ball with her small pocketbook tucked in by her waist and her pepper spray by her side. She felt a tap on her shoulder and heard the words, "Do you need help, ma'am?"

Barbara looked up and found two skinheads on either side of her. One grabbed her arms while the other picked up her pepper spray from the ground and sprayed her in the face. "Stupid bitch!" they screamed as they ran to find their next target. Barbara returned to her fetal position, furiously rubbing her eyes. By the time the violence came under control, several others had joined her on the ground as they too became incapacitated for different reasons. Barbara thought, *If this was a battle, we just lost.*

CHAPTER 46

On the Way

AT ELEVEN, THE City of Charlottesville declared a state of emergency and, within an hour, the governor of Virginia would follow suit. These two determinations made the rally an unlawful assembly and it was officially over before it had even begun.

A hard-core pack of about a hundred protesters devised a plan to relocate to their original staging area, McIntire Park, in an attempt to run their program at this alternate location. The anti-fascist organization, Antifa, countered with, "We go where you go." Another scuffle ensued as the counterprotesters tried to block the protesters from beginning their walk back to McIntire. The blockade didn't hold and far-right figurehead Richard Spencer was sprayed with pepper on his way to the park. Spencer's repeated screams of the mayor's name in his microphone as he expressed his displeasure with the town's handling of the rally fueled the ongoing chants of "Jew! Jew! Jew!"

The fury of the protesters was matched by that of the counterprotesters. The authorities may have called an end to the event, but that did not quell the animosity of both sides or disperse the crowds. Charlottesville was in a state of chaos.

⊷⊷ ⊶⊶

Barbara remained behind the protection of the pickup truck for some time. She rubbed her eyes raw trying to soothe the effects of the pepper and had difficulty seeing. Her pocketbook was long gone, but her phone was still by her side. Every time she stood to figure out her next move, she quickly retreated behind the truck. After an hour in her spot and no sign of help from the police or any trustworthy source, she texted her location to a group of friends who lived in the area. Her message: I'M AT THIS SPOT ON THE MAP HIDING BEHIND A PICKUP TRUCK. I'VE BEEN ATTACKED AND SPRAYED WITH PEPPER. CAN'T SEE WELL. NO POLICE HERE. I NEED HELP.

She sent the message to five people and received three responses. The first assured her that they would inform the police of her location. The second recommended that she stay put until things calmed down, and the third was from Charlie, who texted back three words: ON THE WAY.

⊷⊷═◉ ◉═⊶⊶

"Don't worry, Charlie. We can be there in another twenty minutes. It's not far at all and, remember, if my latest dream about the location of the attack is correct, it doesn't sound like downtown Charlottesville. I don't think there will be so many lonely houses in the woods with prominent chimneys and red mailboxes. The most important thing is that we stay together, no matter what. Understood?"

Charlie nodded as she navigated her mapping software on her phone. "I've got her plotted. Let's try to park as close as we can. Hit the gas, twenty minutes is too long."

The car lurched forward as Dustin followed her instructions. Fifteen minutes later, they parked on a side street a few blocks away from the heart of the action. Dustin grabbed Charlie's phone, checked Barbara's location again, and said, "Follow me, she's close."

⊷⊷═◉ ◉═⊶⊶

Atticus and Waylon headed around the corner to their parked pickup truck, which featured a painted Confederate flag on the tailgate. They each chugged a beer from their cooler in celebration of the day. The voice came from behind as the two men were joined by three Klansmen, including their new friend Merl Miller. "What are the two of you celebrating?" Merl asked.

"We just mixed it up a bit," Atticus said. "Felt good. Right, Waylon?"

"Sure did, big brother."

"Still a lot more that needs to be done," Merl added. "Where did you boys say you came from?"

"Little Rock. Drove all the way up and we're glad we did. We always respected the Klan. Nice to be side by side with you."

"Likewise. Here, ditch those Nazi signs. Two boys from Arkansas should know better than to get involved with that foreign bullshit. Take these Confederate flags. This is what proper Southern men should carry."

"Yeah, you're right. Thanks a lot."

"How would you like to receive a recommendation to join your local Klan chapter in Arkansas?" Miller said.

Atticus elbowed his brother in the side. "Nothing would make us happier."

"Things may be breaking up here soon, but there should be lots of action all around town for the rest of the day. Stay close and if you continue to impress us, we'll see about that recommendation."

Waylon tossed each of the Klansman a beer and offered a toast. "To the Invisible Empire."

They all chanted, "Here! Here!"

⊷▻ ◅⊶

"Barbara, it's me, Charlie. You can raise your head. The fighting is over. Are you okay?"

Barbara stood and rubbed her eyes yet again. "Thank God, I didn't know what I was going to do. They sprayed me with my own pepper. I can barely see."

Dustin ran over to the emergency personnel attending to dozens of people who had been sprayed and brought back a bottle of water and an eyewash kit. "The EMS folks are spread pretty thin, but I watched them and helped myself to one of these kits. We need to flush your eyes with the water a few times and then things will improve. Let me try."

Barbara's eyesight gradually returned and the trio decided to head back to Waynesboro in Barbara's car, which was parked closer than Charlie's rental. They approached the corner of Fourth and Water and fell in line with a massive band of counterprotesters marching up the street. "Let's follow them for two more blocks," Barbara shouted. "My car will be on one of the side streets to the right."

Dozens of people filled in behind them and soon the trio felt as if they were somewhere in the middle of the tight pack of marchers, who seemed to start and stop in irregular intervals creating an accordion-like effect. After one of these stops, the line began moving forward, and Charlie pointed toward the rear as she tried to move backward against the flow of the crowd. Dustin realized this was the scene from one of his visions. He grabbed Charlie and Barbara by their collars and roughly pulled them into a nearby doorway.

A flood of people was thrown horizontally past their position. Their screams were deafening. Dustin tried to pull a young woman to the safety of their spot but lost his grip on her hands as she was bulldozed by a man who thrust her back into the throng. Barbara covered her eyes and Charlie held onto her brother for dear life. Once the forward momentum of the crowd stopped, a chaotic frenzy commenced as people tried to get off the street. Intuitively, people ran forward instead of escaping to the side. Anyone who lost their footing was trampled and any good Samaritan who stopped to help regretted that decision.

After some time, Dustin looked out and saw the immediate cause of the violence: A minivan propelled into the marchers, pushed by a sedan, which in turn was projected by a Dodge Charger. They later learned that the neo-Nazi protester who had driven the vehicle that began this chain reaction was arrested soon after the attack. Dozens of people sustained injuries and one, Heather Heyer, a thirty-two-year-old local paralegal, died hours later at the University of Virginia Medical Center.

CHAPTER 47

Someone to Count On

THE RIDE BACK to Waynesboro was filled with a combination of relief that the wait for the attack was over and mortification about the depths of racial hatred the trio had just experienced. The Charlottesville event might have been local to the small town, but it was national in scope, as people traveled from all over the country to participate on either side of the issue. Barbara didn't understand the conversation about *the vision* but congratulated her two friends on having survived their challenge and thanked Dustin again for pulling her out of harm's way.

The mood became pensive as neither sibling attempted to continue their dialogue after they arrived back at the lodge. Dustin sat on the couch and thumbed through a magazine while Charlie scanned her social media accounts. She broke the silence. "It wasn't what we thought, but if you hadn't spotted the minivan coming our way, we would have been hurt. Thanks. I always knew I could count on you."

Dustin stood and walked over to give his sister a hug. "So nice to hear someone say that to me."

"The more you put yourself out there, the more you're going to hear things like that. You never really let Paddy and me get to know you and, with all of your moving, you're always the mysterious new neighbor and never the trusted old friend. Do you get that, Dustin?"

"Yeah, I do."

"Now that these things are clear, you can change your life."

"But I'm fifty-seven."

"Hey, I'm sixty-two, but I feel like I'm forty and, damn, I look good." She extended her right arm in front of her as she struck a pose and knocked over the floor lamp. Charlie laughed as she picked up the lamp. "Well, you get my point—you've still got some prime years left, make the most of them." Charlie hugged her brother and then pushed him away. "Jesus, you stink. Go take a shower!"

"Take a gander at yourself in the mirror."

"Oh my God, it has been a bad day. You go first, I need a cold drink."

⊷═◦ ◦═⊷

Charlie left the room to fill the empty ice bucket as she heard the water turn off in the bathroom. Dustin stepped into the living area barefoot and bare-chested— just in a pair of jeans. He dried his head with a towel and bumped his foot on the bed. "Shit! That hurt! Charlie, did you see my blue pullover shirt?"

No answer.

He removed the towel and realized his sister was not in the room. Her drink was on the counter and he noted the empty cooler. Two or three minutes later, she still hadn't returned. Dustin got dressed by the back window and noticed that the massive truck parked outside had pulled away. As he took in the view from this back window for the first time, he saw a house in the woods on the other side of the parking lot with a prominent long chimney and a bright red mailbox.

⊷═◦ ◦═⊷

Merl Miller instructed the Willard brothers to hold Charlie in place against the wall next to the ice machine. Atticus pulled her arms behind her back. The Klansman leaned in within inches of her face. "I think you owe me an apology, Miss New York. What did you call me? KKK trash?"

Charlie kicked Miller in the leg and screamed, "Yes, you piece of shit! Let me go, right now!"

The Klansman took out his switchblade and held it to her face. Atticus yanked her back and said, "Now hold on, no need for that. Just get your apology like you said."

"Damn backwater Arkansas hick, who the fuck are you to tell me what to do?" Miller shouted.

Atticus released Charlie and started to walk away. The Klansmen grabbed her by the hair. Waylon hesitated but then followed as Atticus screamed, "Keep your fucking recommendation."

The Klansman leaned into Charlie's ear. "It's better this way. I want to make a little mark on that pretty face of yours all by myself, so I'll truly be special to you." He laughed as she squirmed.

Dustin darted out from the lodge and tackled Miller into the garbage dumpster. They rolled together on the ground. The Klansman was caught by surprise but was both younger and stronger. Miller soon gained the advantage.

Dustin cried out, "No, stop. Grace—no, Charlie. Leave her alone."

The Klansman jabbed his knife into Dustin's side, then jumped to his feet as Charlie ran to her brother. Three older women came onto the scene and one of them yelled, "The cops are on their way. You better hope he lives."

CHAPTER 48

Waiting on Dustin

THE EMS WORKERS noted the amount of lost blood pooled on the pavement and assumed that the knife had nicked an artery. They applied pressure to the wound but were unable to slow the bleeding and determined the best course of action was to get the patient to the hospital as fast as possible. Charlie sat next to her baby brother as the ambulance raced the five-mile stretch to the nearest emergency room. They arrived within minutes.

The trauma team assessed and prepped him for surgery. His blood pressure was seventy over fifty and falling and he needed to be stabilized before surgery. The doctors worried they didn't have the time to do so, because if they couldn't stop the bleeding, nothing else mattered.

Charlie offered to donate blood and did so in the outpatient lab after determining she was an appropriate match. By the time she had returned to the ER, Dustin had already been wheeled into the surgical suite.

Charlie sat by the window of the waiting room on the fifth floor and looked down at all of the people entering and leaving the facility. A mother and a child played on a bench while a young couple snuck behind a tree to steal a kiss. Everyone went about their activities while she watched from above. *This is how Dustin lived his life.*

Dustin came out of surgery an hour later, but his sister was not permitted to see him. Charlie asked to speak with the surgeon.

"Ms. Murphy. My name is James Wellwood. I operated on your brother. We stopped the bleeding and stabilized his blood pressure. Your donation helped, thank you."

"I'm sensing a *but*, Doctor. Please tell me what the problem is."

"The procedure ended over an hour ago, but we're having trouble waking him up. This happens from time to time. You can see him briefly if you like. We'll continue to monitor his condition and provide you with updates."

"He's okay, right?"

"Yes, we patched him up, but not waking up is a concern. This is all I can tell you for now. I'll take you to him."

⋆▬○ ○▬⋆

Paddy hopped in his car to make the long drive to Virginia. His boys, Anthony and Matthew, would continue taking care of their grandmother. Everyone agreed that she shouldn't be told anything about Dustin's condition, as she was often out of touch with reality and there was nothing to be gained.

Eight hours later, Paddy arrived, but without jokes for nurses, engineered falls, or funny dances. He took the seat next to his sister and put his arm around her back.

She leaned into him. "It should be me lying there. I'm the one with the big mouth. I caused all of this, Paddy."

"Don't think like that—he'll be okay. I'm sure he just needs time. Dustin's probably having one of his dreams. Let him rest and enjoy his adventure. He'll come back. He always does."

⋆▬○ ○▬⋆

Ilva jerked up from the easy chair in her den and called out to the aide. "Give me my car keys. I've got to go."

Corinda rushed into the room. "Mrs. Murphy, you don't own a car. Don't you remember? You sold it a long time ago."

"What do you mean I sold it? I need to go. You don't understand and if you won't help me, I'll do it myself."

Ilva stood and then fell back into her chair. On her second attempt, she got to her walker and headed for the front door. Corinda blocked her exit and sent Anthony a text: YOUR GRANDMOTHER IS ACTING UP. WANTS TO LEAVE THE HOUSE. I NEED HELP.

Anthony arrived fifteen minutes later, while the confrontation at the door was still playing out. Ilva kicked Corinda and tried to scratch her. "Get out of my way. I'm calling the police. You have no right to stop me."

Anthony took over. "Hi, Grandma, I'll take you wherever you want to go. Why don't you first change out of those pajamas before we leave? Corinda, you can finish up for the day. We're going out. Did my grandmother take her afternoon pills yet?"

"No. Not yet."

"Okay, I'll get them."

He returned minutes later with her regular pills along with a dose of a sedative that the doctor prescribed for this type of episode. The medication helped to change the activity from dressing to resting. Corinda left and Anthony sat by the bed and talked his grandma to sleep. Before she closed her eyes, she said, "Dustin is in trouble and needs our help."

⤝▒◯ ◯▒⤞

Charlie tapped her brother on the knee. "Paddy, this is Doctor Wellwood. He was the surgeon."

The doctor extended his hand to Paddy and then suggested that they all sit. "It's been almost nine hours since your brother came out of surgery. His vital signs are stable but we're concerned about his inability to regain consciousness. We moved him to the ICU a while ago to better monitor his neurological status. We'll give him a short while longer to wake up naturally, but if he doesn't, we will need to have a different conversation."

"Different in what way?" Paddy asked.

"We'll talk about other options, but that conversation is still premature. We're still confident he'll come out of this on his own. Please try to think positive thoughts."

Charlie squeezed Paddy's arm and said, "Thank you, Doctor. We'll be right here by his side."

⤝▒◯ ◯▒⤞

Dustin hovered in the clouds, alone and frozen in place. No way to move backward to observe old memories or forward to gain insights about the future. No way to go down to return to his life or up toward the sun. The intensity of the light blinded him every time he tried to look up, but the heat warmed his bones, like toes in the sand. Dustin heard some chatter. "Who's there?" he called out. Perhaps someone or something was above him, but he couldn't maintain his gaze long enough to discern who or what it was. He was stuck in both time and place.

Then he wasn't alone. The first red bird gave him hope, and the second and third gave him reason for optimism. He moved, albeit slowly, with one bird on either side and one in front. After some time, he hovered above his current apartment in Manhattan. His last girlfriend, Josy, stood on the terrace. Then on the move again to his place before that—another girl, another terrace. Finally, back in Queens and able to go low enough to see The Castle. *Why didn't I stay there? Why did I keep moving year after year?*

Travel resumed again . . . back in college and then back at home in Hicksville, stopping again over the motel where he was being administered to by the smelly man with the heavy beard who flipped the switch, convulsing his little ten-year-old body with surges of electricity. His mother, right there by his side, crying.

Back in Hicksville . . . his father screamed at his mother, "He can't stay in this house. He isn't right in the head. We have two other children to think about. I know where we can send him . . ." Then the speed increased and he hovered above Aunt Rita's apartment. She lectured her brother. "Bruce, nothing is thicker than blood." Finally, he was over Montserrat, then down on the ground tied to the wheel, taking his punishment . . . *sometimes it's how much you can take, not how much you can give.* The whipping ended and Grace sat with him, cradling his head, blood dripping from his back. Dustin moved again at warp speed and was back behind the lodge in Waynesboro, Virginia. Charlie's arms were covered with his bright red blood. She covered her eyes with her hands and the blood smeared on her face. Dustin looked to the left, the right, and straight ahead. The birds were gone. Once again, he was alone but on the move back to the motel room.

The smelly man with the heavy beard repeated his mantra in a loop. "You're not connected to anyone . . . you're on your own. All alone. You're alone today and will continue to be alone tomorrow. You have your mother, Dustin. Always your mother."

Ten-year-old Dustin sobbed, "Why do you hate me, Mama? What did I do?"

Ilva sat by her son's side, crying. "I love you, Dustin. This is for the best."

The man flipped the switch again. Dustin reacted, screaming, "It burns! I don't want to sleep, not ever again. I don't want to dream, not ever again. Please make it stop."

Then it did.

Everything stopped.

The memories gone, the future of no consequence.

"Finally, I can rest."

CHAPTER 49

One Final Jolt

TIME SLOWED TO a crawl. Charlie stared at the clock on the wall and thought the second hand had taken a break from its continuous motion. She leaned into Dustin's ear and whispered, "I hope you're having fun with whatever you're doing, but do us a favor, come back for a while to say hello. Please, we just need you to say hi."

No response.

Her eyes focused again on the clock and the hands continued to be uncooperative. She lowered her head and concentrated on the floor, making little semicircles with her feet as she outlined each individual tile. Charlie remembered her room as a child and how she had spent hours writing the initials of her boyfriends in the corner of each tile. Her floor was covered with names by the time she'd moved out and became her walk of fame, kind of like her personal Grauman's Chinese Theatre.

Charlie smiled as she remembered her fun in school, but then the tears came. "I called him so many bad things, Paddy. I'm so ashamed. Wake up, Dustin . . . please."

"Give him time. Like I said, he's probably off on an adventure. Maybe he's back in Nevis. Who knows? He sure does get around. Let's sit and wait. Don't worry about the name-calling from years ago. He'll be fine, Charlie."

Paddy moved his sister's chair closer and patted her on the back. The monitors caught his attention—the blood-pressure reading had been a hundred twenty over eighty when he'd come into the room and now was just seventy over forty. He pressed the call button at the same time the alarm went off on the monitor and a nurse ran in. She shouted back out to the nursing station, "Code Blue. We need the crash cart."

The nurse slid by Paddy and Charlie in order to attend to Dustin. "You folks better go on outside and let us do our work." The siblings hustled out of the way and Charlie cried hysterically once in the hallway. "He has to live . . . he never got his chance!"

The five-person medical response team stormed into the room. Everyone had a job to do and they went right to it.

The doctor took charge. "His heart rhythm is abnormal. We need to shock him. Clear." He looked to the other four members of his team, who all responded, "Clear."

⊷▬◉ ◉▬⊶

Dustin's peace was interrupted and he no longer observed from above. He was down below, inside the motel room on the bed. The bearded man to his right and his mother to the left. The man flipped the switch and the jolt overwhelmed his ten-year-old body, which stiffened like a board. He screamed, "But I'm not dreaming!"

The man disagreed, "Yes, you are."

Dustin pleaded, "Please, sir, I'm not dreaming now and I won't ever dream again. I won't even sleep. I promise."

The man didn't acknowledge his pleas or look his way. Dustin turned to his mother. "Please tell him to stop. Please. I'll be a good boy. I promise."

⊷▬◉ ◉▬⊶

The medical response team regrouped. One nurse performed CPR while the doctor ordered, "Point-three milligrams epi," and a nurse delivered the prescribed dose. The doctor announced, "The rhythm is still abnormal, we need to shock him again."

⊷▬◉ ◉▬⊶

Dustin turned to the bearded man before he reached for the switch. "Please, sir, stop. I can't handle any more. Please stop."

Ilva's voice came from above. "Sometimes it's not how much you can give, it's how much you can take . . . hold on, Dustin . . . you can do it. I know you can."

"I can't . . . it's too much."

Ilva Murphy's voice softened. "It's time, Dustin. Time to go."

The darkness lifted and now Dustin's mother was stuck. She called out from above and became frozen in place. The majestic red birds with the black masks left her side and traveled down to him, but they were confused. He sensed it. One yearned to go back, another wanted to return to the light, but the bird in front insisted and led Dustin down to finish what he had started. Ilva blew him a kiss and waved.

⊷⇒ ⇐⊶

The doctor called out, "Again. Clear."

All four team members called back in unison. "Clear."

The smelly man returned to the recesses of Dustin's mind. No more begging or promising. This jolt would be the last one and it didn't punish or burn . . . it energized. Dustin popped up in the bed, gasping for air.

The doctor greeted him. "Welcome back, Mr. Murphy."

The staff exchanged congratulatory glances as the nurses removed the equipment and made sure he was comfortable. Charlie and Paddy rushed back into the room, each grabbing one of Dustin's hands. They looked up and gave thanks. Paddy moved away from the bed to give his big sister a moment. Once she had waved him over, Paddy pulled his hair straight up into spikes and said he'd touched one of the paddles by mistake. It wasn't especially funny or clever. It was, as Paddy always said, all in the delivery, and he delivered it well.

Part Nine

New York
October 2017

C H A P T E R 5 0

Did I Ever Tell You?

"Mrs. Murphy, please use your walker when you move around the house. You could fall."

"So what if I fall! Big deal, Corinda. It happens all the time. Not exactly a major news story."

"Maybe not a story for you, but it will be for me, even though this is your house. I'll be in trouble if you fall without your walker. The agency will fire me. Sorry."

The aide knew she'd made a mistake the moment she said *your house*.

Ilva sat down. "What do you mean, *my house*? This isn't *my house*. You people keep telling me this lie. Do you think you can fool me? It looks like my house—even has some of the same furniture, but I see right through you. Did Charlie put you up to this? I know it was her."

"You didn't touch your breakfast, Mrs. Murphy. Do you want something else?"

"Don't try to change the subject on me, Corinda. Charlie is a liar! She set this house up to look like mine, but where's my stuff? I keep my newspapers right over there. Dustin always told me I took too long to read them, but I picked up the pace. He'll be so proud of me, my Dustin. He doesn't write so well, though, always had a problem with his handwriting. I told him for years that no one could read his chicken scratch. Do you know what he tells me?"

"No, what does he tell you, Mrs. Murphy?"

"He has the nerve to say my writing is as bad as his! Can you believe that! Then we start to laugh and say together, *I guess it's okay as long as they can read the numbers on the checks!* We think it's so funny—always laughing, me and my Dustin, my little baby." Ilva reached for the napkin and dabbed her eye.

Corinda moved the box of tissues by her side and said, "Just in case."

"He comes every Sunday. I make a meal for him and we pay the bills." Ilva's tears flowed freely and she stared out the window as she blew her nose. "He's such a good boy, we laugh all the time." She smiled and turned to her aide. "He comes every Sunday."

Corinda put a shawl around Ilva's shoulders. "Your son sounds very nice."

"He is. He's my baby."

"I hope to meet him one day."

"Just be here on a Sunday when I cook for him."

"I'm sure I'll meet him soon."

"How's this for an idea? I could prepare dinner for both of you? Would you like that, Corinda?"

"Yes, I would."

"Okay, but when we do the bills, you need to excuse us."

"No problem. I'll give the two of you all of the privacy that you need."

"Did I tell you about his bad handwriting?"

A car honked twice as it drove by the house. Ilva raised her eyebrows. "Could be him. He always honks two times. Always two honks, never three, never one. Did I ever mention that, Corinda?"

"Once or twice, Mrs. Murphy. Time for lunch."

⊷▧◉ ◎▧⊶

"If you're trying to stay away from us, you may need to find some new restaurants, Uncle Dustin," Anthony offered.

The bartender interrupted. "Last time you came here, young man, you insulted fútbol and now you want to send away our best customer ever? You are nothing but trouble! Two beers coming up!"

Dustin hugged his two nephews and made room for them at the bar. "Sorry I was out of contact. I had lots to sort out. How are things?"

Matthew patted his uncle on the back. "Dad told us what happened. You protected Aunt Charlie and Dad said you solved some mysteries."

"Well, if ignorance is bliss, what is remembering after fifty years?"

Anthony suggested, "About time."

Dustin laughed. "Wise guy!"

"We want to help you find a new groove," Matthew said.

"What, like the movie?" Dustin joked.

Mathew rubbed his chin. "What movie?"

"Never mind. What do you mean?"

"Dad said you understand things now, but you're used to doing things a certain way and old habits are hard to break," Matthew said.

"Your father is a smart man."

Anthony cut to the chase. "Dad wants you to do two things: one for you and one for him. You've been back in New York a month and you haven't been out to Hicksville to visit Grandma. She makes less sense with every passing day, so you should visit her soon. Dad says whatever the meeting is going to be, just let it happen so you can move forward."

"What's the second thing?"

Matthew handed him a flier. "My father is finally going to do an open mic night out on the Island in two weeks. He says he can't do it without you. We'll all be there."

The boys finished their beers and headed out. Dustin moved to his outdoor table overlooking Forty-Sixth Street. A fresh Macallan arrived as he took his seat. A family passed by and he admired their sense of connectedness. Couples, old and young, strolled by holding hands. He thought, *The boys are right. It's time.*

C H A P T E R 5 1

Sunday

"What day is today, Corinda?"

"Sunday, Mrs. Murphy."

"Dustin should be here soon. He comes every Sunday. Did I ever—"

"Yes, Mrs. Murphy, he visits on Sunday, writes badly, and accuses you of having the same problem. He honks two times when he leaves."

Ilva smirked. "I guess I told you that a few times. Am I right?"

Corinda offered her own grin.

"Remember, when we sit down at the table to do the bills, we need privacy. I didn't make anything, so he's going to be disappointed. Maybe some takeout? Yes, this will be our plan. Please help me dress to greet my son."

"Of course, but why do you think he'll be here today. Did he call?"

"He doesn't need to call. I told you, he comes every Sunday, but I didn't cook. We could order something."

"Yes, Mrs. Murphy, takeout for sure. Let's get dressed, but please remember the rules of the agency and use your walker. I'll pick out an outfit for you."

◦═◉ ◉═◦

For many years, Dustin's Sunday visits to Hicksville helped to ground him and provide a sense of belonging. It was the one time and place that someone outside of business expected him, looked forward to seeing him, and appreciated his help. He always told his mother that the home-cooked meal was the attraction, and while there was some truth to that statement, this was just his cover story. When the research about the family began, Sundays also meant discovery, excitement, and storytelling—three things that Dustin enjoyed immensely. This Sunday, however, wouldn't likely be any of those things.

⊷⊶ ⊷⊶

"Corinda, please stop. My hair is fine. Open the door for Dustin."

"Mrs. Murphy, perhaps we shouldn't get our hopes up. He might be busy today. I can—"

Ding ding.

"There he is. Let him in. We'll sit at the dining room table. Remember, we need our privacy. You can take a break upstairs."

"As you wish. Let me answer the door."

Corinda stepped into the living room as Dustin let himself in with his key. "Are you Dustin?"

"Yes."

"I'm your mother's aide, Corinda. Boy, have I heard a lot about you! Your mother will be out in a minute. She wants to chat with you in the dining room and she's upset that she didn't cook anything. I hope you realize she hasn't cooked in a long time. She's been talking about takeout."

Dustin offered a half-smile and looked away. "I'm not so sure how long I'll be here."

Corinda's shoulders slumped. "Oh, I see. She'll be disappointed. I'll be upstairs if you need anything."

Dustin sat at the table and remembered all of the family dinners during his childhood. He got up from the head seat, which was his father's, and repositioned himself in his old spot—one seat down and to the left. The thumping began in the distance and got louder as it became closer. The tennis balls at the bottom of the walker appeared first, followed by his mother. It had only been about ten weeks since his last visit, but she was much more hunched over and twisted than before. He gave her a peck on the cheek and helped her into the seat at the head of the table.

"Been a while, Mom. How are you?"

Ilva didn't answer right away and started to cry. She blew her nose in a tissue from the tabletop and straightened up in her chair. "I tried to prepare for this conversation. I'm so sorry. I did my best, but I made some bad choices for you."

"Let's just promise, no more secrets. Both of us are too old for that kind of thing."

"God yes, Dustin, especially me. I never thought I would be this way."

Dustin stacked the placemats into a pile and lined up the salt and pepper shakers in the center of the table. His mother took hold of his hand. "Stop fidgeting. Ask me what you want to know."

"Fine. How well do you remember what happened to me when I was ten?"

"I can't remember what I told someone five minutes ago and I rarely know what day it is, but I recall everything that happened years ago."

"Tell me what you think I should understand."

"Where should I start? You discovered so much, why don't you ask your questions?"

"I'm more interested in why those things happened than what happened. I remember a lot of the details, so I don't want to rehash them. So, why did I go through this back then and why did you wait forty-seven years to fill me in."

"I'll start by saying that I may be an old senile lady, but don't think I missed the fact that you're sitting in your old chair and I'm in your father's spot at the head of the table. I was in charge of this family for many years, but I wasn't in charge back then. So you need to understand that the *why* forty-seven years ago was more about your father. As for why I didn't tell you until now, I take total blame for that, but I'll still do my best to explain."

"Fine. I'm listening."

"We've had some mental illness on both sides of the family. Your Uncle H.O. was never the same after he came out of the Navy during the Korean War and several people on your father's side struggled with issues. We tried to help H.O. without committing him to an institution and he lived a long life, but not a good one. I am happy, though, that we made the effort, because at least he had the love of his family. If we would have institutionalized him, things would have been worse."

"Is that what Dad wanted to do with me?"

"Yes, we took you to several doctors and they all felt that you would be better off in a controlled environment."

"You mean an institution. What was I doing that was so bad?"

"It was the dreams, it was always about the dreams, Dustin. I didn't under-stand them back then. I have a touch of your ability as well, but not like you. The yelling and screaming at night in a small house became too much for your father and when I hinted that you saw some things in the future, he flipped and wanted you out."

"My own father wanted me out. Wow . . . did he always feel this way about me?"

"It wasn't about feelings. Believe it or not, your father loved you. He believed that to do right for all of his kids, you couldn't be around."

"So, my father is to blame. Is this why you drugged me in a motel room while some quack of a doctor gave me shock therapy? Was that his fault as well?"

Ilva broke down and sobbed with her head almost touching the table. Dustin moved to her side and kissed her on the shoulder. "I'm sorry, Mom. I shouldn't have said that. No need to say anything else."

"No, I want to explain. Your father gave me a month to *fix* you, but I knew you weren't broken. I had to find a way to make your dreams stop at least for a while, so I could protect your life—an institution would have been the end of you."

"But electric shock treatment on a drugged ten-year-old boy?"

Ilva slapped her hands down on the table. "I had no way of knowing how bad it would be! That isn't fair!"

"Again, I'm sorry. I guess I just don't understand."

"It was like torture, but I thought I was saving your life. Once we got started, it became clear you would associate dreaming with the electric shock, which the doctor thought would generally discourage future dreams. The other suggestions about being alone and having no connections with people were meant to fight the strength of the specific dream that made you scream every night."

"But why didn't you tell me when I became an adult?"

"I kidded myself into believing that you were high-functioning. Not at all like your Uncle H.O.—he couldn't even handle everyday life at a low level. You started making lots of money and did well for yourself. Your Aunt Grace was the one who pushed me to speak to you sooner, but I didn't listen to her. I decided to drop both of my bombshells on you at the same time."

"Mom, I'm fifty-seven and I have nothing. No children. No wife. No friends. No life. It's too late for me. You waited too long."

"Yes, I did wait too long, but you're wrong about having nothing—you have Charlie, Paddy, Anthony, Matthew, and you still have me. I'm hoping I'm still in the group."

"Of course you are, Mom. Of course."

"You deserved more from me, and as for the background regarding the family, the discoveries you made answered so many of the questions that we had over the years. You were the right person for the job. I just waited too long to give it to you."

"With all that said, Mom, there were other lessons learned that served me. Aunt Rita taught me that there's nothing thicker than blood." He reached out for his mother's hand. She sighed and then smiled.

Dustin sat back in his chair and continued to hold his mother's hand. He remembered his discussion with her at this same table about ten years earlier after the passing of Aunt Grace. The thought that his aunt's presence was everywhere in the house provided comfort and helped them to deal with the tremendous sense of loss. He squeezed his mother's hand and realized that no matter where he went or what he did, she would always be present for him as well. She made tough decisions for herself and her children with good intentions and lived with the consequences. He was part of her, and she the essence of him.

He let go of her hand and returned his attention to the arrangement of salt and pepper shakers and placemats. After they had all been positioned just right, he said, "I think I'm going to leave now. I'm not mad or upset, but I feel like I have a tremendous amount to do and only a little time to do it. I'll arrange for some takeout for you and Corinda. Don't give her too hard of a time. Okay?"

Ilva nodded and walked her son to the door with her walker. She crossed her fingers and called up the stairs, "Corinda, turn off the TV and listen." She stood by the door and braced herself as Dustin tapped his horn twice before pulling away. Ilva clapped her hands. "See, I told you. This is what we do. He comes over every Sunday. We didn't do the bills this week and I don't think his handwriting improved much, but he honks the horn two times when he leaves. That's what we do, me and my Dustin. You heard it, right?"

"Yes, Mrs. Murphy. Two times. Heard it clear as day."

"Do you know what he had the nerve to tell me?"

"No, Mrs. Murphy, what did he have the nerve to tell you?"

CHAPTER 52

Stand-Up

DUSTIN ARRIVED AT the Joke Mill about thirty minutes before showtime. His family was seated around two tables pushed together. Ten comics were scheduled to perform and Paddy drew the last position, which was either good or bad depending on a host of factors. Only five of the twenty tables were occupied.

Charlie tapped her spoon on her glass. "I have an announcement to make. Listen up. This is serious. I turned down dates from two particularly handsome men to be here alone, so I could give Paddy my full support and attention."

"We probably could have used another person in the audience, Aunt Charlie. You may want to give one of those particularly handsome men a call! Maybe both if it wouldn't get too awkward for you!" Anthony said.

"Anthony, Anthony, Anthony," Charlie quipped, "Don't worry about the turnout." She reached for her phone and started to broadcast live on Facebook. Within minutes, a dozen people commented that they were en route to the club.

The first comic came out and only his small following laughed at any of his jokes. Paddy tried to be supportive but turned to Dustin and whispered, "Tough crowd."

Dustin put his hand on his brother's shoulder. "Don't worry, Paddy, you'll knock'm dead." He became worried, however, when he spotted Paddy reviewing a large stack of index cards. Matthew noticed his concern and picked up the deck and rifled through them in Dustin's direction. They were all blank.

The second act was a little better as the club filled up with Charlie's Facebook friends, who started calling out, "We want Paddy! We want Paddy!" The club didn't stand on ceremony and changed the lineup so Paddy could go third.

Paddy tripped on the corner table as he neared the stage and his stack of index cards went flying in the air. He made a funny face as he took the opportunity to drink a stranger's beer while steadying himself against the front table. The audience gave him his first laugh, perhaps slightly muted. Anthony ran onto the stage and scooped up the deck. "Please put them back in order for me. Thanks," Paddy said. "All hundred and forty-two, yes, all hundred and forty-two."

"Sure thing," Anthony called out.

"Hi, I'm Paddy Murphy. Now, I want you to be straight with me. Did my entrance make you worried? First impressions, right! Am I right?"

Paddy waited for some acknowledgment from the audience. "Okay, so you saw me walk out and . . . let's just see . . . clap your hands if you thought male model?" He struck a pose and got a few laughs. "Okay, so maybe that's a stretch. How many thought, what a charming fat fuck?" Paddy raised one eyebrow while rubbing his impressive pot belly. The audience applauded loudly. "Okay, the charming fat fucks have it. All right, so I fell and you either thought, *Holy shit, this is going to be some asshole or maybe he's a physically gifted comedian?* The real reason I fell, actually, is that I needed one more beer before I performed. Sorry, buddy. Somebody should have told you—never, ever, ever sit in the front row in a comedy club. It is an actual rule, I believe." The crowd chuckled. "Okay, back to the question. Show of hands—did you think, *some asshole?*" He paused and gauged the applause. "Ooh, more than I hoped, not good. How about *physically gifted?*" Another pause as he measured the reaction. "I believe the physically gifted has a slight edge." He smiled.

Paddy took another sip of the stranger's beer. "Thanks, fella, but you know, I really would have preferred a Heineken." The man held up his hand and a waitress appeared and rested the bottle on the table. Paddy held the microphone to her lips.

She looked at the stranger. "Eight dollars, please."

The man raised his hands and laughed. Paddy took back the microphone. "Listen, buddy, don't be a cheapskate . . . give her a nice tip, and hurry up, will ya, I've got a show to do!"

The crowd laughed again and Paddy took a sip of his fresh beer before he continued. "Okay, where were we? Oh yeah, the index cards. You spotted my index cards, yes, all hundred and forty-two of them and this fine young man over here scooped them up and offered to put them back in order. Come up here, young man. Did you get those cards ordered right?"

"I guess so," Anthony answered.

"Great." He turned back to the general audience. "So when these cards flew in the air after I fell, you figured you dodged a bullet. There is nothing worse in the world than a person making a speech or doing comedy reading from cards . . . am I right?"

The crowd nodded and offered a group groan.

"I see I'm on point here. Young man, why did you say 'I guess so' when I asked you if the cards were in order?"

"They're all blank, so it doesn't matter." He held up a few of the blank cards and turned to the crowd. "See?"

"Blank cards . . . interesting. Could it be that you're dealing with someone who lacks total content, hence a hundred and forty-two blank cards?" He paused and moved his hands up and down in response to the volume of applause. "Or, am I a master who dazzled you with his comedic misdirection?" Paddy did a little dance that had nothing to do with anything but brought down the house. He waited for the applause to subside and tried to determine the stronger reaction to the two choices he proposed. "To be fair, the clapping was a little weak for both options, but since this is supposed to be funny and I did get a big laugh for my dance after the second choice, let's pick that. So, let me summarize, we've already agreed that I'm a physically gifted comedian"—he made a muscle—"master of comedic misdirection"—he twirled—"who happens to be a charming fat fuck"—he stuck out his stomach. "Okay, is this a fair summary?" The applause provided his acknowledgment.

"Great, what else can you say about me? My name is Paddy Murphy, I have red hair, and I enjoy a beer or two. Okay, so with those additional clues, ask me another question—one, two, three."

Anthony and Matthew screamed, "What are you?" Others joined in with other questions, but many seemed a little confused.

"Okay, let's go with 'What are you?' I guess I could answer with one of the things we've already established, right?" He paused and gave the audience a chance to consider their answer.

"I'm physically gifted, an expert at comedic misdirection, and of course, a charming fat fuck." He turned to Matthew. "Is that what you meant when you asked that question?"

Matthew answered, "No."

"That's right, to be honest, what people want to know when they ask that question is how they can file you away, because until they can, they don't know how to deal with you. Am I right?"

"Yes," the audience screamed. People started to whisper to one another as they found themselves alternating between smiling, laughing, and thinking.

"Now, I could answer, *Why do you ask?* Boy, would this change the dynamic! But given that this is a comedy routine, I think we have to take that response off the table for now." Paddy smiled at Dustin. "Does it help if I tell you that this young man next to me is my son, Anthony, and his brother, Matthew, the one who asked the question, is right over there. Come on up, Anthony and Matt. And my sister is over here—stand up, Charlie." The crowd roared, spurred on by Charlie's personal fan club. She curtsied. Paddy offered, "What the hell is she, right? And my brother is over there. Stand up, Dustin." He received a smaller round of applause.

"Let me take a second to say that my brother over here is a hero. He saved someone's life during the incident in Charlottesville in August. He took a knife in his side to save—guess who—Sis over there." Dustin received a standing ovation and Paddy asked his family to sit. He called out to his brother, "Dustin, if that doesn't get you laid tonight, I'm not sure anything will!" The crowd erupted again. "Anyway, back to *what are you?*"

Paddy continued, "So you really can't guess, can you? The reality is I'm mostly Irish, but I'm also twenty-five percent Black." He paused. The crowd was unsure how to react. A few laughed, some smiled, and many fidgeted in their seats. Paddy continued, "My sons' mother was Puerto Rican, so think about what they are, but the thing is when you're a comedian and you're telling jokes, are you allowed to joke about groups that you don't obviously own?" The audience became awkwardly silent for a moment and Paddy answered his own question, "No, you can't—so what group do I clearly own? In other words, what group can I make the brunt of most of my jokes?" The audience started to whisper and Paddy knew he had them moving in the right direction.

Anthony provided the answer as he called out, "You can own the fat fucks all over the world, but I'm not so sure about the *charming* part!"

Paddy made a fist. "Why I oughta . . ." And with that he fell again and drank another stranger's beer before gathering himself up from the floor. He closed his routine with, "Thank you, I'm Paddy Murphy. Enjoy the rest of the show." Paddy got the best round of applause of the night.

Dustin stood as his guest arrived and he pulled out a chair for her. "Guys, this is my friend, Surita."

"Sorry I'm late, everyone. I hope I didn't miss your show. Paddy, right?"

"The one and only. I just wrapped up. I think I did okay."

Three people from the bar walked over to congratulate Paddy on his set. He shook their hands and thanked them for their kind words.

"From the look of things, you did better than you think," Surita said. "I'm sorry I missed it, but I'll catch the next one. I was finishing a job in New Jersey and the traffic was horrible coming over here, but I was determined to make it and I'm glad I did." She flashed Dustin a smile.

Charlie jumped in. "So how do you know Dustin?"

"I'll say it this way. I knew of him years ago during his first run in that fancy apartment of his in Queens and then he vanished for years. I saw him again when he returned and then he vanished once more, but this time only for weeks. When he knocked on my door the other day with this invitation, I just had to come out to spend some time with the person the neighborhood likes to call *The Man in The Castle*." She leaned over and gave Dustin a kiss on the cheek. "I'm hoping that this time he won't vanish at all."

Charlie clapped her hands. "Oh my God, this is your first date!"

"But definitely not the last," Surita said and offered Dustin another peck on the cheek. "What are we drinking?"

Dustin motioned for the waitress to come over and continued to smile and laugh but didn't say much. He reflected on the accomplishments of his brother and sister. Paddy had done it. He had finally followed through on what people had suggested his whole life and performed a stand-up comedy routine. Not only had he put on a good show, he'd done it in an intelligent and thoughtful manner. Regardless of whether his night of stand-up led to anything else, he could be proud of this achievement.

Charlie had done it as well by coming to grips with the things in her past that needed to be reconciled, measured, and, perhaps, atoned for. She still *stirred the pot* on Facebook, but with a new appreciation for those in the middle whom she was determined to move forward in order to create change. Both brothers would now be the recipients of her trademark shoulder punches and Dustin had no doubt that she would seek the title of New York's hottest seventy-year-old when the time came.

Dustin took in the moment and wished his mother were there to see him in the world trying. *Better late than never*, he thought as his gaze went from his siblings to his nephews and then back to his lovely date. He realized the negative assessment he had made of his life to his mother was wrong. He had a whole lot to be thankful for and so much that he was connected to. Dustin smiled and drained the last drop of his scotch as he waved again for the server.

"Waitress, another Macallan please. Make it an eighteen."

Surita smiled and added, "Make that two."

Part Ten

The Bronx
November 2020

C HAPTER 53

Woodlawn

DUSTIN WAITED FOR Charlie and Paddy by the entrance to the building and laughed as his sister tripped on the curb at the edge of the parking lot at the Woodlawn Cemetery. Paddy caught her before she fell to the ground.

"Nice entrance, Charlie. Paddy, good catch," Dustin called out.

"Are we ready to do this?" Charlie asked. Both brothers nodded and the trio entered the mausoleum. The first stop was Great-Aunt Rita's niche, where her ashes had resided since her passing in the 1970s. Each sibling reflected in their own way on their colorful and energetic relative. Paddy still couldn't get over the fact that she had worked with the infamous New York crime figure Bumpy Johnson. Charlie admired her strength and the fact that she had lived her life at full speed, refusing to slow down for anyone. Dustin traced the etching of her name on the stone wall with his index finger and said, "Nothing is thicker than blood."

Aunt Grace's resting place was just a few locations to the right of Aunt Rita. Paddy said hello and asked his deceased aunt if she had already shown her big sister around. The siblings became silent, as if they needed to give her time to respond. Grace had been a big part of their lives growing up, but her role after her death in starting Dustin on his journey of discovery may have been her most lasting contribution to the family. Charlie walked up to the niche, which was at eye level, and rested her palm against the surface. "Thank you and don't worry," she said. "Dustin is taking good care of Grandpa Joe."

The group moved to the end of the aisle and came face-to-face with their mother's new home for the first time. Paddy was the first to shed a tear. Charlie reached out to him with her right hand and Dustin took hold of her left. Cries turned into laughs as Paddy told the first story. Each do you remember when tale was followed by reflection as the siblings realized the deeper meaning in much of what their mother had said and done over the years. An hour later, Charlie suggested it was time to go. Paddy concurred, but Dustin wanted to stay a few more minutes. "Let's give him a little alone time with Mom," Paddy said as he grabbed hold of her arm. "Don't worry, Charlie, I'll help you navigate that dangerous curb." Charlie bit her tongue and punched Paddy in the shoulder as the two older siblings walked away.

Dustin wasn't sure where to direct his eyes or his voice but was confident that he would be both seen and heard. "I want you to know that I understand why you did what you did and I forgive you. That's it—I'm not adding even one *but* or *if only*. You sacrificed for all of us and couldn't have been a better mother." Dustin's words lifted a weight off his shoulders. He started making circles around the lettering of his mother's name with his index finger as he continued. "I'm not sure what I'm going to do with myself on Sundays, Mom. You know it was always my favorite day of the week." Dustin smiled and pressed his hand against his heart. "I do want to ask for one favor, though. Is that okay, Mom?" He paused. "I've got so much that I still need to do, but I want to know if you'll wait for me. You know where—we've both been there before."

Dustin stepped back and looked for a sign. He accepted the *whoosh* of a sudden rush of air as a positive response. "Thanks. The red birds with the black masks will keep you company while you wait. And don't worry, when my time comes, I'll honk two times to let you know I'm outside. Love you." Dustin sank to one knee with his last word and put the palm of his right hand against the wall.

Charlie and Paddy returned a few moments later and helped Dustin to his feet. A sense of optimism and satisfaction enveloped the three siblings as they exited the building. They had met the challenge of their mother's final few months together and provided her with all of the love, comfort, and respect that was humanly possible.

The brothers each grabbed one of Charlie's arms and lifted her up and over the parking lot curb, which was only tricky for their accident-prone sister. She punctuated her feigned protest at being manhandled with two of her signature punches. Paddy rubbed his shoulder and claimed injury, but Dustin loved how it felt. The trio offered each other both a hug and a smile.

Dustin considered how far they had come as a family once they'd uncovered and resolved the mysteries of their past. The idea of future possibilities filled him with excitement and anticipation. Charlie and Paddy waved back at the building to say goodbye, but Dustin turned and waved toward the sun, certain his mother was settled in its warmth, looking down and keeping an eye on all of them. He whispered, "Thanks."

Notes & Liberties

Part I—Long Island, 2009 & Part II—Harlem, 1934

The Sunday meetings between mother and son were real and consistent over a period of twenty-five-plus years. The main character, Dustin Murphy, was loosely based on the author and his mother, Ilva Murphy, was inspired by the author's mother, Gloria Ilva Allen. Grace Iles was also a true character and her death and relationship with Ilva and Dustin were all accurately portrayed.

The portrait of teenage Ilva (below left), which was painted in 1938, still hangs behind the head of the dining room table in the Hicksville house. The portrait of Joseph Julian (Grandpa Joe, below right), which traveled from St. Croix to Port of Spain (Trinidad), London, New York City, and Long Island over the last hundred and seventy years, now hangs in the author's residence. Joseph Julian (1822–1872) was part of a long line of merchants who originally hailed from Europe. Their earliest known ancestor in this line, Abraham Henriques Juliao (1661–1692), was born in Oporto, Portugal. The surname was Anglicized from Juliao to Julian in the mid-1700s.

Ilva and Francis Murphy (Gloria Ilva Allen and Edward Francis Allen) are pictured below. At left:1955, in front of the family's first bar, Allen's Alley, and in the 1980s to the right.

The Sisters: Grace and Ilva (Grace and Gloria) in their midtwenties and early fifties.

The Iles children: Gloria, Grace, and Horatio (H.O.) pictured below (left, circa 1930 and to the right in 1945). Ilva is on the left in both pictures.

An exterior view of the main character's residence in Queens (The Classic Kew Gardens) appears below to the left. The concrete extension that appears to rise above the roof (in the upper right corner in the photo) is what is referred to as The Castle in the novel. The picture to the right is the view of the greenery in the cemetery looking out from one of the cut-out windows inside The Castle.

Rita Muñoz-Iles (Aunt Rita): Harlem, 1934

Rita Muñoz-Iles was a prominent banker in the numbers racket in New York during the 1930s. She and her husband (Tito Muñoz) ran the bank out of the apartment where Ilva grew up as a child. Rita later became "The Fixer," as described in the book. Her close working relationship with Bumpy Johnson (a well-known figure in New York from the 1920s to 1960s) and Queen Stephanie St. Clair (the head of the numbers operation Rita served) was true. In addition, the theft of the bank, which was kept hidden in a hatbox, by two policemen in the family apartment, was also factual.

By 1937, Rita Muñoz was working with a different policymaker by the name of Henry Miro. They both ran afoul of the law and fled to France. Rita returned three years later and resolved her legal issues. Her marriage to Tito ended with her departure to France.

The family composition as described in Harlem in 1934 was accurate and all characters residing in that household were based on actual relatives. The actual names of all family members were used in the book. The relationships and family tensions were also accurately portrayed. Aunt Rita's Diary, however, does not exist. The stories from this period were cobbled together from oral histories, pictures, and other research. No group photo of the adults in the Iles family from the 1930s was available. The picture that appears on the left below was taken in the 1950s. In the back row, left to right: Aunt Rita (Rita Muñoz in the 1930s) and Bruce Mackinnon Iles. In the front row left to right: Olga Iles and Julia Grace Iles. The photo to the right was taken on Long Island in the 1970s and includes Rita Muñoz standing between Olga Iles and Gloria Ilva Allen.

Tito Muñoz

Rita Muñoz (Iles)

Two additional pictures of Rita Muñoz appear below. The photo on the left was taken in 1938 in France during the period that Rita had fled the country with Henry Miro, who is also pictured in the shot. The image on the right shows Rita with her trademark fur coat in the early 1930s.

Bruce Mackinnon Iles appears below to the left with two of his grandchildren and his wife, Olga Iles, appears to the right.

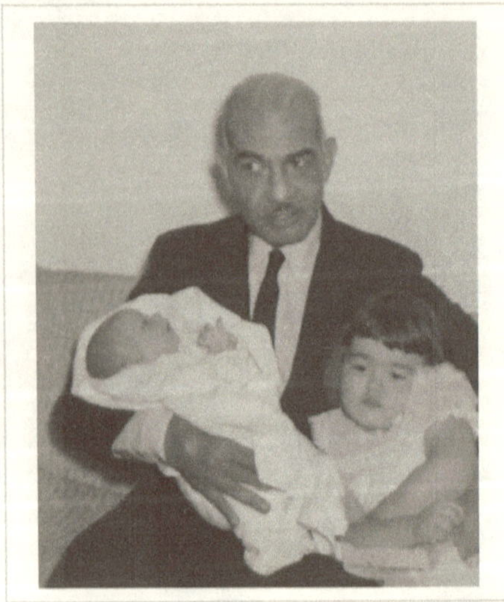

Part III—Long Island, 2009

The highly unlikely coincidence of the portrait of the father (Joseph Julian) being placed almost a hundred and seventy years later directly across from the burial plot of his daughter (Ilva Julian) was true. Ilva Julian is buried in the Maple Grove Cemetery, directly across from The Classic Kew Gardens. All of the details about the migration of the Julian family from Portugal to Amsterdam, Recife, Curacao, St. Domingue, and finally St. Croix were accurate, as was the story of Joseph and Julia Julian, a Sephardic Jew and a mixed-race woman who waited more than twenty years and eleven children to formally become husband and wife. Much of this information about the Julians came from distant cousins that the author met while doing his research on Ancestry.com. The Nevis Historical Society did, in fact, provide the additional information that helped explain the double-barreled Mackinnon Iles name.

During the period from 1920 to 1940, the family had been classified as Black by New York State and White by the federal government during the periodic census as indicated in the novel, although it is doubtful that they were aware of this fact. Finally, the stories related to the ownership of mixed-race bars in the 1950s were also true, as well as the donation to the NAACP. However, the name of the first family bar was not Murphy's Mayo; it was Allen's Alley.

Charlotte (Charlie) and Patrick (Paddy) are based on Diane and Frank, the author's siblings. Anthony and Matthew, Paddy's children in the novel, are actually the author's sons. The photo below to the left was taken in 1970. The author (leftmost in the photo) was about ten and his brother, twelve. Charlie (Diane) appears in the photo to the right (age twelve).

Below left: The author is seated next to his mother with his siblings standing behind (2010). Right: The same group without the author on the Manhattan terrace, across from the Greek Orthodox church, as described in the novel (2011).

Anthony Bruce Allen (Anthony Murphy) is pictured below to the left and Matthew Edward Allen (Matthew Murphy) to the right (2019) with his son, Matthew Allen Jones, who has the first double-barreled name in the family since Mackinnon Iles.

The story regarding the conversion of a racist Irish bar into a mixed-race establishment through a public relations spectacle was true. The donation to the NAACP by the Allen brothers (Edward Allen, the author's father, second from left, and Jack Allen, the author's uncle, second from right) was documented in this photograph that appeared in the *Amsterdam News* on April 6, 1957 (below, left). The photo to the right was taken in 1958 at Allen's Alley. Edward and Gloria Allen are standing behind the bar with a partial picture of a sign in the background that advertises Allenburgers for $.85.

Part IV—Nevis, 1815–1845

Horatio Iles was a prominent planter in Nevis in the early 1800s and he did marry Grace Mackinnon, a free woman of color, in the mid-1820s. The story about the Mackinnon Iles double-barreled name was true, as was the sale of a slave by the name of John Day by Horatio Iles to Grace Mackinnon. Horatio Iles's son from his first marriage, John Alex Iles (referred to as Alex Iles in the novel), did become a prominent government official in Nevis during the mid-1800s. The description of the racial balance in Nevis and the scarcity of eligible White women as partners for the wealthy planter class were also accurate.

The names Horatio and Grace would be used several times in the family based on the prominence of these two individuals, but the significance of the double-barreled last name (Mackinnon Iles) was something that had been lost on recent generations and discovered during the author's family research, as indicated in the novel. Two characters—Grace Mackinnon's father, Bruce, and his brother, Sinclair—were not based on documented fact. Luky, Grace Mackinnon's mother, who was a slave, was documented by research.

The record of the sale of a slave by the name of John Day on August 22, 1818, from Horatio Iles to Grace Mackinnon appears below and to the left. This document was obtained from the Slave Registers of Former British Colonial Dependencies, 1812–1834. The monument inscription (below to the right) appears on the Iles gravesite in Nevis on a stone vault containing the remains of both the father, Horatio Iles, and his eldest child, John Alex Iles. The fictitious family plantation in the novel was named after the island from which the Iles family came, Montserrat.

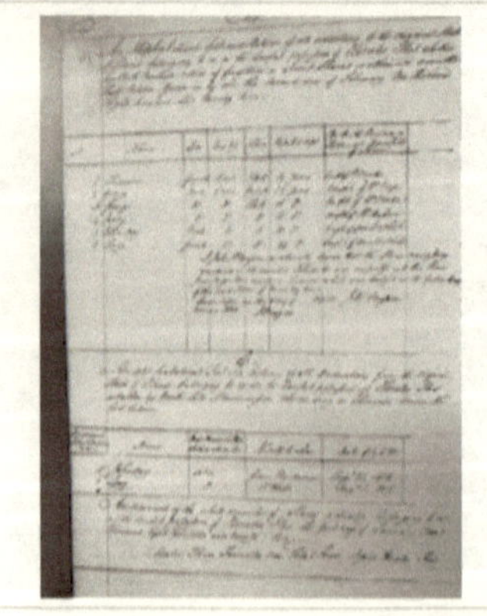

HORATIO ILES
DIED 5th JANUARY 1834
IN THE 51st YEAR
OF HIS AGE
1862, DEC., John Alex Iles became a
Member of the Executive Council of
Nevis. The family was from Montserrat.

Remaining Parts (V–X)

The buildup to the Unite the Right rally in the book was inspired by the actual events during that time, but all of the characters and locations in Waynesboro were fictitious. This portion of the book also chronicles the decline in the physical and mental health of the matriarch of the family after her fall. While there are bits and pieces of truth related to the family in the surrounding pages, much of this part of the book is fictional.

The description of the more prominent groups present on both sides of the Charlottesville conflict was accurate, as was the general description of the car attack that resulted in the death of Heather Heyer. The following two leaders of the protest mentioned in the book were, in fact, present: David Duke, the former Imperial Wizard of the KKK, and Richard Spencer, the chairman of the National Policy Institute. The sequence of events the night before and the day of the rally were also accurate. No member of the family was present during the Charlottesville rally.

About the Author

A. Robert Allen has published five novels and two short-story prequels in his Slavery and Beyond series. All are stand-alone stories connected by theme. He writes historical fiction that transports readers to times and places immediately before or soon after the end of slavery. A. Robert is a long-time higher education professional and resides in New York. The first volume in the series, *Failed Moments*, is a fictional account of Allen's ancestors in 1790 during the slave revolution in what would become Haiti and of, later in 1863, New York's Draft Riots. The second volume, *A Wave From Mama*, immerses readers in racially charged post–Civil War Brooklyn and gives an interesting look at the building of the Brooklyn Bridge. The third book in the series, *Minetta Lane*, takes place in 1904 in a downtown New York neighborhood that lives by an unusual race-based code. The prequel to this third volume, *Minetta Mornings*, takes place twenty-five years earlier. His fourth novel, *Living in the Middle*, involves the most violent and significant incident of racial violence in U.S. history, the Tulsa Race Riots of 1921. The prequel to this novel, which takes place in 1896, is entitled *Ticket to Tulsa*. Allen's most recent release, *Sundays*, is another fictional account of Allen's ancestors which transports readers to the island of Nevis in the early 1800s and Harlem in the 1930s. This novel also features the Unite the Right Rally in Charlottesville in 2017. Find out more about the author and his works at his website: http:// arobertallen.com

Get Exclusive Materials

The author writes prequels and sequels to his books and also provides other content including a guide to the Slavery and Beyond series which outlines all of the novels as well as the important historical events that are embedded within each story. All of this free content is available to readers on his mailing list. Go to http://arobertallen.com to join and pick up this free additional content.

Also by A. Robert Allen

Failed Moments

What if the only way to survive your life is to go back in history and right the wrongs of two other men's lives? Patrick Walsh finds himself in this precarious position as he goes back in time to the French Caribbean in 1790, just before the slave revolt that created Haiti, and to 1863 NYC during the Draft Riots. Tackling race relations from a unique perspective, FAILED MOMENTS is a thought-provoking adventure through four centuries that questions the measure of a man not by his decision to do no harm, but his willingness to act on what is right.

http://www.amazon.com/dp/B00TOXIZ10

A Wave From Mama

1863 Weeksville, Brooklyn: The free Black community of Weeksville becomes home to an unusually small boy and his mother who fled Manhattan during New York's Draft Riots. When his mother succumbs to her injuries, the boy swears revenge against everyone and everything that contributed to her death. His diminutive size and acrobatic climbing abilities make him a spectacle to behold, while his awkward social habits make him an outcast to everyone in Weeksville, except the adopted family he swears to protect. The boy becomes embroiled in a battle between the Irish Gangs and Whiskey Kings of Irishtown while the corrupt Metropolitan Police sit on the sidelines. All of this action is set in the backdrop of the building of the Brooklyn Bridge and the racial tensions of the period.

http://www.amazon.com/dp/B01JHKC5JW

Minetta Lane

1904 New York City: Bodee Rivers, who has always run from the major challenges in his life, moves to the most dangerous block in the city, MINETTA LANE. He struggles to find the strength and courage to survive in his new surroundings, which are governed by an unusual race-based code. Police in pursuit of criminals often give up the chase as they approach the entrance to Minetta because even they know better than to test the hardened criminals who hide in the shadows.

Bodee's circle of family and friends help him successfully manage some initial tests of his perseverance, but when he finds himself alone and confronted with an overwhelming challenge aboard the General Slocum Steamship, he isn't sure he's up to the task. Stand and fight or cut and run? Running is what he knows. Running is what will keep him safe. Will Bodee find the courage to fight, or will he simply do what he has always done?

http://www.amazon.com/dp/B0792MQ7QX

Minetta Mornings (Prequel to Minetta Lane)

1879 New York City: Juba, a former slave from New Orleans, and her seventeen-year-old daughter move to Minetta Lane, the most dangerous block in the city, where both the roads and the rules curve in unusual directions. Juba's stepson, Marcus, comes to their rescue when they are attacked during their first day in the neighborhood. Soon thereafter, mother and stepson assume control of the block and institute a code that must be followed by all. When Juba's daughter falls in love with a neighborhood rival, the resulting conflict threatens to tear the family apart. Will Juba's brains and Marcus's brawn be enough to meet the challenge?

MINETTA MORNINGS is a short-story prequel, which sets the stage for events that will transpire twenty-five years later in the associated novel, MINETTA LANE.

http://www.amazon.com/dp/B07F8JSTXP

Living in the Middle

New York & Tulsa, early 1900s: Jimmy Montgomery comes from old New York money and grows up among the Manhattan elite. At the age of eighteen, he discovers his whole life has been a lie and he follows his roots back to Tulsa, Oklahoma, to answer the burning questions in his life. Who is he? What is he? Where does he belong? He finds love and friendship along the way, but full acceptance from either the White or the Black world eludes him. When trouble pits the White population of Tulsa against the Black community of Greenwood, Jimmy must finally make a choice—he must stop LIVING IN THE MIDDLE. His decision to live in either the White or Black world will alter the course of his life and those he's come to love. What will he decide?

https://www.amazon.com/dp/B07PP5K4D8

Ticket to Tulsa (Prequel to Living in the Middle)

1896, New York City/Tulsa: James Montgomery fails in business but succeeds in love with a woman from the other side of the tracks in racially divided Oklahoma. He loses all his money . . . a child is on the way. An unorthodox proposal offers a solution. What will he do?

TICKET TO TULSA is a short-story prequel, which sets the stage for events that will transpire eighteen years later in the associated novel, LIVING IN THE MIDDLE.

https://www.amazon.com/dp/1096579235